CW01630717

CAN'T EAT YOU FOR SUPPER

Roxanne Remy

B.F.F.

Edition License Notes

All rights reserved. This ebook is licensed for your personal enjoyment only. This ebook may not be re-sold or given away to other people. If you would like to share this book with another person, please purchase an additional copy for each recipient. Thank you for respecting the hard work of this author.

THEY CAN'T EAT YOU FOR SUPPER

Copyright © 2020 by Roxanne Remy

Publisher's Note: Although is work was inspired by actual occurrences outside the author's personal experiences, this is a work of fiction. Names, characters, places, and incidents are a product of the author's imagination. Locales and public names are sometimes used for atmospheric purposes. Any similarities to the name, character, or history of any person, living or dead, or of any actual event, is entirely coincidental and unintentional.

Please direct inquiries to B.F.F. Publishing at bffpub@gmail.com

For content warnings please go to :

http://www.roxanneremy.com

Book and Cover design by Vila Design Book Cover Design

ISBN: 978-1-7364917-0-6

First Edition: April 2021

To the all the alienated children, parents, grandparents, stepparents,

and others who dare to keep love in their hearts.

Justice will not be served until those who are unaffected are as outraged as those who are.

-Benjamin Franklin

CHAPTER ONE

The rearview lights of a departing restaurant patron caught Kristin's attention. Streetlamps cast hues at the beginning of their shift, as she whipped her van into the vacant spot. Her weak arms clicked the gearshift into Park. Noticing the time, she rested her forehead over clasped hands on the steering wheel and released a long sigh. Interstate 75's sea of travelers delayed her northward commute home to Alabama, and she had arrived forty minutes late.

A buzz from the cradled cell phone on the dash prompted her to glance at the caller ID. Ten years after their divorce, and her stomach still pitted when she read his name.

"Hello," she said, with a dab of pink lip balm to her faded complexion.

"Kris, listen. Things were hectic at the drop off; I wanted to speak, but—"

"We never speak at the drop off," she interrupted. "What do you want, Hutch?"

"I felt like I should take a minute to say thank you."

She flipped the driver's side visor down and pinched her cheeks in the mirror. "You've already thanked me."

"*Again*, then," he said with a firmness that reminded her why her stomach still sunk after all this time. "I felt like I should thank you, again," his tone softened. "I really appreciate you doing this for me."

"For Olivia and Lennon, you mean."

"Right, for the girls. I know it's not easy. You, with your husband and dogs. Me, Peyton, and our four children—"

"Two."

"What's that?"

"The twins, they're two children. So, you moved your wife and *two* children seven hundred miles away from the *two* daughters you had with me." Kristin gave a one-sided shrug to the reflection in the mirror then flipped it back into position. "So, here we are."

"You were always better with details."

An extended break in her ex-husband's conversation returned her to a familiar setting; her lungs filled awaiting his response.

"Well, like I was saying, thank you for keeping our weekends on track while I get things sorted." She released her breath through an open mouth, as he continued. "I know it was abrupt, but this promotion was just the kick my career needed. I'm thriving," his low tone lulled a lifetime of sales experience.

"I'm sure Peyton wanted to move closer to home, too."

"This move benefited my entire family, Olivia and Lennon included. If I can be a better provider for them, they'll only be more successful in the long run."

Of course, more money, more success. It's the Hutch Camek motto.

"Well, congrats. No additional thanks required. Just get a

new plan in place. My *dogs* need me," she said, feeling her "gray-rock" reply was in line with her therapist's recommendations.

"Kris," his smoky voice re-invited her attention. "You know you're better than your mother. Let's keep this up a little while longer, for the girls."

"Gotta' go. Good chat." Ending the call, she realized she was now an hour late to dinner with her in-laws. She rubbed the blistered edges of her elbows, worn from their fixed position while driving through late-afternoon storms. Her chipped, nude-coated nails came into view; she recalled when their sheen once competed with that of the wood-grain steering wheel she'd gripped for hours. The woman's round, toffee eyes focused on her overgrown cuticles while she smoothed the sunset-tinted whispers of hair around her face. This would have to suffice. Grey expected her at dinner, and she couldn't let drive time disappoint her husband again.

When her ex moved to a suburban utopia on South Florida's luxurious coastline, he feared missing precious time with their two daughters. She agreed to a temporary fix of a complicated situation. For months now, the former spouses crossed state lines to an agreeable half-way spot. Two days of travel whittled her weekends down to a single day, giving her little time to recoup from the wanderer's lifestyle she'd adopted.

The weary mother stretched for a pair of decent flats she kept on reserve in the rear floorboard. Her lower spine popped when it realigned. She held her shaking muscles in position savoring their release. Opening the car door, Kristin rested her sneakers on the frame and rounded her back over her legs.

Her creased eyes admired the progressive renovations of her hometown's historic district. This area was a blighted community during her youth. A resurgence of dining establishments and nightlife added foot traffic to the brick alleyways. Neighboring kitchen grills intoxicated the night air, signaling Ellington's inaugural First Friday Night celebration was underway. Early birds crinkled their carryout bags while getting into their cars. Vendors lined the sidewalks offering fresh poured craft beers to thirsty customers; a strong sign the younger crowds approved of the new open-container law.

From the driver seat, she viewed the Mardi Gras-themed exterior of the restaurant where her husband awaited her arrival with his family. Despite Grey's support, her in-laws disapproved of any arrangement infringing on the youngest Murphy son's marital rights—late appearances to family dinners included.

The establishment's corner location anchored the revitalized district, but its average health scores made her question the sister-in-law's choice of venue. Vy was a serial planner and designated hostess for most Murphy family gatherings. From weddings to wakes, she wasn't one to overlook a detail. With her husband poised to receive a handsome payment for joining his National Guard company on assignment overseas, Kristin doubted the party coordinator spared expenses either. She suspected the military wife would say Grey's brother enjoyed the live music, but Weyman liked anything Vy told him to. An abandoned acoustic guitar propped on a wooden stool outside suggested the first set had wrapped.

Taking an owner-like stance on the front sidewalk, the plump woman stretched her neck scanning the crowd. The reluctant guest ducked, shielding her face from her sister-in-law's scowl. As the violet and emerald beaded door sealed shut, the weary traveler swung her feet back into position and slammed the car door.

I can't deal with this tonight.

The dashboard illuminated the interior, and she hoped her husband gave them a suitable cover story.

The caller ID flashed a perfectly angled platinum-blonde pixie onto her screen. "Vy, I hope you're not waiting on me. Traffic is horrendous," she said, watching the restaurant fade in the rearview mirror.

"We started to worry."

Kristin imagined her sister-in-law's Botoxed brow not cooperating with her fabricated look of concern. "I'm sorry, it's still hard for me to gauge the drive."

"I can only imagine driving that far each weekend. That's—," she paused, "something. Our soldier leaves tomorrow. We wish you were here. Wey and I love the live music. Maybe you can make his welcome home party in October."

"I hope."

With a hurried breath, "I need to catch our server. Everyone's finished eating and he hasn't taken the first dessert order. I'm not sure if he's dumb or just oblivious," she said, as the phone went dark.

The home screen refreshed, and another familiar name appeared. It was the first phone call of the night Kristin welcomed. "Hello, my only friend," she said, letting the clicks of her turn signal fill dead air until her closest confidant replied.

"Hold on." Audric's no nonsense tone cut to the point.

When Grey introduced the two mothers they formed a bond commiserating with having a backstage ticket to the Boys Only Club they wed. The women shared emotional scars from first marriages and supported each other's new commitments. Protecting their daughters from becoming the sacrificial lambs of parental egos was always a hot topic. Audrie's own past a key contributor, her heart bled for children caught in the middle of adults vindicating a dissolved relationship. Most times, she made a hurried check on her stepnieces when her husband was out of earshot. A bold move, the friend recognized. The Murphy sons followed their father's lead and supporting a non-blood-related family member over their own was disloyal. Though she missed their extended conversations, Kristin respected her sister-in-law's promise of a unified home for her daughter. Secret carpool chats would do. Besides, how could she judge another woman's sacrifices?

"Sorry about that, I had a visitor," Audrie said. "Heads-up, Grey just left."

"Any chance he grabbed a to-go box of beignets on the way out?"

"Nope, not tonight."

"Thanks for the tip." Kristin considered lying to her too, but she knew she'd see through it. "I'm just exhausted, Aud."

"I know you are, friend. The girls will appreciate you for doing this, one day."

"One day feels a long way off."

"Do you see an end in sight?"

"Hutch says he's working on it. He wants to do it without lawyers, if possible."

"Can you trust him?"

The exes' relationship had been complicated for a lifetime. "Trust is a strong word," she said, giving a single-beat laugh. "I can say, wholeheartedly, court is not the place for family decisions. Attorneys just want the money. And judges have no obligation to preserve anyone's dignity except their own."

"Well, foster kids grow up in the system. My whole childhood was one big courtroom movie scene and you're right, nobody wins." Audrie's life experiences deemed her the legal mastermind of the family, without question. "I'll call tomorrow on my way to the store."

Her exits were always abrupt.

As the city lights grew distant, the stars peered from behind passing clouds. Her tires splashed through remnants from an earlier storm as she recalled the velvety kill shot Hutch used to nick the artery of her guilty conscience.

You know you're better than your mother.

His statement was spot-on. She was a better mother than her own; Rosalyn Irvine would have killed him and been done with it. When it came to preserving a father-daughter relationship, Kristin reigned supreme, but he knew his ex-wife's past. And he loved reminding her of the monster she refused to become.

Her father remarried three years after her parents' divorce. She remembered her first visit to his new home when she was thirteen, the same age as her daughter, Lennon.

***

While packing her Dukes of Hazzard backpack for the weekend, her mother dictated marching orders, "Do you have everything, Krissy?"

"I think so," she said, giving a sharp tug on the laces of her pale-pink Tretorns.

"Keep an eye out for me when you're there. This wife of his, she's a real piece of work. I hear she's been around the block a time or two before she landed your dad. He never could say no to a woman." Rosalyn lit a cigarette, watching her daughter skip across the bedroom. "You know she's the reason for our divorce, don't you?"

"I do." Overlooking her mother's repeated accusation, she zipped the duffle shut and wafted smoke from her face.

The mother continued to speak to the back of her child's head. "She was the control desk operator, and he was the telephone repair tech. He met her calling in to get his next job assignment. She's trash. She probably doesn't even use Duke's mayonnaise." Kristin's mother rolled her eyes and flicked her cigarette in a crystal ashtray near the sofa. "I'm not even from this godforsaken state, but I took one hint from your grandmother on how to make potato salad."

The child stood at the window, awaiting her father's arrival while the bitter ex-wife continued to agonize. "And don't get me started on this new pre-shredded cheese. How lazy does a woman have to be to not grate her own cheese?"

Kristin's allergies surged with her mother's fiery drag on a Benson and Hedges 100.

"I have a right to know what you're being subjected to," she said, her militant tone softened. "Take your own personal products. Her two girls are so young, they're still in diapers."

"Wouldn't she have something?" The daughter dared not mention her new stepmother's name; fearing her mother would cancel the trip altogether.

Her bottomless emerald eyes mirrored the rejection she still clung to. "Be careful poking that bear, child. Your father left us when you started puberty because he couldn't handle you growing up. Asking him to go to the Piggly Wiggly for pads could trigger him to leave again. You wouldn't want that on your head, now would you?"

The young girl sensed a need to pacify her mother's Irish temper with an agreeable response. "You're right, Ma. I just want to blend in," she said, burying paper wrappers into the deepest corners of her overnight bag.

The mother-child dynamic duo was all she'd known since her parents separated. Her mother led the charge for wives of other promiscuous utility workers and coached them on how to restore their dignity.

Lighting another cigarette, the scorned woman angled her glare toward the ceiling. Her flame-colored layers feathered across her brow. "That coward of a man. Leaving us to be with a tramp operator. Why? To make him feel younger, sexier, richer? He never loved us, Krissy. You'll see that hasn't changed." On an exhale, she forced the toxic fumes away from her child's delicate senses.

Seeing the dented white hood of her father's Datsun truck, the child tapped her hands together then leaned to kiss her mother's delicate cheek. "I know, Ma. I'll be alright. See you Sunday."

"Lucky stars above you. Sunshine on your way."

Joe's horn announced his arrival, and young Kristin floated through the door.

Sliding inside the truck flooded her with fond memories. "Hi, Daddy." Her dimples pitted into her cheeks.

"There's my girl." His warm, Southern drawl wrapped around her.

Her pink fingertips brushed over healed cuts on her dad's sun-drenched forearms. "What happened?" she asked, pulling her hand back. Her mother's warning rambled through her head.

"Life of a 'polecat' you know." He laughed, pulling the tattered stick shift into reverse. Creases along his chestnut eyes deepened as he studied his path through the back window. She bounced in the passenger seat watching him look over his broad shoulder. "I swear this driveway gets longer every time I come here."

Leaving the sleepy neighborhood together reminded her of many Saturday morning trips to the hardware store she and her father took when they lived in the same house. The eight-track player he'd let her play The Gambler, on repeat, was dark from years of her absence as DJ. She missed their weekends together when he lived in apartments, and hotel rooms after the divorce. Kristin welcomed her father's sporadic visits to her tennis matches, but his work schedule made his appearances hard to predict. This was what her heart longed for; time with him uninterrupted by her mother's siege.

"So, what are we doing today?" she asked.

"I thought we'd go back to the house first. Angela decorated a room for you, and I thought you'd want to meet her two daughters."

"My sisters, right?" she hesitated to apply such a foreign label.

"Technically, yes. You have two new sisters. Kate is the oldest one, she's four, I think. Kinsey will be three soon. They're sweet girls, like you. You'll be the big sister, so teach them well."

Arriving at Joe's house, Kristin delighted at the idea of having the large family she'd dreamt of. She noticed two tiny, towheads peering through the glass doorway as the lights of her father's truck illuminated the front stoop. One child in diapers, as Rosalyn predicted, and the other clutching a teddy bear.

An only child, she had few interactions with little ones. She channeled her favorite television mom from "Family Ties" and took the lead. "Hi, I'm Kristin. You must be Kinsey and Kate."

Shy, giggly responses relieved her, as the twin-like sisters led the way to the end of the dark, paneled hall. Her hands looked bleached against the wood-grained door when she twisted the scratched brass knob. A quaint bedroom invited her with the same décor Rosalyn had spent considerable funds removing from the former marital home. The dimmed lamp highlighted the latticed, white headboard of a twin bed. Delicate curtains matched a flowery patterned quilt and whispered in the gentle comfort of the ceiling fan, a mainstay in any Southerner's bedroom. Snow globes her father collected from traveling storm-stricken areas in need, adorned the inside shelves of a linen-painted chifforobe. Each served as a reminder to his idolizing child, she was on her father's mind. Stylish, multi-colored beads replaced the standard bifold closet doors and showcased new outfits hanging inside.

"I hope you like it," the new stepmother said. Her fuchsia-colored fingernails twisted blonde ribbons of one child's hair. "The girls helped me decorate."

As Angela stood in the doorway, young Kristin noticed the mother's eyelashes tapped the edges of layered bangs hiding her love of electric-blue eyeliner. The child mentally proclaimed allegiance to Rosalyn and tempered her full elation for a hung poster. "The Duke Boys! Cool."

Joe's smile spanned across his face. Giving a one-armed hug to his youthful wife, he said, "Well, you know Daddy had to have something in this 'flower power' room."

The diapered child presented a new teddy bear to her new stepsister. "For me?"

With a bounce of her flaxen curls, the toddler shrank deeper behind her mother's legs.

"He's so soft. I love his collared shirt. What's this say, 'Preppy Bear'?" Kristin held the plush gift close to her face. "How cute, he reminds me of Paddington. Do you remember those books, Daddy?" She hoped her childhood memories still mattered to him.

"Yep, that bear knew how to start trouble."

"Thank you, Kinsey. He'll sleep in my bed tonight, okay?"

"Okay."

The weekend brought expected adjustments for Kristin. She felt awkward seeing her father with a woman other than her mother, and uncomfortable, because it made her happy for him. Rosalyn's words rang in her ear, she'd remain diligent to monitoring this new union for anything unusual. Of note, her stepmother washed dishes balancing on one foot with the other perched onto her opposite thigh. While too frivolous for her mother, it still didn't seem like a deal breaker. A trip to the refrigerator for a Coca-Cola, exposed an unopened bag of pre-shredded cheese; she'd have to see how that played out. Overall, she struggled with what horrible things she would come up with to tell her mother when she returned home.

The morning started with church and ended with a family dinner before Kristin's dad drove her home. With a kiss on his cheek she said, "I love you, Daddy. I had a great time. I mean, really great."

His rugged chin tightened. "I love you too, Kris. I'll see you in two weekends, okay?"

She hopped out of his truck and gave the dented door a firm shove. Climbing the brick steps to the carport entry, her unbridled excitement of meeting his family stirred in her head. Rosalyn listened to the sultry sounds of her favorite crooner, which was her usual Sunday afternoon cleaning routine. The daydreaming child eased across the lemony linoleum kitchen floor. Each creak of the seventies-style ranch home's wooden floors announced her arrival.

From a small, quilted bench her mother stared through the picture window at her ex-husband's truck leaving the drive. "How was it?"

Immersed in the sounds of her father's rattling muffler fading away, her mother's question startled her into reality. "It was—okay. You know, weird. I missed you."

"I missed you too, dear." Rosalyn exchanged her feather duster for a freshly lit cigarette and quieted the music awaiting her daughter's report.

"Well, I'm just gonna hit the sack. Tired you know, little crumb snatchers don't sleep late."

Her mother's house smelled of fresh paint and wallpaper glue. She laid her bag on the mauve-and-blue comforter selected for her as part of the remodel. Her mother believed she needed to eliminate the flowery bedspread and move into grown up decor.

"Well, did you see anything?"

"We didn't eat potato salad, so I didn't notice if she was a Hellman's user."

Her mother smacked her lips together and widened her eyes.

Young Kristin's mind sifted through a joyful weekend, for one negative thing her mother could latch onto. "There was a bag of pre-shredded cheese in the fridge."

"I knew it! She's pure trash. Women, these days. They always go for the latest and greatest."

A wave of relief crept in; she was hopeful she'd get approval for a future visit.

"Anything else?"

"Not much." She returned the unopened sanitary napkins to the bathroom closet continuing her update from over her shoulder. "The girls are kind of annoy—"

Returning to her room, she froze seeing her mom at the bedside, holding her stepsister's gift. "What's this?"

"Just some lame toy." The child huffed. "Stupid right? I'm thirteen. Too old for teddy bears."

"Why didn't you return it to its rightful owner?"

"You wouldn't want me to be rude, would you?"

Rosalyn's crimson peaks shifted across her forehead. Studying the stitches that held the bear's playful, glass eyes intact she said, "It's a sign he still thinks of you as a little girl, Krissy."

"For sure. I'll just toss it in the back of my closet. Kill me if my friends see it."

"You're too old for toys."

As Kristin attempted to take the bear, her mother gripped the plush arm in her fist. "You don't want this reminder of how they are putting you down, do you?"

Rosalyn's voice grated through her clenched jaw.

"I said I'd hide it."

"You don't have to hide anything, dear. Let me handle this, Ma Kelly's way."

"Ma Kelly hasn't been here for a long time. Let me toss it under my bed."

Marching through, the other half of her dynamic duo slung the teddy bear on the dining room table. "Krissy, I'm aware my own mother is dead. I'm going to teach you how The Family handles an insult from a trashy woman."

The child accompanied her gift as clanging echoed in the kitchen. Running her fingers across the plush leg, she thought to herself, "But, the kid gave it to me."

Emerging with a pair of steel-handled scissors in her hand, the mother's face wore a rash-like pattern that engulfed throat and face. "Get me a bag from the pantry."

Kristin retrieved a paper sack embossed with a faded, red Piggly Wiggly logo and joined the assassination at the table. She watched the silver, sheared edge of her mother's weapon slide to the bottom of the bear's plump neck. With multiple pumps, the severed head plopped, jarring the bag out of the child's quivering hands. The assistant scrambled back into position.

Rosalyn continued to destroy the memento from Joe's home, snipping one appendage on each side of its torso. Then, with masterful precision, she trimmed the shirt, leaving the identifiable logo in place. "Let it serve as a reminder to the new wife; our Irish roots run deep."

The remaining scraps plummeted to the bottom, each with a jolting pop that sickened her child.

"Let's go," Rosalyn instructed.

Crimping the edges into a rolled handle, Kristin followed, wondering how she could stop this from getting worse.

With a fresh cigarette dangling from her lips, Rosalyn adjusted the gearshift of the white station wagon. After thirteen years of leaving their football-field-length driveway, Kristin knew her mother navigated reverse better than most people drove forward. The enraged ex-wife aimed her ambulance-shaped vehicle at the neighborhood road and stomped the gas.

Thick magnolias shadowed lingering, golden light from the father's home. The living room lamp filled the front window of the darkened porch. Rosalyn's headlights spanned over a tricycle lying in the front yard.

"They just moved here. How did you know where he lived?" the child asked.

"I have my ways. It's best for you not to know everything."

Desperate to normalize the moment for a fraction of rational thought to enter her mother's mind, her voice filled the car. "Ma! Please don't."

"Stay here."

The mother tiptoed through the grass with the ease of a serial killer. She glided over three steps to the front stoop where she delivered her signature 'return to sender' message. With the one-eared, one-eyed, severed head hung on the doorknob, she placed the makeshift body bag in the recipient's full view. Her delicate finger chimed the parcel's arrival, as she waltzed back to the wagon still running. The scent of a new cigarette meant the terror had ended. Kristin hoped the diapered stepsister was in bed.

"I can't believe you did that," the child shamed quietly.

"Oh, Krissy, you're just like your tenderhearted father. Weak."

"I'm sorry. It's just scary to think he's going to see that." Her voice cracked, stumbling for words that wouldn't infuriate her mother again.

"You're making this a bigger deal than it is. What's the worst that can happen?" she asked. "He'll get mad about it, and they'll have a little ruck tonight on my account."

"What if they think it was me?"

"So what? They can't eat you for supper."

Her father's truck did not pull down the driveway for several weekends to follow. Kristin tried re-establishing their relationship, but his responses lessened with time. She imagined it didn't take her stepmother long to remove the door poster and give her stepsister the bedroom. Rosalyn continued to intercept packages intended for her daughter. As a child, she watched her mother shred blouses, ruin sneakers, and burn professional family photographs in effigy of her father's memory. If a birthday card made its way through an ocean of changed addresses, she scrutinized postmarks for late mailing dates. All acts were for her benefit, her mother would tell her. Each done in the spirit of full transparency, so the child knew she was merely an afterthought to the man she called Daddy.

Chapter Two

The crunching gravel welcomed the driver home from each interminable commute. She drove on a winding path through thick loblolly pines and native rhododendrons barricading their sanctuary from the main road. Her somber mood lifted as the warm glow of their wraparound porch came into view. Even the handicap ramp was a part of their family's journey; she wasn't sure when her husband would take it down.

Spending an extra minute in the car, she gratefully embraced the end of another safe journey. Working from home gave her a week of no driving until the girls returned from Washington, DC. Although the trip hosted Olivia's fifth-grade classmates, Hutch offered to chaperone, and somehow convinced the school to allow her older sister to tag along. The mother appreciated his enthusiasm for a father–daughter opportunity and was a smidgeon relieved to share her chaperone duties.

The mother cleared her kids' road-trip snacks from the rear seats, wincing through a sharp punishment that radiated to her upper back.

I'll roll my shoulders more, next time.

While passing the warm hood of Grey's truck, a rolling growl served as a reminder she'd bailed on his family dinner. She floundered, balancing on the brick stoop while shuffling bags from arm to arm. As the door unlatched, Kristin's eyes narrowed hoping to glimpse her husband's mood before entering. With no sight of him, she heaved her things on the kitchen floor and ran back to close her car doors.

"It's just Mama," the woman said, surrounded by a pack of wagging tails.

Her husband's evening had concluded. Squeaking coils followed by a clinking glass announced he'd retired to his chair in the living room. Self-medicating his irritation had become routine. His resentment crept over her like the exhaust from an old truck.

Taking her shoes off for the first time all day, the stone tiles felt as cold as his shoulder. She drug her travel cooler across the kitchen to the pantry. "I know you were counting on me to be there to say goodbye to Wey, but traffic was a nightmare." Her voice gave way, pushing through the sinking feeling in her chest. "I'm sure it was nice; they usually have a good house salad."

Iced shuffles filled the room as she immersed herself in the chest freezer to sift through weeks of premade meals. Mondays had become her time to plan and create days' worth of healthy dinners for both Grey and the girls. She said it made her feel motherly when Olivia enjoyed a homemade, modified, sugar-free brownie instead of the gas station pre-packaged one. It was a small gesture to help ease her mind during their hectic schedule.

She emerged with two tin loaf pans in her hands and stomped into the living room where her husband studied his phone. Shaking the pans, she tilted her head at him, "You didn't eat the chicken pot pie?" she asked. "Or, the meatloaf? You love my meatloaf."

Grey cleared his throat. "I didn't feel like cooking," he said. His voice was still gravelly.

"*I* cooked it."

The steel in her husband's eyes replaced his usual variant of oak and fern. "I didn't feel like eating it, I guess."

With a huff, she returned the pans to the pantry. She grunted, pushing the lid of the freezer with her frigid hands. Her fingers slipped out from under the door handle, popping her already tender tips across her palms. She leaned on the top and pulled at her bottom lip with her teeth.

With a deep breath, the wife returned to the living room. "Can you open the freezer for me? It's sealed shut again."

Her husband sat still; she wondered if he heard her. With ease, he rested his phone on the side table next to his leather recliner followed by a two-handed pat on his dark denim. Standing to meet his wife in the kitchen he asked, "Why was traffic heavy? Was there a wreck?"

"No, just a lot of rain. There were semi-trucks everywhere. I felt like I should have taken the boat instead of my van."

Grey shoved the lid open, using the heels of both hands.

"Thank you," she said.

"Okay."

Using the back of her hand, she wiped her brow to resume placing the medical ice packs in the deep freezer. "It's just that, I make the meals, so it feels like I'm here."

"But you're *not*. Even when you are, you're consumed with planning your next trip."

"It takes a lot to coordinate."

"Oh, I know." Pacing in the kitchen, he looked to the ceiling while he counted on his fingers. "Planning for gas, groceries for two places, and the perfect kid-to-snack ratio for the car ride. It's a full-time job."

"Olivia has dietary needs. I can't just throw a Slim Jim at her."

"I give her the shots too." His tone strengthened. "I fully understand *our* daughter has diabetes."

"Then, you understand dosing for high-sugar snacks in the car means stopping for an extra insulin shot. Her endocrinologist says Liv can get a pump once she's out of the honeymoon phase, remember? That's when her pancreas completely stops making its own insulin." The wife looked down at the hardwood floors dusted with Champ's gold and silver fluffs after her husband's no-housework weekend. "We're still adjusting to the diagnosis. The low-carb meals help keep things simple; planning them takes time."

"I understand that, I do."

"This is hard on all of us—"

"You say that like I haven't watched you drive the kids every weekend for eight years. First it was halfway to Birmingham. Now, it's halfway to Miami. If there's a Camek family event, within a sixty-mile radius, your van is on the road," he said, turning his palms to the ceiling. "Even when I got laid off from my job, you left me here, alone, at my lowest. No meatloaf can make that better."

"Don't give me a pity party." Standing with crossed arms, she scrunched her face. "Audrie said your brother was with you the entire weekend. When the corporate rat race ended for you, he celebrated." Her eyes widened, "She came over too, and the three of you planned the store's new layout, remember?"

"I think we know Higgs would have handed the keys to a talking monkey, by that point. He's not known for his people skills."

Both chuckled.

"Yeah, his wife was glad he still had a job, when you came on full time," Kristin said.

"Well, that's because we all know the store would crumble without Audrie. She'd never forgive me if I fired her husband."

Grey's wife stood in the pantry doorway with her foot turned inward.

"I just miss you," he said.

"I miss you, too."

"And it infuriates me to see Hutch take advantage of you."

The couple walked into the laundry room where her husband helped unpack the girls' overnight bags. "Careful," she said. "Those are their clothes from his home, and these are from ours." Mixing wardrobes between households was the cardinal sin of divorced parents.

"Tell me, again, why you had to meet him this weekend. Aren't they going on a field trip with the school?"

"He wanted to fly them to Washington, DC, to meet the class."

"Why couldn't they just ride the bus, like all the other kids?"

She shrugged and continued to unravel socks from the depths of cuffed, skinny jeans. "He said he wanted them to spend time with his family before going."

"It's a rite of passage for fifth-graders to do a final school field trip together. Who does he think he is?"

"He says he's letting them ride home." She shook her head hearing herself rationalize her ex-husband's motives again. "It's his money; what do we care?"

"Have you talked to Tom? What does he say?"

"For $250 an hour, Tom says he's not my therapist," she

said. "I'll call him when I need legal advice, not a bestie."

"The sooner you can get on his calendar, the better. Hutch chose to move to another state for money. You're not obligated to make him feel less guilty."

"I don't—," she stopped, feeling her heart rate climb again as her fists clutched a striped t-shirt. She didn't want to end the evening this way. She took a deep breath and stared into the basin of the washer. "If all that stands in the way of their relationship is my comfort, I can deal with it for a few more weeks. And I suggest you find a way, too."

The washing machine lid clanged shut.

"Honey, your situation has changed since the girls were two and four."

"We're humans, G, not lamps. Of course, our circumstances change. Our parenting plan allows for adjustments."

"His salary has skyrocketed since then." Grey followed her to the living room, calculating. "He was already a trust fund baby, but somehow he pays the same amount for two kids that I pay for one, how's that fair?"

"So, you want me to take him to court every time one of us gets a raise?" she asked, throwing her hands in the air. "Besides, he's away from his kids 180 days out of the year. It's not like he's getting a coupon."

"You're away from them, too. Don't forget what you sacrifice."

Grey returned to his chair and resumed scrolling his phone. His wife made her way to their bedroom. She could feel the tension in her neck loosen knowing the conversation was over until another day. Clean laundry, piled on her side of the bed, greeted her when she flipped the light switch in the master suite.

She knew this wasn't the gig he signed up for.

They met at a cookout his sister-in-law hosted for fellow

coworkers. Kristin worked night shifts to supplement her single parent income; Vy was a unit secretary and a notorious busybody. His recent divorce made her brother-in-law her next project. A usual occurrence, Hutch made a last-minute cancellation for his parenting time, leaving two elementary-aged children in tow on their mother's blind date.

When Grey told the story, he claimed loving his future wife the minute he saw her with the girls. He was learning to navigate the roads of being an every-other-weekend dad to Browning while managing a high-pressure corporate position. The two hit it off and vowed to never give their sister-in-law the matchmaking credit she craved.

After leaving a chaotic first marriage, he felt comforted by Kristin's traditional values. The family routines she learned from her father were the ones Grey experienced during years spent on his grandparents' farm. Home-cooked dinners, family time in the evenings, and nightly rituals all resonated with him. Back then, bedtime stories followed warm baths, and each night ended with sweet kisses on foreheads. Her determination to establish a new life inspired him. He considered his wife's willingness to move home, after twenty years away, as evidence of her humility. A mother's creativity made children giggle and warmed his reserved heart. Over time, the man trusted again and stepped into the role of a loving stepfather.

Now, the qualities he used to celebrate in his wife seemed to grate him. Time spent decoding legal jargon to unveil her custodial rights, replaced actual parenting. Late-night runs to and from state lines scattered methodical bedtime routines. She didn't blame him if he questioned his place in her new life.

It had been months since their last getaway. She would settle for a simple child-free weekend again. They used to alternate activities—his choice and hers. Grey made her go to the hardware stores.

He'd joke, "No complaints."

They enjoyed listening to songs from their high school years and reminiscing over simpler days. It wasn't anything extraordinary, but it was time together and she missed it too.

Being a divorced mother was a noose around her neck. With each question he asked, she felt him ratcheting the tension. The exhausted wife was relieved to be out of the range for failed relationships within five years of a second marriage. But, with only 33% of them surviving the lifetime odds, she knew she needed to get the "his and her" weekends back on the calendar. Complicated factors around children from previous relationships seemed to be the biggest stressor of those attempting love again.

With the final clasp of the wardrobe door, Kristin decided to make a quick call to her daughters before she laid down. The school's itinerary said campers should be able to contact them in their hotel rooms after nine o'clock. Settling into the oversized chair in the corner of her bedroom, she selected Lennon's contact first. Ringtones cycled with no answer which had been the theme for her eldest child on her weekends with Dad. After experiencing the same response from Olivia's phone, she texted Hutch.

Kristin: Are the girls avail?

Just as her eyes closed, the phone rang with Hutch's caller ID on her phone.

Twice in one day, what did I do to deserve this?

"Hello."

"Hi," a gentle voice said.

"Hi, Livvy," she said, with relief hearing her ten-year-old answer. "How was the flight?"

"Gooood," Olivia lingered.

"Where's Leonard?" The mother attempted to draw a giggle by using the nickname for Olivia's sister, which they both knew she hated. "I tried to call her first."

"She's...busy."

"Okay, well tell her I love her," Kristin paused. "Why d'you call from Dad's phone? Did you lose yours already?"

"It's charging. Dead battery."

"Well charge up, Buttercup. I see a lot of walking between sites on the agenda." The mother probed her child as she dismissed the student's lack of enthusiasm on a long travel day. "Are you excited to see anything in particular?"

"I guess the Smithsonian."

"There's so many. Which one?"

"The natural history one, I think. The dinosaurs look cool."

"The coolest. Remember the fossils Mama found?"

"Yeah!"

"My dream was to have them on display at the Smithsonian, but that didn't happen."

Olivia snickered. "True. I doubt there'll be anything with your name on it. How are you doing?"

"Well, aren't you *thoughtful* to ask?" Kristin reinforced empathy with both girls at every opportunity. Emotional intelligence was a key leadership skill she wanted them to possess. "End of year exams, for my students, have kept me busy, but it makes the day go by fast."

"Do you think you'll ever go back to the hospital to work? You know, now that we're older."

"Well, I haven't thought about it." The mother stumbled for an answer to her daughter's surprising question. "I loved my job at the hospital, but it was time for a change."

"A change?"

"Nursing is a physical job. When I was five months pregnant with you, a confused patient kicked me in the stomach while I helped him move onto the CAT scan table."

"What? Was I hurt?" Olivia's voice tipped.

"No, you were fine."

"Why would anyone kick a pregnant woman with a cat?"

Kristin muffled her amusement. "His disease made him confused. It comes with the job. Anyway, I went to the OBGYN."

"O-What?"

"The baby doctor. She did scans on you the next day and said you were still swimming around in there."

The child giggled. "I bet I was cute."

"The cutest," she said, obliging with a forced compliment. "That incident and working twelve-hour shifts made me consider a job change. Leaving the house when Lennon was asleep and getting home when she was in bed was tough on a new mother."

"She still sleeps a lot. She's lazy."

"It wasn't long after that I started teaching nursing students. Working from home let me have more time with my giggly baby."

"But we're growing up."

"That's for sure," the mother paused. "Right now, I'm happy. I like teaching and these are parents going back to school, improving their lives. I like being a part of that."

"I just want to make sure Mama has something to do when we're gone."

"Gone?" Kristin asked. "Is this the way you tell me you're joining the circus? I knew the day would come."

"No circus," Olivia giggled. "You know, college and stuff."

"Oh, *that* day." Kristin held the phone to her face, while she loosened her hair tie with the other. Her strands fell on her shoulders like maple leaves in late fall. "You mean when you're away at nursing school."

"Really, Mama?"

"It's a flexible career, is all I'm saying."

"Well, I better go. We have to get up early for another long day of walking through boring museums," the child said through a long sigh. "I love you."

"I love you, Livvy. Say hi to the President for me."

Chapter Three

Removing her headset, she untangled black wires twisted at the base of her crimson bun. The squeal of a neon highlighter striking through another course topic signaled a break in her workday. Her fingers massaged the bridge of her nose, relieving pressure from pinching eyeglasses. She rolled her neck after another restless night of positioning achy muscles in the right spot.

The desktop buzzed under her phone.

Remind Message: Parents, we're running about 40 minutes behind schedule.

Another text rushed in behind the school's which she recognized as the recently relabeled name for Hutch, "Just Breathe." Kristin smirked. Her therapist would be pleased to see her using visual cues to rein in her emotions when dealing with him.

Just Breathe: Running late.

Kristin: Okay.

Just Breathe: Okay to take the girls to my mom's tonight? She'd like to see them before I go back.

Kristin: Not today. I'll get them to her soon, though.

Just Breathe: The church youth director is at her house. She hasn't seen them since their days at vacation bible school when they were little. It would mean a lot to Mom.

She rolled her eyes. *Why does he complicate everything?*

Just Breathe: Want to talk?

Kristin: No. Fine. Get them to the house early tomorrow.

Just Breathe: Rosemary will bring them. Thx.

With her head supported by her fingertips, she looked to her loyal office partner curled at her feet. "Grey will say I caved again, won't he, Champ?" His white muzzle and doe-like eyes looked up to her. "I'll remind him I'm home this weekend. That may help ease the blow." The dog lover patted her old friend, sensing he understood her predicament, torn between loyalty and instinct.

Tonight, she'd overlook another iced response to her leniency, understanding her husband's frustration stemmed from feeling helpless in the solution. Kristin knew it was difficult for him to sit back and watch her shuttle kids like a pack mule. She tired of carrying the load, too.

Guilt for following her mother's example of failed marriages was her penance; her abhorrence of her mother's cruelty was the emotional bolt in her ex-husband's wrench. Hutch leveraged his knowledge of her scarred childhood pushing her to the brink of every ledge she stood on. She was punished for not being a devoted wife to him, despite her own misery when she was. Kristin's fear of becoming a bitter divorcee overshadowed her truth, and he delighted in pulling the cloak for her.

After the divorce, she tried forming a united front with

the father of her children. Self-help books touted successful co-parenting required a level of cohesiveness; however, her attempts became an open invitation for her ex-husband to poke holes in her psyche. Every interaction left the mother sorting through copious accounts of her inadequacies. Seeking her legal partner's permission felt like searching for the center of a Tootsie Pop for a simple, "Yes, No, or Maybe." Collaboration on the kids' activities was a forum for his plight against Ellington's lacking resources. A simple communication informing him of an ill child turned into relentless reminders she was a washed-up ICU nurse with a mediocre affinity for teaching at best. Partnership invited ridicule. Her whipping post was trusting he'd change after the next pay raise, insult, or marriage.

Information was shared in a written format, per Hutch's demand. He filled the screen with personal opinions of his ex-wife, ripping her self-worth with each keystroke. If she received an actual phone call, his tone waivered from corporate professional to the seething sounds of Gollum with every door creak. Scathing rolls of whispered insults regulated his stern monologues, depending on the audience. Her moral ground governed the information she shared with the children. The mother believed, in time, they would see it for themselves.

His campaign against her was subtle with the girls, at least when she stayed close. On nightly video chats, she cringed hearing him dismiss shared adventures from school or home. If a dreary day allowed them time for a mother–daughter activity, he'd end their sentence for them. Olivia was a school athlete, but the outcomes of her games were insignificant compared to those of his son's that he coached. Lennon was an accomplished musician, but the similarities to her mother were more than the father could tolerate. He wove her achievements into a web he could boast ownership of. Kristin listened to him steal the spotlight for years, paying no attention to life outside of his reach.

A few years after their divorce, he tired of living a bachelor's life and asked Kristin to reunite their family. Offers for a new home, new cars, and a fresh start with a changed man enticed her, but he drew her in with a promise to restore peace to their relationship. Unpacking her suitcase at his home meant the demeaning, underhanded comments had ceased. Dignity gifted back to her in exchange for living the life he wanted her to live. But she knew the calm would be fleeting.

At gala events, she'd return to masking her anxiety with a pretentious smile as she excused herself to purge sampled appetizers. She'd hope her supple cheeks hid the cracked edges of her lips while she wrenched her hands to cover blistered knuckles. Her protruding collarbones would be softened by bold jewelry and no one would know her menstrual cycle had been absent for months.

He'd insist she resume tennis lessons, so she didn't embarrass him at doubles matches. Luncheons with potential client's wives would replace volunteering at the diabetes clinic followed by obsessive running to negate the calories. But she'd have full discretion when selecting an au pair. Caring for their daughters never interfered with her more visible responsibilities as his wife. In the end, she knew it was a pitch to trade one hell for the other. When she refused his offer, he vowed to make her regret it.

For a decade, she resisted his attempts to provoke the villain she'd abandoned in that Piggly Wiggly sack on her father's porch. Anyone who knew the Camek girls would justify her actions. They didn't fit society's mold for children of divorce. These girls differed from other friends caught in a crossfire of high conflict and egos. Most children want both parents in one home, but that wasn't a gift she could offer.

Therefore, her commitment lay in creating a success story for other blended families to model.

For now, they appeared to overlook his undermining seep of insecurity, but the mother feared their tiny taste buds were acclimating to his slow-burning pot of hatred. And, she wondered how long before they showed interest in the brand of mayonnaise she used.

***

Late spring mornings on the front porch offered her a meditative reservoir to tap into during phone conversations with her mother. When the serene background noise sparked a rant from the former UMass grad on how much she missed Boston's conveniences, the daughter could lose herself in the pond ripples left by dipping thrashers. In the eighties, after her parents divorced, she expected her mother would move them to the birthplace she pined for. Rosalyn surprised most by staying in the slower-paced South and keeping her married moniker, Irvine. Both things she loved to criticize.

The sharp inhale from the other line indicated she hadn't quit smoking, like she'd told her daughter. "How many more weekends will you give up, Krissy?"

"I'm complying with our original agreement. He's had the girls every weekend since we divorced. We agreed, since he traveled with work, they would go to school from my house."

"I remember. You were too generous then, as well. The concern is, now, you're not meeting him halfway to Birmingham. You're driving to another state."

"It's temporary. The school year ends in a few weeks. If he hasn't done anything by the time the girls go to his house for summer break, I'll go to my attorney."

"The chubby one that lost Grey's case against

Browning's mother. What will he do?"

"First, he didn't lose, it was a shady judge—"

"Define shady," Rosalyn said, through a forced exhale.

"And he'll write a new parenting plan that works for out-of-state households." Her jaw clenched giving the explanation.

"I'm with Grey!"

"Are we choosing sides?"

"I'm on your side. But I agree with his family, this arrangement has gone on long enough."

"Do I want to know what you say to my in-laws?"

"Most days, your life is not that exciting, but this topic piqued interest at dinner the other night. The soldier left for his assignment, you know. Pity you couldn't make it."

"You went to Weyman's going away party?"

"Certainly. Vy invited, and I accepted. You never know, dear. This could be the end of 'Wey-vy.' " Rosalyn's drag lingered in the dramatic pause.

"I didn't realize you spoke Yiddish."

"No, '*Wey*-vy.' You know, the couple that are really one—they're enmeshed."

"That doesn't work for them, but yes. Weyman and Vy will be apart for six months, which won't phase her. She's a self-proclaimed, military brat."

"Do tell, dear."

"She made him quit his job at the rec center. He loved refereeing basketball games, but Vy wanted those government benefits. As soon as Wey zipped his fatigues, she was at the commissary with her mother, reliving her childhood."

"Well, he is going to Europe, it's volatile there."

"He's a healthcare specialist stationed at an army base in Germany. Wey has a better chance of getting a hangover at Oktoberfest than dying on this assignment." Kristin grimaced hearing the crass words leave her lips. Her mother had a way of teasing the malicious side in everyone.

"Spoken like a true Kelly." Rosalyn gave pause to her family's name. "Nonetheless, the Murphy kids are quite concerned. We all agree, Hutch is using Olivia's diagnosis to make you feel guilty. He knows you'd never sacrifice their well-being for your own."

"That may be true. I just have to do what I think is best, no offense."

"Please," the mother dismissed. "I'm just saying, he didn't have to move to Miami. He was quite successful living close to his daughters, he could have waited until they were older."

"He has a new family he has to consider, and we didn't have a clause about moving in our divorce papers," she said. "Peyton was raised in that area, she was somewhat of a local celebrity. Maybe she wants to resume her career again, too."

"As a cheerleader?"

"She cheered at the University of Miami, as a student. After that I think she did some modeling and television ads. Olivia says she lets the little ones dress up with her beauty pageant crown.

"Just like your father, sacrificing a relationship with his children for a woman, ten years his junior," said Rosalyn. "He's trash."

"You realize, I'm ten years younger than him, right?"

"Well, she's certainly younger than you, her skin is flawless."

Kristin shook her head. "They're good for each other. The kids say he's home more and he helps with the twins who'll start elementary school soon."

"You shouldn't have to guess. His move affected your kids' lives, these are things parents talk about. It requires more than an email notice."

"He would never ask my permission."

"It's not about permission, it's about respecting the other parent."

"Well, that's not something he can find a lot of, I'm afraid. So, we speculate."

"Continue to make excuses for him if you want. He's the one who chased prestige over parenting. His daughters live here, not in some beach town. What about his poor mother, left here alone? Ronny—"

"Rosemary."

"Rose-*mary*," she said. "Boy, don't you go out of your way to keep her involved with her granddaughters?"

"I know she's lonely, her only child living so far away."

"And she never remarried after her husband passed? A work accident, wasn't it?"

"Yes. He was head of sales for a chemical company. His team was demoing a new product on a construction site when a beam fell from one of the structures. Hutch said it killed his dad and another man, I think."

"And he was young, you said?" Rosalyn asked.

"Thirteen or fourteen. Close to Lennon's age."

"My heart aches for his widow. I couldn't imagine telling you your father had died."

"You would've worn red to his funeral."

"False, my dear. If two people share a child, they're never completely divorced. I would have grieved for your loss, and my own."

"I don't think Hutch ever got over it. Rosemary said he took his job seriously as 'man-of-the-house' after that day. He was determined to be the successful businessman, loving husband, and provider like his dad. I know she misses her son and the girls, which is why I try to take them to her family things. Besides, grandmothers are important; I never got to see mine."

"*I'd* like to see my grands more, if you're asking."

"They bake cookies with her," she said, tempering her words. "That's not exactly your specialty."

After a sharp flick and a strong pull, Rosalyn coughed. "Let me know when they can learn how to make a Tom Collins." The two women chuckled. "If Hutch wants to follow in his father's footsteps, why didn't he stay close to his family?"

"Ellington isn't the right fit for him. He moved home once before when he was struggling to make ends meet."

"I'm sure the settlement was substantial; I thought he was a silver-spoon-fed only child."

"It was a large amount. I don't recall the actual figure, but it paid for his boarding school tuition and their home. Rosemary never had to work a day of her married life; Kirby had his affairs in order."

"So, he blew it all away?" Rosalyn asked.

"No, nothing like that. Rosemary told me he met a woman a few years older than him, not long after he started college. Her dad was a financial planner with a local branch under his management, and Hutch was eager to learn the ropes of trading stocks. She convinced him to drop out of college and apprentice with her father, which lit Hutch's fire for the rich life. Problem was, it takes time to become a licensed advisor and build a book of business. Girlfriend was ready to have the lifestyle her parents enjoyed. Rosemary said Hutch mentored at the office during the day and bartended at night, but the girl's impatience only made things more difficult. He was young and eager for independence; we all learn lessons in our twenties," she said. "After girlfriend almost bankrupted him, she left, and he had to move home."

"Fascinating," Rosalyn hummed.

"It was the best thing for him though. He finished college, paid off the debt she'd left him with, and climbed his way right to the top. Lennon gets a lot of her determination from him. It took a little time for his goals to gain traction, but he was destined to have an accomplished life. I just think he regretted his father dying before he could prove his full potential."

"It's an interesting theory, but I think we know where Lennon gets her ferocity," the grandmother said. "Well, your in-laws are all filled with concern. Especially that precious girl with the long black hair. She says you've become quite close."

"Audrie."

"Yes, her daughter was there, sweet girl. Looks like our Livvy," Rosalyn said. "But, her dad was, you know, off to the war in his head, I guess."

"Ma!" Kristin gasped. "He was diagnosed with PTSD after two Gulf War tours."

"I'm just saying he wasn't there, but..." The mother retracted. "Audrie doesn't seem to mind representing his interests at family gatherings."

The daughter's feelings remained tender. "She understands I'm in this for the girls' sake."

"Her story is something, isn't it? Talk about a survivor," she said. "That first husband of hers was a real POS."

"Audrie talked to you about that?"

"It may surprise you to know other people, besides my daughter, find me to be a good listener."

Kristin gave a thin lipped smile to a butterfly fluttering across the railing.

"It sounds like those meth-heads did to him, what she only wanted to," she said with a puff. "Hm...I can't remember if she ever mentioned going to the funeral."

"Well, Mother I'm glad you had a nice time."

"Yes, I really did. It was delightful to see Ches again. Twila, too."

"Ches?"

"Grey's father, did I get his name wrong, too?"

"No, you're right. I'm just surprised he made it," she said. Her forehead creased counting the months since she'd seen her father-in-law.

"Tall fellow, I see where the sons get it."

"I'm fairly certain they all hate me right now."

"Hate is a strong word, Krissy. They just think you're walking over your husband, their brother and son, so you don't have to confront your ex." The mother's voice strained.

Her nurse assessment skills recognized it to be a grunt of a smoker reaching to snuff out a smoke in a nearby ashtray. "Well, that's specific feedback, Roz."

"Just deal with this dip. You're the mother, what can he do?"

"It's not the eighties anymore."

"Suit yourself."

The two women discussed the grandchildren's expected return home from the school field trip. Although she was positioned in her usual spot overlooking the pond she decided to skip telling her mother she allowed the girls an extra night with their dad; even dipping thrashers wouldn't bring Zen to that conversation.

After the call ended, she rocked on the porch taking a minute to decompress. Their relationship was complicated, she'd admit, but nothing like the one her husband had with his father. Or, could it be they were both accustomed to their own line of misguided advisors? Both husband and wife floated through life's stages on sole motivation of proving both dominating parents wrong.

She remembered the first time she met her father-in-law when she and Grey returned from their honeymoon. Ches had been a no-show at the wedding. Touting a 52-year marriage to Grey's mother, his lack of enthusiasm for their second union came as no surprise. Eventually, he and his wife, Twila, graced the newlyweds with a postnuptial dinner.

That night the former high school quarterback commanded the group's attention from the head of the table. Ches's long arms spanned the corners with his emphatic accounts from the football field to the battlefield. He boasted his self-made success story: a war-torn infantryman started his freshman year at the University of Alabama, and became a walk-on, tight end for the beloved Bear Bryant, a story that drew a few "Roll Tides" from eavesdropping fans at other tables.

Despite his father's sometimes violent disapproval, Ches stayed his course of leaving the Murphy lineage of row croppers in the dirt their tractors tilled. A four-year business degree was the young entrepreneur's first step toward career success miles from the fields he plowed as a child. His tone touched on regret admitting his father never attended a game; his new daughter-in-law believed that upset him more than Pops missing his graduation.

She couldn't remember Twila saying anything during the dinner, other than the standard pleasantries. Her husband's replay of their love story merely drew a forced smile. He, the recognizable athlete on campus. Twila, the demure office clerk who helped him order his cap and gown. It was love at first sight, according to Ches, although his story contrasted Grey's version. His account included a future Weyman making a surprise appearance in the young undergrads' budding relationship and ended with a sharp ultimatum from Twila's father. Kristin reminded herself the patriarch was storytelling, not writing a memoir. Regardless of all the details of their courtship, she gave her mother- and father-in-law much-deserved credit for staying together for over five decades.

Ches became the owner and CEO of a local software company, which he traveled the world promoting while his wife raised their three sons. Kristin found it ironic his wealth accumulated from years spent price gouging charitable organizations for computer programs, all in the name of helping the less fortunate. When Grey, the youngest son, was in his senior year of high school, the father relinquished his executive chair, vowing to contribute as owner while he eased into retirement. He still eased. She'd seen his truck at the office just last week. A mint condition, indigo blue, vintage Ford Bronco with offset Mickey Thompson's; it was hard to miss.

He steered the conversation like a Ferrari, sharing embellished memories of being a devoted father on the fields of his sons' athletic events. She suppressed the urge to arch an eyebrow when his eyes welled, sharing the pride he felt on the gridiron with his sons, who relied on his expertise. One of the best inside jokes running the brothers' conversations, was Dad's slurred game-time speeches which sounded closer to a John McEnroe outburst than a Vince Lombardi half-time huddle. The Murphy sons' unwavering loyalty to their father's complex parenting style remained a mystery to her.

One instance, she remembered, piqued Twila's attention: Offering an anecdote to his unorthodox coaching methods Ches commented, "Sometimes you got to piss a kid off to get him to do what you want."

Twila clenched her jaw and narrowed her eyes at her husband's statement, which snared her husband from his raucous laughter. Kristin watched her father-in-law's forehead flush through to the harvest oak edges of his receded hairline. His wife's visible disapproval was stifled by his returned glare.

The knit and purls of the veteran couple's display was familiar to the newest member of the family. An audacious husband restrained his response in public, but his wife's humdrum reaction would likely bring chastising behind closed doors. Kristin knew how these men destroyed their wives without raising a hand. Syllables hid bruises and maintained their illusion of an agreeable union. Secretly, she wondered how long they were together when Mrs. Murphy earned her own bedroom?

After eight years, Kristin had found her place in the Murphy family's pecking order which seemed to rise and fall with Ches's opinion. When her trips to the Alabama-Florida state line started, she noticed her father-in-law distancing himself from her and his son. He seemed to forget she arrived at the hospital before any other family member after his emergent open-heart surgery. The former athlete no longer asked about her personal best matches, nor did he brag regarding his latest handicap.

He vocalized his stance on several occasions. "There are no mulligans in marriage."

She had to assume he believed this life on the road was her punishment for not sleeping on the couch when things got bad. The inconvenient hell she lived was petty compared to the suffering her children endured. She knew he placed her a few rungs below Grey's mother, who still delivered homemade pear cobblers to her sons every Sunday. If Ches resented her for making his son cook his own chicken pot pies, how could she blame him?

Chapter Four

The evening passed as the wife predicted. Grey left for the store before daylight, again. She sipped her coffee on the porch, wiping the tears of yet another argument from her cheeks. A buzz from her phone startled her from watching the sun crest the pines.

Just Breathe: We need to talk.

Kristin: Shoot.

Just Breathe: No, we should meet for this. The girls are okay.

Kristin's stomach churned reading Hutch's demand.

Why would he want to meet in person? If he were terminally ill, he'd make his doctor dictate his prognosis in an email.

With her back straight, she moved to the edge of her chair. Her response stalled as she recalled several bombshell moments since their divorce, each communicated by email or text.

His grandmother's death. Olivia's interest in a girl at church. The terms of our divorce. Why is this different?

Kristin: Why?

Just Breathe: This is big.

Kristin: Come by the house. I'm working today.

Just Breathe: No, we should be somewhere neutral.

Kristin flung the screen door open and marched inside. She paced in the living room, clasping the phone in her hand. Repeating the "gray-rock" mantra her therapist recommended.

Be boring, bland, calm. Be boring, bland, calm.

Placing her hands on the desktop, with eyes closed tight, she filled her chest with air and imagined herself blowing the flickering wick of a birthday candle.

She returned to her text conversation.

Kristin: Are you ill?

Just Breathe: No. I need to talk to you before I leave for Florida today.

Kristin's office chair squeaked as she leaned against the seatback. Her glasses reflected the warm-up screens from her monitor. Hutch's insults to her character, worthiness, and parenting skills, all delivered when he couldn't see the whites of her eyes. She bit her lip and leaned in as the home screen appeared.

She heard a knock from the carport door, followed by Audrie's voice. "Anybody home?"

"In here." Feverish tapping made her location known. When her visitor stepped in the doorway, she asked, "What'd Grey forget?"

"The keys to the storage sheds. He asked me to come by on my way to the store. You look serious."

"Hutch. He's up to something." Fixated on the monitor, she continued to type. "The keys are hanging on the keyring next to the pantry."

Just Breathe: R U there?

Audrie looked toward the vibration coming from the desk. With creased eyebrows, she asked "What does he want now?"

"To meet with me. In private." Kristin peered over her glasses.

"Is he dying?"

"That's what I'm looking up."

"Can't you ask him, 'Are you dying?'"

"I asked. It's not that."

"Co-parenting shouldn't be this hard. A real father wouldn't have time for these games."

"There, I'm in," she said, sliding her glasses into position.

"In what?"

"Peyton's Instagram profile."

"Hutch's wife, Peyton?" Audrie leaned in over her sister-in-law's shoulder. "You're looking for clues about your ex-husband's imminent death on his wife's Instagram page?"

"She's an influencer. If something happened in their household, she'll blab about it to her fans." The mouse wheel clicked, each roll rotated images of Peyton and Hutch's life together.

"I can't believe she lets you follow her," Audrie said. "No offense."

"She doesn't. I blocked her. This is Mom's account."

"Does Roz know you're logged in as Roz?"

"It's fine. She never gets on Insta. Peyton has thousands of followers, she's a big deal."

"Why snub the stepmom?"

"Anytime I'd disagree with one of Hutch's outlandish requests, his wife would post a not-so-subtle meme."

"A meme?"

"Yeah, about how daughters need their fathers or

infringing stepparents' rights."

"She knows there're funnier memes, right?"

Kristin adjusted her hunched posture. "Yeah, like the one about how her husband's ex stalked her."

"Well . . ."

"She's a *public* figure." With a shake of her head, Kristin's shoulders rounded over the keyboard again. "Anyways, I had enough when she started adding clever hashtags to pictures of Len and Liv. She'd say, '#likemomlikedaughter' or '#bonusmomsrule.' She tried taunting me, so I blocked her."

"Passive-aggressive much?"

She questioned which one of Hutch's wives her sister in law's comment referred to. "It wasn't worth risking 'the Roz' slipping out of me online."

"Is that her?" Audrie pushed her thick, black hair around her ears and leaned closer.

Her sister-in-law stayed silent.

"Quite the spectacle."

"All for the 'Gram', right?" Kristin's response was as blank as her face staring at the signature photograph of her children's stepmother. The endless reach of the woman's white breeches, tucked inside black jodhpurs, straddled the gunmetal girth of a blue roan mare. With her shoulders relaxed and spine straight, 14 karat gold waves fell across the shoulders of her black riding jacket. Holding a velvet cap and leather whip in one hand, the reins in the other, her effortless smile was dimmed only by her piercing eyes. A tropical colored banner, strung between two palm trees, announced her completion of a USDF competition."

"Why is that horse wearing a hat?" Audrie asked.

"It's dressage," she said, noting her sister-in-law's raised eyebrow. "It's an equestrian competition. The outfits are part of the rules."

"So, she's gorgeous, rich, and rides horses with hats. Some girls just have it all," said Audrie.

"Her parents have a horse breeding operation in Central Florida."

"And you know about them because ..."

Kristin returned to studying the photo. "She's an influ—,"

"Do you think she uses that whip on Hutch?" Both women chuckled. And Kristin almost forgot Hutch was awaiting her reply. She returned to her investigation.

The only sign of exertion the formal model displayed was her rose-hued cheeks. A full mouth of blinding-white teeth encapsulated her brilliant joy only to be outmatched by the dainty pink ribbon pinned to her horse's bridle. The center read, *Baby on Board.*

"Pregnant?" Audrie's mouth dropped. "Is that even safe?"

"This woman rode before she walked. And dressage is kind of like ballet for horses. I'm sure she's fine to ride in her first trimester."

"But pregnant? How old is your ex again?

"52."

"So, let me get this straight," said Audrie, flopping into an oversized chair in the corner of the room. On her fingers, she counted. "He has two daughters with you. Twins with Peyton and another one on the way?" she paused, looking at Kristin. "That's a packed house."

"It could be another set of twins."

"Now, that's a reality show."

"Maybe *that's* why he wants to talk to me."

"Yeah, he probably needs a pale redheaded ex-wife to make a guest appearance," Audrie said, giving her sister-in-law a thin-lipped smile.

Leaning back into the chair, Kristin said, "No, really. Maybe he's worried the girls are having a hard time with things. Think about it, the dodgy teenager."

"Not really a shocker, there. I mean she's thirteen."

"The ten-year-old's concern about her mother's future career plans."

"Olivia's a sage."

"Maybe he just wants to talk about things. You know, make sure we're on the same page on how to handle any questions the girls may have," said the ex-wife.

"You think he wants your opinion on how the girls feel about another sibling? That would be a stretch for him."

"I don't understand what he wants from me. I've done everything he's asked me to do since he moved to Florida." Kristin sifted through any possible angle that would give her the upper hand. The last thing she wanted was to give him the satisfaction of dropping a bomb on her. "Something was off when he called me the other night. Sugar wouldn't have melted in his mouth."

"Well, you know when he calls you, he wants something. Remember when he asked you if the girls could call Peyton, 'Mom'?" Audrie huffed. "Talk about a schmooze-fest."

"Yeah, I thought he was proposing again," she said, puffing air through her lips.

"I'm still impressed by how you handled that one."

"We make it work. They don't call her 'Mom' around me, and I pretend they don't use that word when they're with—," she threw her hands over her mouth, giving a blank stare to the floor.

Audrie's feet fell to the floor. "What?"

"That VBS director-friend," the mother said, wagging her finger in the air. "She's a notary. Hutch and I used her for many things when we were married."

"He needed something notarized after hours. What would he need legal sign off on …Oh my God," the sister-in-law said, mirroring Kristin with her hands over her gaped mouth.

The mother's cheeks started to burn as tears welled. "He's taking the girls from me."

"He's setting you up," said Audrie.

"He's moved his queen into position and my pawns aren't even on the board." Her eyes darted toward the buzzing phone.

Just Breathe: Hello?

The ex-wife's trembling hands returned his message.

Kristin: Congratulations, all my best to you and Peyton.

Just Breathe: What are you referring to?

Kristin: Your life unfolding on Instagram. Congrats to Peyton on her latest competition. She's as impressive as she says she is."

Just Breathe: We still need to talk.

Kristin: I get it. You're having a baby. And you want the girls to complete your family picture.

Just Breathe: Some things need to take place here.

Kristin: Let's give things a year to settle down and see how they feel. I'm sure this is exciting news for all. Good for you. Best wishes.

Just Breathe: The girls want this to happen. We can avoid the courts and lawyers if we can agree to something. You have my word; whatever visitation schedule you want, we'll agree to.

Kristin: If we could have done this without lawyers, why did you consult with yours? Any modifications you're seeking should go through mine.

Just Breathe: You leave me no choice.

The mother's lungs collapsed, lobe by lobe with each message sent. Had he convinced Olivia and Lennon their best option was leaving the familiarity of home to join his enmeshed seven-top-for-life?

"There's no way the girls are going along with this," said Audrie.

"They already have." The mother's shoulders slumped as she walked through the hallway to the living room and sunk into the couch.

Her sister-in-law followed. "Is he still coming by the house?"

"No."

"It's a good thing. I've got some choice words for Hutch Camek."

She listened to her friend put the pieces of the puzzle together feeling the cool leather touch the back of her neck.

"Remember with Browning's case? Grey's lawyer said the legal age for a child to make a custody decision change, in Alabama, was fourteen. Lennon is only thirteen."

"He also said most requests were granted with little to no resistance. As we learned first-hand."

"Don't get me started on the circus in Vidalia County." Audrie rolled her eyes. "Liv is ten. Ten! I mean, I love my niece, but her last big decision meant blowing her Christmas money on a candy lamp from that tween store in the mall."

"Grey sprayed for ants for weeks," the mother said, blowing air through her nose.

"You're a nurse. Is it true the human brain doesn't fully develop until we're in our mid-twenties?"

Kristin nodded yes.

"How can a judge burden a child with a choice like that? I mean, it's dessert furniture one day. Life-altering decisions the next." The children's aunt threw her hands in the air.

"Well, the reality is we can respect the state laws as much as we want. He'll stretch laws like taffy, turning and twisting the standard until it's a melted pile of goo."

"Like that lamp."

"This is *so* my ex. He couldn't care less they're making a permanent decision to walk away from friendships they've had since kindergarten. What about their grandparents that live here?"

"What about—*you*?"

The mother's eyes watered imagining her trusting daughters had been roped into a custody coup d'état. Dog barks interrupted her worry. "There's Rosemary with the girls. I need to get my act together before they walk in the door."

"I'm going into the store. Call me later," she said, fidgeting with the keys.

Standing in the laundry room, she watched Audrie's truck leave. Both kids waved to her from the back window of Rosemary's car. Her heart wrenched seeing their smiles through the glass. She blotted her weeping eyes and nose with a tissue, watching their arrival through the white, slatted shutters. Nausea prevented her from engaging her former mother-in-law in friendly conversation this time. It was customary for her to greet Rosemary, especially if she provided the girls with a meal or took them to a special event. She knew anyone in his family was burdened with his demands. And his poor mother couldn't muster the strength to tell him no.

The two sisters piled out of the vehicle, both wearing bright, colored, tie-dye sweatshirts with Washington, DC, logos across the front. Plastic bags dangled from their arms, overflowing with American flags and patriotic souvenirs. When they were close to the house, she stepped outside to offer help. The grandmother opened her mouth to speak; Kristin pretended not to notice.

"Wow," she said, clearing her throat. "Look at you. I don't think the Statue of Liberty wears this much patriotic gear all at once."

Olivia gave her mother a body wrapping hug, while Lennon fumbled through her souvenir bag. "I missed you so much, Mama," she said, burying her head into Kristin's chest.

"I missed you, baby." Her shoulders relaxed for the first time since their father's text. "Tell me all about your trip."

The eager child filled Mom in on every detail of the bus trip home from the capital city, which included two kids getting in trouble for kissing in the backseat and one kid's mom getting carsick.

If I chaperoned, would you still tell me you were leaving me?

"Bet that kept you awake on the way home," she said, forcing a smile. "How were the tours?"

"Boring," the youngest child said. "Oh, we saw the President."

Lennon's head jerked from her goodie bag. Her eyes wide open. "Yeah, his motorcade zoomed by us when we were walking to the Hard Rock Café."

"Hey!" Olivia scowled at her older sister.

"There were sirens and security guards everywhere. I tried to get a pic, but I couldn't get my phone out of my pocket fast enough."

"I wanted to tell you that part of the story, Mama."

"Incredible." She rubbed the youngest's back in return for letting her older sister deliver the news. "So, Len, you *did* have your phone. Every time I called it, I got voicemail. Which you need to set up by the way."

"Mom, nobody uses voicemail," the teen said with an eye roll. "It was charging. The battery *always* dies. I need a new one."

"A new battery?" Kristin asked.

"Phone!"

"I want an 11R," the younger sibling said.

"You're in 5th grade. I didn't get mine until the 7th. You're a brat."

"No, *you're* a brat, Leonard. Mama, she's been irritated the whole trip."

"You both have what you need. These are your first phones. Grey and I gave them to you because we knew you were traveling to your dad's house in Florida. It's a long way and we wanted you to have some means of communication."

With the mention of their father's name, the girls stopped bickering. "Yeah, about Dad," a tiny voice said. Olivia cut her eyes to the silent sister. "Can we talk to you?"

"If it can wait," the mother said, hiding her shaking hands with idle tasks at the kitchen island. "We should change our clothes. Grey planned to leave work early today, so we can plant the spring garden."

"Okay, I love putting the seeds in the ground," the fifth-grader said.

"What? Do I have to?"

"Yes, it's a family workday. It won't kill you."

She bit her nails while waiting on the front porch for the girls to finish unpacking. Their procrastination didn't bother her on this day. The spoon-fed proxies for her ex were primed to deliver a Conor McGregor-like shot; she was in no hurry.

As the bluebirds chimed in Bradford pear trees' first blooms, Kristin studied the golden vines of honeysuckles winding their way toward the sunlight.

The girls love the first honeysuckles of the season. Do they realize what they're leaving?

There was another time when the father's script was hand-delivered by her child. She and Grey met him to pick up the girls before attending a game-day football party at a mutual friend's home. Lennon jumped from the car to her mother's van wearing a vibrant sports jersey.

On cue, when Grey complimented the six-year-old's spirit, she gave a firm point at her puffed chest. Through a snaggle-tooth smile she said, "My daddy told me to tell everybody at the party my dad gave me this shirt. And he's the best dad ever."

A twinge ran through Kristin's spine watching the new stepfather shrink in the driver's seat. The bubbly first-grader gave an emphatic thumbs-up through the back window. Her ex-husband sat, poised like a director watching a live audience react to his masterpiece. She imagined his only failure with this performance was not having a front-row seat.

Chapter Five

Grey revered the first day of each planting season like a child does Christmas morning. He came from a long line of farmers whose chocolate waves changed to a salted-caramel mix early in life. On a visit to the centuries-old farm where his hands first callused, the husband and father shared the place where his passion for agriculture started. His grandparents had a meager 200-acre homestead dedicated to operating as the sole source of food and income for themselves and their three sons.

"We were farm-to-table before it was chic," he'd say.

Over time, uncles and cousins helped grow the business to a 1000-acre operation which made them a key supplier for grocers along neighboring states. When his grandfather fell ill, the farm was more than his grandmother could manage on her own. She pleaded for help from all relatives with an ounce of experience.

Ches vowed he wouldn't plow a field after leaving the homeplace in his twenties, but he drafted his three sons when his parents' business was in jeopardy. For three years, he shipped the Murphy boys to their grandparents' house during school breaks. They joined uncles, aunts, and cousins on tractors bound for various tasks to salvage the heritage the Murphy patriarch started. Spring breaks meant calving season and bottom plowing pastures into watermelon fields. With the end of each school year, the sons returned to harvest the fields they planted. Weyman, Higdon, and Grey formed an assembly line to load melons into auction-bound trailers. Passing through town on one trip, he showed his wife the parking lot where he learned his first economics lesson. Row croppers knew the name of the game was getting the produce to market before anyone else. He and his uncles shuddered remembering how they missed the bust one year. Watermelon prices dropped from 8 cents per pound to 2 cents while the Murphy men sat atop their trailer piled high.

After one summer of cutting hay, Ches stopped sending his laborers. His father had died, his mother was ill, and his brothers were downsizing the business to meet their immediate needs. Weyman and Higdon occupied their fall seasons with high school football games and girlfriends, but Grey returned to the fields to harvest wheat and late-season corn for the hogs. While his brothers celebrated spring breaks on the Gulf of Mexico's beaches, he ripped the land for another crop. As they prepared for college, he helped ranchers band steers. When his siblings enlisted, he spent his summer evenings waiting on the last buyer to make a bid. Grey's heart poured into the soil, along with his sweat, while he found his soul in the very dirt he tilled.

It was no surprise to Ches when his youngest son graduated, he moved to his grandparents' so he could farm full time. When a virus eliminated chickens on poultry farms in the tri-county area, the eager 19-year-old convinced the veteran farmers to quit dabbling in crops and livestock and specialize. Money came in rows of cotton. Though the business surged beyond any previous success, he never asked for a cut above what he needed. His pay came from living out his legacy.

Two years in dusty fields led the young man to a small-town girl with sights set for anywhere but there. Like his father, Ferryn needed a ticket out, and the Murphy son had made a name for himself in her hometown. When she told Grey she was pregnant, they married, and his father convinced him dirt was best used to bury the past.

"Farmers aren't reliable providers." Ches scoffed at his family heritage. "You can't take care of your new wife and child trying to beat the market bust. You're already failing if your paycheck depends on the weather report."

It wasn't long before Ferryn's desires exceeded his humble earnings, and the son took his father's advice and embodied the pressures of a performance culture. Workaholism became a convenient way to avoid fixing his failing marriage. His wife used his commitment to the office as an example to Browning of her dad's failures. An expensive divorce and a significant panic attack later, he refocused on a way to bring joy back to his work life.

If the oldest and youngest sons inherited their father's height, it was Higdon who mimicked Ches's notorious temper. The middle brother became stuck in the vicious cycle of post-war trauma. Vivid memories of tragedies, mixed with his inherited paranoia, left his wife tiptoeing through a mixed state of volatile emotions. Audrie sacrificed complacency for a peace, which meant overlooking her husband's worsening marijuana addiction. His inability to hold a steady job added to her stress of raising their young daughter, Savannah.

With Higdon jobless and Grey's corporate pressures

mounting, he proposed a business opportunity as a meaningful method of therapy for both men. Together, they became co-owners of Brother's Feed and Seed, anchored in the county seat of their hometown. The youngest brother was a silent partner at first, while his partner maintained the day-to-day business. A corporate surplus offered severance packages to mid-level executives, but Grey struggled to release the identity his father insisted he maintain.

His second marriage was strengthening, and Kristin supported the opportunity for him to relax back into his farming heritage. Letting go of Ches's unattainable respect, the son returned to his passion despite his father's disapproval. With Audrie managing the ledger, the sons' business grew into an integral part of Ellington's rural community. Non-farmers sought Brother's fresh eggs, hothouse peppers, and touted their Better Boys as the juiciest in the county.

Kristin and the girls walked into the high tunnel. "I'm a blessed man. What a gift to share my favorite hobby with my favorite girls."

"You like free labor," the teen stepdaughter said.

"It helps." Her stepdad chuckled as he brushed the soil from his weathered pant legs.

"I hear the tractor," said Kristin, assuming her familiar catcher's position and sifting the black soil through her fingers. "Higgs must be running it."

"That's him. He's on the 4240, turning the pasture for watermelons. They do better out in the open." Grey gazed at the top of the metal structure he designed to filter harsh rays. "Oh Len, I saved the squash for you. I know it's your favorite." The stepfather smiled, shaking a crinkled paper bag with a hand-scribbled label.

"It's the easiest," she said, grabbing the bag. Raking her fingers through the tiny white ovals, she assumed her planter's position and recited the instructions her stepdad had engrained, "Scoop. Seeds. Spread." The young teen repeated it aloud as she sprinkled the divots with the kernels and cradled them with a top layer of dirt.

"That's right. Then watch your money grow." He continued with his mini economics lesson while sorting through plastic trays of young bell pepper plants. "You can turn dirt into profit just like our ancestors did."

"I promise, I will never need farming for money," his stepdaughter said.

"Never say never. Success comes from the will not the skill." He laughed while walking the next tray of seedlings to his wife.

"G, how 'bout I just come to you for the money?" Olivia asked.

A tight-lipped smile inched across the stepfather's cheeks, extending his wrinkles past the creases of his sun-soaked eyes. "I won't be around forever."

"Then, I'll ask my husband," she declared.

"You and Lennon are tough like your mama. My grandma was the same way. She'd never depend on a man for money," he said, giving a wink to his laboring wife.

"Someone else's money comes with strings attached," the mother said. She dabbed her eyes with a towel while she counted the remaining plants leading up to Hutch's message.

"What's that mean?" Olivia asked.

"Like, you're a fish and the money's the bait. If you bite too hard, you'll get hooked." The oldest sister never hesitated to share wisdom gained being on the planet two whole years before her sibling.

"Not bad for someone who hates fishing," he said.

"It's the worm I hate. Not the fishing." Her phobia justified by a shiver. The stepfather's zing drew a laugh from all the planters. They recounted the events of their family outing, which resulted in Lennon screaming while her little sister held Red Wigglers in her face.

Kristin's nurturing heart filled watching the three of them kneel in the dirt while their quick-witted banter ricocheted off plastic tarps. Like the moisture on the greenhouse walls, the heaviness became trapped in her lungs when the child handed the spade to her stepdad. "I call the shower first."

"You need it, Leonard. Mama, can I take a bath in your big tub?"

"Of course."

"Can I use the jets?"

"Please do. Enjoy," the mother said, as her voice cracked. Tears recoiled watching her youngest rocket off to the house.

Old tennis joints clicked, forcing a drawn lower lip with each extended knee. Kristin watched her youngest stop to admire a vibrant box turtle inching across her path; her older sister gave up first place to join her. Despite having two homes with opposite lifestyles, her daughters had lived every day together since their birth. She lost herself in their laughter. The sunlit Forsythia hedges along their walk, reminded her of new beginnings. The mother felt her husband's hand rest on her shoulder. With her head on his chest, the warmth of their work pressed into her cheek. She whispered, "I'm not ready."

"Me either."

The couple believed great pleasures were the least complicated. While they enjoyed an occasional splurge on a spa weekend in the city, this modest life was richer than they could explain to the Hutches and the Rosalyns of the world. They taught all three girls that humility was a strength and a core value to anything they'd endure as adults.

She had watched her rugged husband melt listening to Lennon recite the steps he once taught to her kindergarten class as an Earth Day activity. She knew he secretly feared losing his stepdaughters so close to losing Browning, but he buried his pain with the roots of each tender plant. Both children had grown up seeing his love for them was as grounded as the seedbeds they molded. As they matured, the mother hoped his gentler approach would resonate with his stepchildren, contrasting their father's overt need for domination. Her pulse quickened, knowing her ex-husband planned to erase the family traditions she had relived this day. Grey wiped the sweat from his brow with his shirtsleeve, then took his wife's hand. Like prisoners, they mustered the strength for an execution.

The mother entered the house as the murmur of rushing water through the plumbed walls ceased. The door of each sister's room slammed open, then closed. Children scurried across the hallway with cell phones clenched to their chests. Kristin's heart raced when the clambering nighttime routines slowed.

"Mama?" Olivia summoned from the hallway. "Can we talk to you? Privately."

Chapter Six

The stepfather offered no reaction to the soft-spoken request. His eyes raised and the couple exchanged glances as she took her place in line behind the ten-year-old messenger. She traversed the tiny, pooled footpath over heart pine boards between the hall bath and her bedroom, noting the floor had never felt colder.

A bedside lamp cut the darkness in the mother's bedroom. She positioned herself on the oversized chair in the corner; Olivia took post on the corner of her parent's king-sized bed.

"Well, this looks serious."

"It's not *serious*, we—" The youngest paused, darting her eyes toward her father's other carrier pigeon on the opposite side. "This is kind of hard to say, so we'll ask you to hold your questions to the end."

With raised eyebrows, the intended recipient nodded.

The tiniest pigeon proceeded. "Lennon and I have been talking to our dad—" she hesitated, "—for a while now—" Her thick voice ended the statement abruptly, when she received an intimidating glare from the obvious ringleader.

The younger sibling collected herself and returned to her line of the script. "We've been talking to Dad and—" the mother wondered if the child would go through with it. "We want to live with him. We've wanted to for a long time now," she said, finishing with the conviction of a Southern Baptist preacher.

Every syllable spoken through her baby's lips ripped her to the bone.

Is the same human who chaffed my nipples for the first year of breastfeeding, saying she no longer needs her mother?

Lennon cleared her throat. "There's a nationally recognized School of the Arts I could attend," she said, glancing over her shoulder to Olivia. "Starting this fall will make me eligible for the high school honors program the following year. It's an incredible opportunity for a child with my skill set."

Kristin's body wrenched listening to the father's words disguised as a seventh-grader's excitement about school syllabi and state accolades. None of which she had ever mentioned prior to that moment. In fact, the child, who had been a teenager for a month, rarely talked about much more than the latest hair straightening tip she gleaned from TikTok.

"They offer an advanced curriculum which colleges like to see on applications," the teen recited, arching her back to adjust her mother's throw pillows behind her.

"Do you have any questions?" Olivia asked.

It was difficult for the recipient to distinguish this monologue from a time-share sales pitch. She sipped water from a glass she had used the previous night. "You're an honor band flutist. Your director says you can make state championships next year."

Looking down at the bed, the musician stayed her course, "I know, but this is something I'm really interested in."

"You've dreamt of playing in the marching band since starting middle school. Next year, as an eighth-grader, you'll have that opportunity. You've been so excited about taking the field with your friends. Why would you let that go?" Kristin asked with the face of a poker player. "If I recall, the Lake Tarpon School of the Arts doesn't have a football team."

The sisters looked to each other with raised eyebrows and shrugged.

"I hear there's a new baby coming. How does it feel to have a new sister—," she paused out of habit. It was difficult for the mother to flip the switch from nurturer to cruel bubble burster. "or brother on the way?"

Olivia froze. Her mouth gaped open.

"Am I correct?"

"We do have a baby coming. He, or she, is due in this fall," the youngest child said.

"That's a lot of adjustments for a year."

"We can't wait to have a baby to take care of. We didn't get to see our brother or sister when they were born."

"You were there every weekend after their birth. I know because I was the driver."

"Right, but it's not the same as living there. We missed out on so much. Now, they're starting school."

"Kids do grow up fast." The mother clenched her fists in her lap.

Turning her shoulders to face Kristin's chair, her firstborn took the baton. "We're looking forward to helping Mom—I mean, Peyton."

"It's all so exciting." She tempered the momentum of the

child's mature response. "You both understand, it's my job, as *Mom*, to make sure *your* lives are fulfilled."

Olivia nodded; Lennon's eyes narrowed.

"As much as I care about the new baby, you're *my* babies. When you were born, I promised to protect you, guide you, and ensure future success for you both. Exploring your musical talent is an opportunity, more so than a permanent babysitting gig."

"We *need* our dad." Lennon's voice strengthened.

"You have him. You have a good relationship with your father and his family because of me. I sacrifice a lot to make sure that occurs. What makes you think this will change if you stay here another year?" the mother asked.

The siblings continued their elevator pitch for the suburban educational offerings, their unbridled excitement for soccer mom mentoring, and a newfound commitment to attend catechism classes at Peyton's home church.

"Since when is your dad Catholic?" Kristin asked. We've never agreed to any ritualized religious program for you."

"True, but you told us we could love God any way we wanted," her youngest child's angelic tone reminded.

Her face flushed at the irony of the daughters using her bedroom as their soapbox for a subpar childhood. She recalled the same child reading her first words aloud, cuddled tight in that very bed. With a tiny reading lamp clipped to the bridge of *Hop on Pop*, four-year-old Olivia formed one-syllable sounds into tiny words. Beaming pride drowned out the thunderous roar of summer outside her parents' bedroom window. The walls could not hold all the Eskimo kisses or cool cloths dabbed on nauseated lips within them. Middle-of-the-night tears, Kristin wiped after scary dreams, would overflow the bathtub. Their entitled speech echoed across pillows that once propped weary heads waiting for fevers to break. A sanctuary that once encouraged her daughters' creative fantasies was now a podium for a pre-teen pitch to move to another state. Cold fingertips loosened her collar from around her throat as the paradox of parenting unfolded on her quilted bedspread.

Lennon delivered the final blow. "Mom, we owe it to him. You've had all this time with us, he should get the rest of our childhood."

"Well…" Her brittle voice hesitated. "I know that was the hardest thing you've ever had to say, in your sweet thirteen years."

She could see her youngest child's lip quivering. Lennon glanced at her wavering partner's emotional moment, then studied the church window pattern of their mother's bed covering. The mother paused for them to sink into the uncomfortable space of adulthood where Dad had abandoned them. "It's certainly the hardest thing I've had to hear in my forty-two years." She continued, "What about Grey? He's as much a part of this family as I am, wouldn't you agree?"

"He is. We know how much he does for us," said Lennon.

"A stepparent loves their spouse's children by choice. He's been in your lives since you were four and two years old. That's not something we can just toss out."

"We can talk to him," Olivia said. "I think he'll understand since he's a dad too. He knows how important it is to have a relationship with his daughter."

"True, he's close with you both. You helped him—us when we lost Browning."

"Yeah, but he's not our *real* dad." The youngest girl's tone softened as she shuffled in her seat.

With her throat tightening, Kristin pressed her fingertips to her chest. "By blood, perhaps you're right, but he's been here when you needed him. Remember when he made those midnight drives to the pharmacy when Lennon had pneumonia, so you and I could sleep between her coughing jags? What about the time he slept on the bathroom floor when you had a stomach virus?"

"He painted my fingernails green while I held onto the toilet because I was worried the St. Patrick's Day leprechaun would pinch me at midnight if I was puking."

Closing her eyes, she sifted memories from years of her husband stepping in as Dad, while their 'real dad' traveled the world searching for success. It was their stepfather bringing Santa Claus, the Easter Bunny, and the Tooth Fairy to life for the wide-eyed wonderment children deserve. Kristin's emotions welled with their irrefutable disregard for the man she loved. She restrained her brokenness, unwilling to concede to Hutch's victory.

Separating her dry lips, she tried not to tear her delicate skin. "Let's include G in this conversation. He's in the living room," she said as she stood.

Both children positioned themselves to retrieve their cell phones from their mother's bed. "You can leave those here."

They looked to each other before they agreed to leave their lifelines unattended, then marched down the hallway to continue their conversation. Exiting, the glow of a new text bubble caught Kristin's attention.

Daddy: How'd it go?

Daddy: Girls?

Daddy: Is everything okay?

Chapter Seven

Olivia sat cross-legged on the corner sofa cushion, her favorite spot for most family meetings. An avocado-patterned fleece wrapped her shoulders. She brushed her sun-streaked waves behind her ears while the others found their positions.

Her stepdad adjusted in his chair, his corporate executive background prepped his response. "How can I help?"

"The girls have something they'd like us to discuss, as a family," Kristin said. Her brow furrowed watching her mirror image roll her eyes at her introduction.

"We want to live with our dad in Florida," Olivia repeated.

Hearing it again, hurt more than the first time; her mother's stomach churned.

"Wow, I didn't see that coming." She appreciated her

husband playing along that this was breaking news. "There's a lot of legal stuff with a request like that. Do you remember what I went through with your stepsister?"

"I do remember and G—please don't think I'm being mean but, I remember she chose to live with her mom when she was fourteen," said Lennon, sitting opposite her sister on the couch.

The mother couldn't help being impressed by her daughter's tactful jab at both parents' hearts. "You're *thirteen.*"

"I'll be fourteen next year."

"I'm aware of how it works. I gave birth to you *thirteen* years ago."

"Why the urgency?" the stepfather asked. His question modulated their intensity.

Turning her shoulder to her mother, the teen addressed his question. "The county has a dedicated fine arts school that offers television acting classes, drama, and graphic art tracks. I'm interested in something other than playing the flute. I've met with the counselors already."

Flashing a lighthearted smile to his serious wife, he said, "It sounds like *Fame.*"

"Like what?" Olivia asked.

Relieved he had moved on from the previous Browning comment, she felt it was still too soon to make jokes. "It's a TV show," she said. "An old TV show about kids who go to a performing arts high school in New York."

"That's *exactly* what it's like, G." Lennon's eyes widened. "Liv, you were right. He gets it."

"Can we land this plane?" Kristin asked. She wondered whose side he was on.

I bet he's humming the theme song in his head.

"Listen girls, I had cousins who lived in the Keys. We drove through Miami every year to see them."

"Dad's house isn't in the city."

"But the art school is," he said. "That's a long way to drive one kid to school every day."

"Okay?" Lennon tilted her head at her stepdad's geography lesson.

"Do you really think your dad will drive you an hour, out of his way, so you can go to an art school?" her mother asked.

"I don't know; he says he will."

"You're right. You don't know because these are things parents think about, not thirteen-year-olds. You can't possibly know all the details involved with this move."

"Dad says he can take me on the way to work every day."

"What about when he's on a business trip?" Kristin rebutted.

"Peyton can take me." Her tone strengthened to match her mother's.

"Do you think she'll have time to drive you between posting on Instagram and raising three children of her own?"

"I'll ride the bus."

I hope she tries out for the debate team next year.

"Will you?" Kristin's eyes narrowed as she leaned back on the sofa cushions, crossing her legs and arms.

"I don't *have to* ride the bus here." The middle schooler released her glare and rounded her back.

"And, why is *that*?"

Pausing to feather her hair from under the collar of her hooded sweatshirt, the middle school honor student drew her legs onto the couch. "Because Grey takes us," she mumbled.

"And, why is that?"

"Cuz, I hate smelling the body odor on the bus."

The mother's temples throbbed. "What do you think you'll smell after riding across the county for an hour, sitting three kids to a seat? Because that's what you're signing up for." Another eye roll response from her daughter sparked a quickened foot tap in the air.

"Lennon, your dad has sold you on a bunch of promises he can't deliver. He's a salesman. This is what he does for a living. When we were married, his favorite phrase was, 'Don't sell the steak, sell the sizzle.' Have you heard him say that?"

Both the daughters looked to each other with the familiarity of the phrase. Their dad had been on the sales force for a medical technology conglomerate for decades. During their marriage, Kristin listened to his stories of schmoozing doctor's on golf courses, in airports, and anywhere he could close a deal. If anyone could convince a person to make a terrible decision and let them think it was their idea all along, it was her ex-husband. His persuasion drugged her daughters and ignited her protective streak.

"Think about it. The server delivers a steak dinner to a customer's table. The customer feels the warmth of the grill rising from their meal on their face. They hear the sizzle. Their nostrils get tickled by the aroma of a slightly charred edge." Kristin closed her eyes and drew a loud inhale through her nose. Using her former stage acting skills, her hands emphasized the scene for her audience. "The customer pokes their fork through the cracked, glazed top making it ooze savory, pink juices. He's convinced this is a premium cut of meat. He's sold." The girls were silent, listening to her tale. "The customer spears a bite and places it in their mouth expecting what?"

Lennon reengaged, "Something delicious?"

"But what they find, with that sumptuous first bite, is an enormous piece of gristly flesh."

Olivia's nose crinkled. "I'm becoming a vegetarian."

"The moral of the story is, it's easy to fool people because they want to believe what they're hearing, seeing, and smelling; but tasting is true," she paused, softening her voice.

"I think your dad means well, but he's a pro at painting a pretty picture."

Lennon wiggled her foot across Champ, who remained curled in his bed undisturbed by his owner's heated discussion, while her sister pulled the blanket tight.

"Liv, you have friends here you met in preschool. What about them?"

"I know. It will be hard to leave," she sighed. "But they're supportive."

"So, they already know?"

"I just said I'm *thinking* about it."

Turning to Lennon, Kristin asked, "What about you? What have your friends said?"

"They're happy for me. They know I've wanted this for an awfully long time."

"Is that right? So, you won't miss them."

"I'll catch 'em on Insta," the teen said, with a one-sided shrug.

"What about your dad's house?"

"What about it?" Lennon mouthed, turning her lips downward and turning her palms to the ceiling.

"Where will you sleep?"

"His house is bigger than your house, Mom."

"So is his family, Len. With the new baby, how will all of you fit?"

"I'm sharing a room with my baby sister," the younger sister said.

"So, you're giving up your own room, to share one with a kindergartener?"

"She's really excited. It will be fun."

"You're buying the sizzle, ladies. Your mom and I are trying to show you what you're in for, but you're not listening."

Her partner's engagement was welcomed.

"If there's anything you can learn from my daughter's choice," the stepfather said, with a strong inhale. "Even the smartest kids need help making big life decisions."

The living room chatter drew calm and Kristin knew the Browning comment still lingered.

"Lennon," the mother said. "You're a regional honor band performer because I took you to every band practice and recital the directors held. Before that, I drove you forty-five minutes each way, for extra flute lessons to give you the edge in honor band auditions." Lennon opened her mouth to respond but said nothing. Kristin's voice intensified with each rung. "*Before that*, I drove you to piano lessons. *Before that*, I played sing-along tapes in the car on trips to see—you guessed it—your dad. *Before that*, I played Baby Einstein music CDs in your nursery; Bella Luna was your favorite," Kristin wiped a dot of spit from the corner of her mouth. With intent focus on the 13-year-old version of herself, she continued, "*You* are a successful musician today because of what *I've* done to get you here. I've earned the right to sit in the stands at the football game wearing a button with your smiling face on it."

"Thank you?" Lennon's voice lifted with her question. "What do you want me to say?"

"I want you to think about someone other than yourself." She planted her hands on the seat cushion.

The mother knew the oldest was the muscle of this operation, but the baby was the emotional gasoline for their engine. From the corner of her view, she saw her sensitive child tuck her feet under her hips. Her bottom lip pulled tight watching the exchange between her mother and sister.

Kristin's face flushed as she forced a swallow. She shielded herself from Hutch's egoic attacks before, but tonight's arena hosted two lionesses, with a fierce loyalty to their King. Kristin refined her tactical approach hoping to avoid another defensive assault. They'd be delighted to tell their handler she'd unleashed her anger or crumbled. Her heart pounded against her breastbone.

"What about your sister?"

"What about her? Her diabetes is fine."

"I'm a nurse, Lennon. She's leaving full time medical care."

"Lots of people aren't nurses and do fine with diabetes."

"So now, you're her endocrinologist?" the mother asked, feeling her jaw clamp tighter.

"Dad can handle it," Lennon grated.

"She hasn't even started her period yet."

"Peyton can help her. It's not that hard."

"You have all the answers, don't you? What about *me*, Len? You're just going to leave *me*?"

"Isn't that what you did to Dad?" Her words daggered her mother for the second time that night, but this time her eyes were absent of self-doubt.

Her younger sister's tears had grown to a full sobbing stream.

"Right? You left Dad," she repeated. "So maybe you're getting what you deserve."

"I think we're done here." Grey held his hands in the air. "Girls, there are still a lot of questions—"

"Lennon Rosalyn." Kristin's cadence slowed enunciating every syllable of her firstborn's name through pursed lips. "I will not divulge the details of my married, adult life to someone who has yet to hold hands with another. Are we clear?"

Without blinking, the child hid her quivering lip behind her teeth.

"Your stepdad and I have both passed on promotions because the job required us to move farther away from your dad. He moved without asking me; nor did he talk to me about options. I continued your weekend schedule, so you could see him."

"I never wanted to replace him in your life," her husband said. "I only wanted to be the best father I could for you."

Olivia wiped her cheeks with the sleeve of her shirt and gave a loud sniffle, "You were—are. You *are* a great father to us."

"We'll continue to support your relationship with him, but we can't promise he'll do the same for us," Kristin walked toward the couch and handed the girls tissues. With a forced exhale, she said, "Let's talk restriction."

"What?" Lennon snarled. "I'm on restriction because I want to live with my dad?"

Her sister's crying jag restarted, given she had never had any serious punishment that the mother could recall.

"One week no phone, because you've been using it secretly to hide your plans from us," Kristin demanded. "This entire plot against us is unacceptable. We should have been brought into the conversation a long time ago. One week of riding the bus to school, since you don't seem bothered by the idea of doing it in Florida."

Lennon huffed and kicked the ottoman beside her.

"Also, a week of sharing a room."

"Olivia's disgusting!"

"Mom, did you hear her?" The sister asked, dropping her jaw.

"Well Liv, you said you won't mind sharing a room with a kindergartener at your dad's house, so sharing with an OCD, neat-freak like Lennon should be a walk in the park," Kristin concluded.

The teen stomped to her room slamming the door behind her. The youngest kissed her stepfather on the cheek and squeezed her mother's shoulders before shuffling down the hall.

“We’ll get through this, I promise,” she said, reassuring her soft-hearted tween as much as she did for herself.

Olivia attempted to open her sister’s door, “I’m your roommate, idiot.” The jiggling knob released, and Kristin stared at her phone with a loss of all emotion.

Just Breathe: Where are my children? What have you done to them?

Kristin: They’re asleep. I’ll have them call you tomorrow.

Just Breathe: Why aren’t they answering their phones? You must let me speak to them. This is my parental right.

Kristin: They’re on restriction for the week.

Just Breathe: For what?

Kristin: For breaking some house rules.

Just Breathe: You will pay for this.

Chapter Eight

It was a rare treat for the family's underage, front-seat passenger to sit next to her mother. While parked at the edge of the drive, she played with the controls and wiggled her tiny hips. "This seat heater is nice." Giving a look over her shoulder, "You don't have those back there, Leonard."

"Whatever."

Kristin smiled at the squabbling sisters and remained in quiet observation of the dawn's unfolding. She savored her coffee watching the red-breasted robins tease their breakfasts from the soft soil. The early layers cackling in their coop reminded her to collect eggs before she went back to the house.

"Mama, I'm kind of excited about riding the bus now. I've wanted to do morning warm-ups in the gym, but you have to be at school so early."

Her daughter's innocent tone stole her attention from a geese flock gliding overhead. "You'll be there by 6:30 a.m. That should give you time to stop by the nurse's office before they start."

"Perfect. It's kind of good we got in trouble, I guess."

"Shut up," the croaky voice from the back seat said.

The mother's caramel eyes peeked in the rearview mirror to see her frowning teen rounding her neck in circles. "Sleep okay?"

"Olivia's a bed hog."

"You snore like a man. You'll make a great husband one day."

On most mornings, school drop-offs were managed by their stepfather while Mom drank coffee in solitude. The carpool referee questioned who this arrangement punished, given he was cozied in the bed. This day, she relished in the moment of normalcy.

Yellow-dotted beacons along the white rooftop cut through dissipating fog. "There's the bus. Get your things."

Screeching brakes followed by a blast of pressured air invited the smile of a familiar face from behind the steering wheel. A woman wearing a tattered Atlanta Braves ball cap called to the mother. "Hey there! I haven't seen the girls lately. What brings y'all out this morning?"

Through a small crack above her driver's side window, she wiggled her fingers hello. "Morning warm-ups. They like to start early." The window's sealed closed and she noticed Olivia's smug appearance. "What?"

The child zipped her backpack closed.

A metal window toward the back of the bus slid open to show the pecan-tanned cheeks of another freshly flat-ironed teen girl. "Lennon? Is that you?"

The voice of the teen's grade school best friend turned the corners of her lips while she scrambled to organize her supplies. "Save me a seat!" she shouted to her friend, grabbing the handle of her flute case just before the van doors sealed.

"I love you, Mama." Olivia leaned over the seat console with puckered lips. Kristin reciprocated, grateful she was still at the age she didn't mind if others saw her kiss her mother. "See you this afternoon at the bus stop."

"I'll be here." She watched her young fifth-grader step up the steep black deck of the yellow bus, her oversized backpack hanging past her hips. As the doors gassed shut for the trip, she noticed an incoming message.

Just Breathe: Are the girls awake?

Kristin: They've left for school. Try this evening.

Just Breathe: Why so early?

Kristin: Morning warm-ups.

The mother stalled her overthrow. Every second with them cut the puppeteer's strings to his marionettes. If she could keep him from jerking their reactions, maybe somehow she could unravel months of him eroding their bond. Soon enough, she speculated, he'd twist her actions' meanings in a show of force to the children. She knew he salivated, waiting for her final bow.

Entering the kitchen through the side door, she said, "We had ten eggs this morning."

"Thank you, I'll wash them and take them to the store." Grey sat at the table sipping from a handmade Father's Day gift Browning made him years ago. "I like this arrangement."

"Don't get used to it." She smiled and laid the eggs in the basket with others from the week.

"How'd that go?"

"Not terrible. They like it better than they'll admit."

"If it makes you feel any better, I heard them giggling in the bedroom last night when I let Champ outside. You're a good mom. It's not torture." His empty cup clanked at the bottom of the copper farmhouse sink.

"Unlike what I'm going through."

"It would help knowing what their dad has filled their heads with."

"I noticed last night he kept texting. Asking them for an update on the situation, but I had asked them to leave their phones."

"He wanted the play-by-play." Her husband shook his head. "Do you still have their phones?"

"Yes," she said.

"Do you know their passcodes?"

"I did, but apparently, they changed them in DC."

"With Dad standing over their shoulders, I'm sure." Grey gave an exasperated puff of his cheeks. "Well, they're kids. They'll slip up."

"I'll keep trying to come up with quirky patterns they would use to see if I can break in," Kristin cringed. "I feel dirty just saying that."

"Hutch compromises everyone's integrity. Let's stay focused on protecting the girls."

"Don't forget Lennon's awards night tonight at 5:30 p.m."

"Okay. I'll come home after work and we can ride together. I love you."

"Love you too."

Stepping onto the front porch, the anticipation of her lengthy to-do list weighed on her. She leaned on the knotted-wood railing. The goats skipped through the pasture toward their morning feed, while her chest sank. She questioned how she, an exemplary mother by society's standards, faced an impending custody lawsuit.

I thought this sort of thing happened to parents who didn't want their kids.

Ten years ago, she exhausted her life savings divorcing her husband, so she could provide the children with a safe, consistent foundation absent of Hutch's elitist reign. Now, her financial security was at risk all over again. Grey's, too. Family court claimed to exclude the spouse's income in their financial calculations, but they never refused payment from either account. Litigation showed no mercy for anyone involved.

She twisted her hair into a quick ponytail. Her attempt to play private investigator and keep her day job had begun. The nurse recalled many acquaintances, from the hospital and academia, forced into FMLA due to their legal complications. Domestic stressors caused some to lose their jobs altogether.

Her phone chimed from the desk. "Hey girl."

"Hey you. I just saw Grey. What in the world?" Audrie asked.

"I've spent most of my day sobbing between meetings and trying to hack the girls' phones. Will I ever have a normal day at work again?"

"The ex makes you feel like you're losing your mind. Can you talk to your boss? Maybe she needs to know what's going on."

"No, I can't go there."

"I get it. I mean, I wouldn't share my business at work, but you know that's what happens when I work with my husband and brother-in-law."

"Zero privacy." The friends laughed.

"Don't let Vy find out. She would have a field day."

"Nope, one sister-in-law's legal advice is enough."

"What did your attorney say?" Audrie asked.

"I have a meeting scheduled with his assistant's assistant during my next session," she said through a loud sigh. "I'll have to juggle something."

"Assistant's assistant? Isn't he important?"

"Family court doesn't offer a court-appointed attorney

to defendants. We're treated like criminals and we get to pay for it. Why not add layers to the process when everyone gets a check?" Kristin's taut sarcasm carried.

"You can represent yourself," Audrie said.

"I'd get skewered, for sure."

"True, damned if you do and damned if you don't. Well, I'm back at the store. Let me know if I can help with anything."

"When you see your brother-in-law, ask him what a Jailbreak is and how can I do it on this phone?" she asked.

"Good Lord, girl. The police department will put you on the force after this experience," Audrie said.

"Right? Nancy Drew never had to deal with cell phones."

"I'll ask him what to do. Hang in there."

It didn't take Audrie long to relay Kristin's question. His response was swift.

Grey: You don't want to do that.

Another dead end left the wife holding her head in her hands.

***

The family readied to conclude another successful year for their middle-schooler. From her daughter's bedroom doorway, the mother scanned framed superlatives of music, academics, and peer recognition hung on the peach-colored walls. Her throat tightened, feeling her joy suffocate at the hands of their father.

"Step away from the flatiron," she said with a smile.

"Just one more stubborn curl that won't..." Lennon tussled with the last sign of her signature hair. The precise variants of red she'd inherited from her mother mixed with haystack-colored curls from her father. She struggled to create the sleek style her friends made appear effortless.

"I love your curls, why do you fight them?"

"Finally," the teen said, tossing the styling tool onto the cluttered surface of her dresser. "Because you love them, duh."

"Let's roll." Grey called from the kitchen, jingling his keys.

Unplugging the warm device from the wall, the mother said, "They want all A-students up front, so let's go. You should call your father on the way." She held the child's phone in her hand, as Lennon emerged from the closet holding a white denim jacket. "That is so cute on you, good choice."

Grabbing the phone from her mother, she flung the summer accessory on the bed.

"Why must you be that way?" Kristin asked.

"What way?"

The mother huffed, following the student outside where the rest of the family waited.

"The way that makes me feel like you'd jump off a bridge just because I told you not to."

Lennon shrugged and climbed into the backseat. With the thud of the truck doors sealing closed, her phone pinged alive.

"Hi. How are you?"

She heard her daughter ask someone on the other end of the phone.

"Yes. Yes. No. I'm fine. She's fine too. She's with me. We're on the way to the awards night. I made all A's—Okay. Yes sir. We love you too." With militant-like compliance, the child took orders instead of celebrating scholastic success.

The mother looked over her shoulder, "If you're done, give it back to me."

"Okay, just a second."

"Mom, she's getting on Insta," the tattling child said.

"We're here now. I'll take that, thank you." Kristin

unbuckled her seatbelt to face Lennon behind her. "You should go inside and get seated."

"Open the door, Leonard. There's Becca. I want to walk in with her and not your lame nerd friends."

"Fine," she said with a grunt, slamming the phone in her mother's palm and jumping onto the sidewalk. "If you see any of my friends messaging me, let them know I'm still alive."

Olivia scooted across the backseat behind her sister's dramatic exit. "Yeah, Mom, reply for Lennon so her *boyfriend* knows she still loves him." From the walkway, she made a kissy face at her sister. "Her password is 08, 01, 98."

Slightly bent strands of blonde strawberries whipped across the sister's shoulders as she jerked her neck glaring at her bratty informant. "I hate you. How did you know my password?"

"It's your celebrity crush's birthday. It's all you ever talk about besides your hair. Duh," the child bemoaned, darting past her revenge-seeking sibling to catch up with her friends.

Voices of the bickering siblings silenced with the boom of the truck door leaving the mother breathless. The driver eased his foot on the accelerator and the diesel engine clambered behind the other cars inching in queue.

"Did you catch that?" he asked, giving a quick-handed wave to parents eager to greet their superstars inside.

"Shhhhhh," Kristin said, monitoring the girls' proximity without moving a muscle. "I'm repeating the numbers in my head until they're out of sight."

With a frozen smile, he said, "There's a pencil and paper in the console."

As the dented metal doors of the gymnasium closed behind Olivia, the passenger sorted through gas receipts and old Red Bull cans to find the elusive writing utensil. With trembling hands, she scratched 080198 on a wrinkled scrap of paper.

"Is that what you heard?" she asked, turning the note in her husband's direction.

He glanced down and nodded yes.

The vehicle came to a stop at the opposite end of the school parking lot. With the same unease of stumbling across an unlocked diary, Kristin tapped the device's cracked glass face. Scrolling through lively Instagram posts, the mother reined in her curiosity to analyze the other material her thirteen-year-old was reading. She felt a familiar feeling in her gut reading his name on her child's phone, "Daddy."

Her matted tongue ran over her cracked lips as she waited for the blue-and-white-bubbled screen to appear. "She hasn't cleared a thing."

"She's a kid. Do you see anything about him making them do this?"

Each screen flipped like a spinning roulette wheel. "I'm trying to get back to the beginning. Here," she read aloud:

Daddy: Len?

Lennon: Yo Daddio !

Daddy: I need your letter. The one the attorney gave us.

Lennon: That essay on why I want to move to your house?

Daddy: Yes, can you send me what you've written so far?

Lennon: It's still at school. I left it in my locker. I had to work on it in class. I'm sorry.

Daddy: This is critical.

Lennon: I know. I'm sorry.

Daddy: What have you written so far?

Lennon: Everything you told me to. The school. The baby. Church..

Kristin struggled to swallow.

Daddy: Catechism?

Lennon: That's on there, church.

Daddy: Write catechism.

Lennon: Ok.

Daddy: We're doing this next weekend. How do I know I can trust you to do your part?

Lennon: You can trust me.

Looking to her husband, his veins bulged above his collar. With tears in her eyes, she said, "It's like she's pledging her allegiance to a dictator."

Daddy: If I can't trust you with this, how can I trust that you really want this to happen?

Lennon: You can trust me. I want this, too.

Daddy: Well, want it enough to finish the paper.

Lennon: Okay.

Daddy: Sweetheart, I'm not mad at you. I just want you to handle it.

Lennon: I will.

Daddy: Then we have an understanding.

Lennon: We do.

Daddy: Good. Get the paper to me, pronto. I love you. Delete this conversation.

Lennon: I love you too. Deleted.

Laying the phone in her lap, her hands steadied. Rowdy chatter of middle-schoolers and their families flooded the school courtyard. She resented their excitement while her child carried this burdensome mission. The mother shuddered at the loss of her child's innocence because of Hutch's selfishness.

"I remember this day." Kristin pulled a ragged leather journal from her purse. "Yes. I thought this was it."

"What day?"

"Mrs. Chapman, her ELA teacher, emailed me saying she failed to turn in required assignments that day. She received zeros on both. The teacher expressed concern. Lennon's not one to underperform."

With his hand on the steering wheel, he motioned toward the school. "She was right to question. Here we are at an honors awards day."

"She said Len acted odd in class, distracted. She gave the students an assignment to complete. Lennon turned in a page with a few lines scribbled. When the teacher asked her what she was submitting, she told her she didn't feel well and apologized." The mother held her index finger over her lip as she continued. "Now, seeing this text, it shows she used her class time to work on her father's special assignment."

"Then he scolded her about being late with his task," he said, lowering his smoky voice.

The water that once quenched Kristin's thirst gagged her as Hutch's scheme came into full view.

Grey laid the device on his lap and used his own to photograph the father's and daughter's text conversations. "I'll try to keep them in order, so the lawyers can see the timelines." His camera snapped. "Here's some group texts that include Liv. Hutch keeps doing these pulse checks." Reading from the device, he said, "Daddy. Everything okay? Any changes? Both girls responded with a thumbs up or *100*." Shaking his head, he looked to his weeping wife. "He's making sure his soldiers aren't going AWOL."

She stared at the sun setting behind the pines, paralyzed by her inability to protect her children.

Handing it back to his wife, he said, "Here, I think I got most of it. Be sure to go back to the screen she was on when you first opened it, so she doesn't see where we've been."

A sickened mother returned the home screen to its original location. Her daughter's tattered phone powered off, and she returned it to the bottom of her purse. Once outside of the truck, she used the passenger- side mirror to refresh her makeup preparing to deal with her mother.

Chapter Nine

"There's Roz." Kristin acknowledged her mother from across the parking lot.

"As another father, I can say this is disgusting," he said, heaving the door closed behind his wife. "I loved Browning and I disagreed with the way her mom controlled her time with us, but I would've never stooped so low."

The blacktop was still warm from the late spring day, as the couple walked toward the dwindling crowd of straggling attendees.

"We're good people. This playing mind games with children isn't in our wheelhouse," she said, still reeling from the texts they'd discovered.

"Tom will have a field day. When do you see him?"

"Not soon enough," she said, as the husband and wife entered the renovated gymnasium. The purple and gold championship banners surrounded the top bleachers where most of the audience were situated, leaving seating closer to the gym floor. She spotted her mother hugging the youngest granddaughter in the lower-level stands. "There they are."

A bright smile spanned her tween's face as she waved her mom and stepdad over to join them.

Making her way through the sea of knees and sibling spectators, Kristin shuffled through to her seat with anticipation of the mother's reaction to her ex-son-in-law's master plan. "You look good, RaRa," she said through a thin-lipped smile while brushing her hand at Olivia to get her to move one bleacher seat in front.

"Thank you, dear. My namesake receives accolades tonight, I need to be on point." The edges of Rosalyn's silver bob flipped as she boasted. Scanning her daughter's face, she said, "You look like you've just seen a ghost."

Waving to a fellow proud parent in the top row, Kristin leaned toward her mother's ear and whispered, "The girls told us last night, they want to move to Florida in the fall."

The grandmother raised her eyebrows with a slow nod.

"We found several texts between Hutch and the girls coaxing them to leave." She could hardly form the words.

"He's sold them a bill of goods," she said. "They are naïve. Trusting. Like their mother."

"They're children." The daughter forced her breath through clenched teeth causing Olivia to turn her head.

Rosalyn patted the child's back, reminding her to improve her posture and cease socializing as the principal's shoes clapped across the wooden stage. "You'll know what to do, Krissy. You always do."

Unshaken by her mother's usual backhanded compliments, Kristin focused on her daughter's achievements. She wanted to take in every second of the awards program, given her future attendance was uncertain. Lennon's family watched as their young protégé received recognition for her educational dedication. Other parents cheered for their prized pupils, but the mother angered hearing their celebrations, oblivious to the turmoil her children were experiencing.

Time slowed watching her daughter accept an award and take her position standing by the other awkward middle-schoolers. Voices muffled. Each clap of her palms together left her slightly more breathless than the next. Her mind flooded with memories of her fearless firstborn who conquered walking at ten months old, reading competitions, spelling bees, and musical auditions. The mother had enjoyed every second of watching her child become a fierce, independent young girl. She feared Hutch had tapped into her psyche, knowing Lennon craved recognition for her delivery in stressful situations. He had started an incorrigible game of flag football and their daughter wouldn't quit until she had yanked the belt from Kristin's waist.

***

The sunlight streamed through the shutters of her home office, leaving a golden patch of warmth on the rug, the perfect spot for Champ's mid-morning nap. The outside dog's incessant rant pulled an engrossed Kristin away from her work. She removed her glasses from her face and tried to recall if a delivery was scheduled. Her old friend's hearing loss left him unaware of the call to action.

"I got this one, buddy," she said, brushing her hand over his white-and-gold coat eliciting a settling groan. Her glasses clinked on the keyboard and she moved toward the front of the house to assess the commotion.

Their gravel driveway announced visitors long before anyone could make out any recognizable shapes. And it usually deterred drop-in guests. Billowing dust parted revealing the headlights of a silver sedan drawing near as the homeowner stepped outside.

A tall, white-haired man wearing gold aviator sunglasses exited the vehicle and straightened his black polo shirt. She watched him stretch inside the car and retrieve a manilla envelope before closing the door. The sewn, yellow star logo over his left chest came into view as he approached the front porch.

"Good morning, sheriff."

"Good morning. Are you Mrs. Murphy?"

She confirmed and extended her hand to accept the package.

"I guess you've been expecting this," the sheriff said, placing the packet within her reach.

Staring at the envelope, she obliged a smile, hopeful her shame wasn't reddening her cheeks. "This is a first, I can say. The only thing I've ever been served is a meal."

"These things are never easy. Can I get you to sign here for me?"

The new defendant scribbled her name with his black pen.

Gazing across the pond and pastures surrounding the Murphy home, he said, "Beautiful place you have here. I hope all works out for you, ma'am." He returned to the vehicle with the engine running.

Me too.

Seated in the armchair at the breakfast table, Kristin took a deep breath and rubbed her hands together. Her stomach did somersaults as her fingers moved over the crinkled edges of the thick paper. The legal office logo in the return address came into view.

She texted her husband, "I got served."

Within a few minutes, he called, "You got served?"

"I did. Just like in the movies. I guess it's official now."

“They aren’t wasting any time with this, are they? What’s in the envelope?”

“It looks like a ridiculous amount of paperwork Tom will have to decipher,” she said, spreading the contents across the knotted-pine table.

Papers stopped shuffling. “Did I lose you?” the husband asked.

“I’m reading the girls’ affidavits now.” Her voice bristled. “Lennon’s testimony is exactly as she replied in her text to Hutch. She wants to move so she can complete her catechism classes, attend the fine arts school, and be with the baby when he or she is born.”

“Word for word, that’s Hutch’s script.”

“Here’s Olivia’s.” Her heart wrenched recognizing her ten-year-old’s scribbled handwriting on such a grown-up document. It was the visual reminder this child was far too young to make adult decisions. The date, she noted, was the day the children returned from Washington, DC. She imagined their father, his mother, Rosemary, and the notary surrounding the tiny subjects like witches huddled over a caldron. With her crippled voice, the mother read the child’s words aloud, “I want to live with my dad and his family because they live in a really cool place. Their house, spelled t-h-e-y-apostrophe-r-e, is close to swimming pools, tennis courts, and I can learn to ride a horse. I’ve always wanted to go to church. I’m excited about seeing my little brother or sister walk and be a baby,” she paused. “I—I can’t finish.”

“Well, it’s bogus. She’s not even the minimum age to make a statement.” Her husband’s tone drew stern.

“Somehow, I’m supposed to work today.” Her voice gave way as the mother’s tears puddled on the legal documents she held.

“I know this is hard, honey. Let me call Tom and tell him where things stand. We’re meeting with him this afternoon, so we should get some answers."

"Thank you. I think I'll lie down for a minute."

The cool pillow of Kristin's bed eased her throbbing head and offered a place of brief respite from Hutch's vitriolic scheme. Her creased brow eased as she pulled the downy throw over her legs.

How did I miss the signs?

While she built a foundation of trust for Olivia and Lennon, their father waited in the wings for an opportunity to steal them from her. She trembled at the thought she'd been robbed of watching her daughters grow into adulthood. Her breath deepened as she succumbed to the ceiling fan's mellow revolutions hovering above.

Chapter Ten

A courtyard of trellising ivy surrounded a black sign at the foot of a live oak which read, *Law Office of Thomas Peavy, Esq.* Grey maneuvered his truck into the designated parking space in front. "I remember when the Grahams lived here."

"I remember when the wife found Mr. Graham with his mistress and she set the house on fire," she said without distraction from recounting the alphabetized folders cradled in her leather brief.

Dried leaves swirled through the parking lot, peppering the hood of the truck as a reminder of the lingering drought. "I'm glad they salvaged the house. A charred eyesore, on this corner, would deter customers from downtown." Grey looked toward the passing traffic behind them. "Although, I hoped we'd never come back."

"It's not a friendly atmosphere," she said.

"Are we sure we want to use Tom again? After the last time . . ." His voice flattened.

"I'm sure I don't want to start from the beginning with some new hot shot attorney. Tom knows we're good parents; he can fight for us. Besides, a different lawyer would charge us $400 for a new client consultation. Tom waived the get-to-know-you fee."

Her husband's concerns were valid, given their single courtroom experience two years prior. Browning's mother was less calculating than Kristin's ex. After leaving her small town, Ferryn became a reckless, c'est la vie brand of attention seeker. She was divorced from Grey for a few years when her party-girl mentality landed her two DUIs. Further investigation revealed an enabling grandmother was the primary caretaker for his eleven-year-old daughter, given his ex-wife's instability. Grey sought an attorney after Browning's teacher notified him the local police had incarcerated the child's mother. Tom came recommended as a bulldog in the courtroom with a pro-dad spin. Upon consultation, he agreed her jail time warranted an emergency custody modification.

Prior to the court hearing, Tom warned his client of a circuit magistrate who had a known soft spot for parents battling addictions. He was notorious for his offhanded deliberations, and judge selection was non-negotiable.

***

When Grey and Kristin arrived at the courthouse, Ches was waiting in the cab of his classic sports utility vehicle reading a newspaper.

Greeting his father through the driver's side window, the son said "Dad, I told you, you didn't have to come to this. There's no telling what time this could end."

"I wanted to be here," he said, removing his reading glasses with his hand stretched over the leather-wrapped steering wheel. "My granddaughter's in danger."

"You're right. Thanks for coming. I'm rattled…"

"Understood, son," he returned his glasses to his front pocket and folded the paper in his hand. "Kristin, how are you holding up, dear?"

"We're both tense today. Thanks for coming, Ches," she said, giving her father-in-law a one-armed hug on their walk inside.

Grey opened the door of the courtroom for his wife, following behind her. The defendant sat on the mahogany bench in front, her ankle monitor peered from beneath a dark-denim cuff.

Ches took a back-row seat, rolling his paper into a tube, which he held close.

The tapping of Tom's leather shoes echoed across the walls of the historic courthouse as he approached his client with a flushed face and jutting chin. "It's Judge Giles. He met with the child's grandmother first. Then had her remove the child from school and bring her here. They're conferencing now, inside his chambers."

"Will I get to talk to the judge, too?"

"Probably not. This is the one I warned you about," Tom said.

"My kid is in real danger—emotional and physical. We can prove it if he looks at the evidence."

"He's not meeting with her either," the attorney whispered, darting his eyes in Ferryn's direction. "Only the child and the grandmother were invited."

Thirty minutes later, a young girl strolled through the courtroom appearing much older than the stepmother had ever seen her. The teen's makeup mirrored those of the influencers she mimicked, her freckles were barely visible.

Soft shades of caramel smoothed her narrow jawline with no visible tangles or unraveled braids. A plump pout was warmed with a tint the same shade as her grandmother's. With her chest out and shoulders back, she looked pleased with her adult-like contribution at the hearing her father said she wouldn't attend. Morning's light beamed across her butterscotch highlights as she hugged her mother's neck. The eighth grader acknowledged Dad with a smug grin then, followed Ferryn's mother to the back of the courtroom.

Both attorneys convened with their clients for a post-mortem update from the judge. Huddled in the corner, Tom advised, "Giles said the child didn't want to change custody, but he's adding an extra week with you during the summer. He's not conducting further interviews."

Grey threw his hands in the air. "Why would the child get to make that call? How does a judge get to make a unilateral decision without evidence?"

"His court. His rules."

Browning held a sucker in her mouth as she waved to him before the heavy oak doors slammed closed.

Parenting time was limited to every other weekend with sporadic weeknight dinners scheduled around work and school schedules. She vacationed with them for a week the summer before her freshmen year was supposed to start. The photo from that trip, the one where Grey's sundrenched shoulders met Browning's wide, brace-filled grin, remained on his desk at work. Kristin matted it in a double frame next to their first Daddy-daughter picture together. The one where she was swaddled in pink and blue stripes, wearing a white beanie. In both, it was obvious which parent's nose she'd inherited.

On a warm, late summer evening, she called her dad from Ferryn's car. It was later than their usual check-in time,

Kristin remembered. As part of their idle chit-chat, the father asked where they were going. She explained they were on the way home from their favorite restaurant.

When he questioned the late dinner hour the teen said, "Dad, Mom just likes their sweet tea."

Grey told Kristin, months after, that was the moment he knew he'd never hear her voice again.

A single chime of his phone jolted his eyes open from their half-closed position. His low tone filled the pitch-black room. An Alabama state trooper accounted for the incidents leading up to the wreck. The mother lost control of her vehicle rounding a curve on county road 39, just outside of Ellington. Browning was restrained in the front seat, but the airbag didn't deploy. Her mother was in custody under suspicion of DUI; she'd refused to blow at the scene. Grey listened with his usual stoicism as the onsite officer detailed his child's injuries, but the sound of the medivac's lift off was more than he could stomach.

Weeks passed and the couple alternated bedside shifts at Children's UAB, but the teen never opened her eyes despite the father's tender pleas. On days when the stepmom was on duty, Dad prepared their home for the day he'd bring his baby girl home. Lennon's bedroom was relocated to the guest suite downstairs. Shower bars adhered to the tub walls. Travel paths widened inside to accommodate medical equipment. And a wooden ramp built over the side entry stairwell. They'd walked past it now, for two years.

Eventually, the fluid inside the child's skull was more than could be shunted away from her brain. Pneumonia from prolonged dependence on a ventilator, infected her bloodstream. Hundreds, maybe thousands of CT scans were done during her admission, each with an associated risk of transporting life-saving equipment to the radiology department. Minimal changes noted on each. Being on the family's side of this scenario was unfamiliar to Kristin, but she recognized the sorrow in the nurse's eyes the day she asked them to conference with the medical team, in private.

The couple followed the nurse around the horseshoe-shaped console in the center of the unit. Kristin watched other families gather behind closed glass doors and pulled curtains. She recognized the shift change in progress. Refreshed daytime workers, listened to the charge nurse report while haggard staff typed their final notes of the night. Brewing coffee filled her senses entering an obscure nook in the PICU. There, she recognized an average looking door, the kind most visitors would overlook, as a reserved space every unit she'd ever worked in seemed to have. Staff called it the grieving room, and she still hated opening the door.

As she suspected, inside waited a group of freshly starched whites. Medical hierarchy was determined by the coat length, the knee-level hemline of Browning's chief neurosurgeon stepped forward first. Soon after, the thigh-length coats of her pediatrician and intensivist offered their insight. She couldn't help but notice a young woman, wearing her symbol of credibility at her waist, poised behind her instructor. Her emotions were as raw as the father receiving the news. Kristin knew she'd get used to it, by the time her hemline reached her thigh. With each exit, the room widened. The final door closed on the dad, stepmom, nurse, and a hospital chaplain who guided Grey down a path no parent should have to traverse.

Tom's office was painful for more reasons than Hutch Camek would ever know, and she hated him for bringing her back.

"Listen, you don't have to go with me, I understand. I'm just trying to move through this process quickly."

"I know, but—" Grey looked down, biting his lip.

"We can't blame Tom for a crooked judge he warned us

about before the hearing," his wife said, stepping onto the truck's running board. She grabbed her brief from the floorboard. Replacing their last custody case with this one was an easy swap. "This is a different court circuit; there's no Judge Giles this time."

They walked into the renovated residential-now-commercial property. Its 1970 brick, ranch-style layout still made it feel like someone's home. A middle-aged woman with a coiffed brown bob peered over the dark-cherry counter. With her glasses at the edge of her nose, she asked, "Are you Mrs. Murphy?"

"Yes, I'm here for an appointment with Mr. Peavy."

"He's expecting you. Please have a seat in the waiting room and I'll let him know you're here."

Kristin sat next to Grey in what was likely the former carport for the ranch home. The exposed brick, painted white, created a deep cold sensation on her back. She shivered, pulling the sleeves of her yellow blazer down over her wrists. A lanky gentleman sat next to the corner ficus tree, sifting through paperwork, his face dazed. The mother assumed he was joining the ranks as a "criminal" parent, too.

A stocky man wearing a collared shirt and black golf vest, stood in the open doorway appearing much larger than in years prior. Kristin questioned if she had booked the right lawyer. "Hey guys. Y'all can come back," he said.

The corridor's walls sucked the air from her lungs as she imagined this was the setting for many of the previous homeowners' arguments. Black, hardwood floors creaked with every step of her worn, ballet flats. As the men caught up on the latest football news behind her, she tried to guess where the fatal disagreement took place.

In Tom's office, the wife said, "We didn't want to be repeat customers, but here we are."

"This time it's you, Kristin. I'm so sorry to hear this jerk has caused issues. You and Grey, you're good parents with some real characters for exes." He opened the envelope on his desk. "Let's see what we have here."

She appreciated his brevity when it came to small talk.

He glanced at his client over the thick-rimmed glasses balanced at his nose's end. "I think I have a good handle on where this is going. Talk to me about Mr. Camek—does he have any criminal background? DUIs?" The attorney paused his red-flag pre-screen of the plaintiff and removed his glasses.

Kristin knew his question had prompted memory of his former client, sitting next to her. As many tragic cases as family lawyers encounter, they protect themselves from becoming too emotionally attached; however, there are those cases even they can't forget.

"Grey," said Tom, "I read about your daughter in the paper. I—I meant to reach out to you, please accept my condolences now."

The two fathers exchanged a glance, and Grey looked down pressing the bridge of his nose between this thumb and forefinger.

Clearing his throat, the counselor continued. "If I recall, Judge Giles remembered the mother, too, when she came to his court for sentencing."

"Well, ten years for negligent homicide still seems light to me. It was my kid who got the life sentence."

"It sure was," he returned his glasses to his nose. "Kristin, where were we? Okay, so no alleged abuse. Is he a job hopper?"

"No, he's the head of sales for a med tech company," his client said. "No skeletons, I'm afraid."

The attorney leaned back, clasping his hands together. His index fingers pointed up, their flat surfaces touching. "Have the children ever mentioned wanting to live with him?"

"No, never. We have a good relationship. They love their stepdad. They're excellent students whose teachers adore them. The oldest is in the school band."

"Mine too. It's a fun age," he said. "Child support. Medical expenses. How's Mr. Camek with that kind of thing?"

"He's late on occasion, but not because they have financial problems," she said.

"But never over thirty days, I bet."

"Twenty-nine and a half." The ex-wife forced a laugh. Sensing her attorney's frustration with dead-ends on Hutch's character assassination, the desperate mother redirected. "You received the copies of the text messages between the father and children that I emailed?"

"I did. What an ass." Tom moved his eyes between the two parents. "I think I can say that with you by now."

She noticed her husband's jaw loosen with Tom's casual approach.

"We have both the girls in counseling now," she said.

"Male or female therapist?"

"Male."

"Do you trust him to be unbiased?" the attorney asked.

"He's a certified professional, I think he can maintain objectivity."

"You may want to make a change. The last thing you want is some guy thinking about his own daughter and steering them back to their dad."

"Is that possible?" Kristin raised her eyebrows and tilted her chin at the hefty man behind the desk. A third-party person interfering with her children's emotional security, she had not considered. However, she didn't think she'd broach the inside of a courtroom again, either.

Maybe I am naïve.

"You'd be surprised. Everyone has a story, and favoritism is difficult to mask. I wouldn't risk it."

"Do I need to change lawyers too?"

Tom turned his back to his computer screen. The soft upholstery hugged his shoulders like a worn catcher's mitt while he held his rimmed glasses in his hand. "Kristin, do you know how to tell the difference between a child who's abused and one who's alienated?"

"The abused one still wants to be with their parent." Grey answered without hesitation.

He pointed his glasses and nodded yes to the stepfather. His jowls flapped with his affirmation. "The alienated child is convinced he/she isn't wanted, cared for, loved, fill-in-the-blank, by the other parent which makes them push away." He paced his words with the cadence of a closing argument. "Often the parent the child pushes away is, in fact, the more stable parent. We saw this with Browning, remember? Healthy people don't push away from other healthy people naturally, I think we can agree. If your ten-year-old daughter claimed she'd rather live two states away from the stable, loving household she's lived in since she was a toddler, we know her brain hasn't developed enough for this concept. It's been planted in her head."

Hearing a legal professional claim her fears as truth, caused his client to sit upright on the chair's edge. His acknowledgement of the abuse pierced the mother's soul.

"Listen, I've defended jerk-moms, jerk-dads, jerk-grandparents—you name it. I would have no issue defending you."

"I'm sorry, I just—" Kristin's voice cracked as tears streamed from the corners of her reddened eyes.

"No apologies. I understand your concerns." Tom adjusted his glasses at his nose's edge again as he sorted papers scattered across his desk. Perusing the handwritten affidavits, the lawyer said, "This guy got to your daughters during a key transitional period in their lives. What's scary is, that's not by accident. Most teenage girls push away from their mother, and he's exploiting it. Mr. Camek has capitalized on their hunger for independence. Living at the beach and weekend trips to Disney World, very enticing to a child. He's playing on your babies' whims. Your ex-husband is executing a plan he's had in the works for months, maybe years."

"We know you'll represent us well, Tom," Grey said.

"I will do my level best. The only barrier I see is that the State of Alabama allows a child of fourteen years or older to decide on the custodial parent they want to live with. You already know this."

"Right, but my oldest is only thirteen."

"His court, his rules, remember?"

She cringed hearing the familiar phrase that somehow was used to justify her stepdaughter's death. "I thought it was the judge's role to uphold the law, not manipulate it."

"They call it discretion, I'm afraid. Presuming the child much like her mother: confident, determined, able to make a good argument?" Tom asked.

"Yes . . . " The mother hesitated, unsure if Tom's statement was a compliment or criticism. "She's mature for her age. But the texts show he's using coercive control."

The lawyer eased up in his seat with elbows resting on the desk. His client tapped her foot on the floor in front of him. "That's where the courts don't always work in favor of good people. The manipulation is just like a fly in your soup. Sometimes the meal is unsalvageable, and the customer sends it back. Other times, you just swat it away and continue to eat."

"So, this is merely a nuisance, not a crime," said Grey.

"Manipulation happens with every custody case on the

books. Fortunately, he's used empty promises. Many parents take a more physical approach."

Kristin's mouth watered, choking her.

"Some judges tolerate it less than others. We'll hope we get Judge Chandler from this circuit. He'll give Mr. Camek a real lashing. For the others, it just comes down to the facts of the case, not necessarily the methods used."

"What facts do they expect us to present?" Grey asked.

The defendant answered in her head with each bullet point her attorney highlighted.

"What are the child's decision-making capabilities?"

Strong.

"What is the father's financial status?"

Rich.

"And, of course, the child's safety."

A guaranteed mental breakdown by graduation.

"No mention of emotional abuse?" the nurse asked.

"It's hard to prove in a court," the attorney said.

"The CDC issues guidelines for preventing adverse childhood experiences, mental abuse being a key contributor. It's science, not opinion."

"We could get an expert witness, but not for a temporary hearing. The judge will make a ruling on a trial basis. If it sticks, and we still want to fight it, we'll ask for a permanent hearing. That's when the real guns come out."

The mother looked down to her feet. "So, there's a good chance the judge will let this happen, is that what you're telling us?"

"I don't like to BS my clients."

"That's why I asked the question."

"There's a good chance the judge will rule in his favor. Again, it's temporary. The judge may be inclined to let the children try it since there's no 'bad' parent here, per se."

"What about the youngest one?" Kristin's lip quivered.

"She still needs her mother."

"The baby is young, even by the state's standards. She was just barely ten when her father forced her to write and sign this statement. This is questionable." Tom showcased the document, pointing to the portion that read, *I, Olivia Camek, hereby certify I am eleven years old.*

"And they knew she was under the legal age, what the—?" Grey clasped his hands behind his head.

"If we can get the judge to agree she's too young, maybe he or she would rule for the oldest child to stay too," Tom strategized. "The courts want siblings to stay together at all costs."

The stepfather pondered aloud. "If Lennon will wait a year, while Olivia reaches the minimum age for election, we can shift the momentum. She'll meet more friends when she starts high school."

Tom nodded his head. "That's what I'm thinking too. That's our best angle. We should get a GAL assigned."

"What's that?" Kristin asked.

"Guardian ad litem. She has a separate retainer. You and Mr. Camek will split the costs."

"So, we're hiring another lawyer?" Grey's eyes widened as he placed his hands back on the armrests. "I don't remember doing that with Browning's case."

"The courts consider this a high-conflict case." Tom twisted his lip. "The guardian represents the children."

"A high-conflict case? All I'm doing is disagreeing with his proposal. I'm open to negotiating more time with him, or even a move when they are older, just not at age ten," the mother said.

"This situation is one where a neutral party is needed to make an assessment. You're advocating for your daughters and Mr. Camek will say the same. It's the guardian's job to find out what's behind the emotions," the attorney said.

"What about mediation?"

"Do you think he'd agree to anything less than what he's proposed?" Tom asked.

"I don't know, maybe. He's a sales guy; he likes to haggle."

"Well, it's expensive to haggle in the legal world, I'm afraid. Mediation requires additional attorneys as well. It's a time-consuming process with value, but only when there's a chance of an agreement."

"Kris, you know he's not going to back down," the husband said.

Tom removed his glasses again to address his client. "These guys know the law and plan for this day. Honestly, it's one thing I hate about our state's domestic policy. It was designed for the children who truly need to leave a parent's home. Maybe they're exposed to abuse, crime, drugs–these kids need another option. Sometimes they trade one situation for the lesser of two evils, but it can be a second chance for them. Its unfortunate selfish parents, like this guy, take advantage of the age stipulation. And attorneys play a part in that, I can't deny. If you think he'll agree to mediation, I'll offer that in our rebuttal. But, I promise he's had this day marked on his calendar for a long time. My hunch is he's committed to seeing this play out exactly the way he's planned."

"You've seen the end of this movie before, I take it. Thank you for your honest assessment. What else can I expect from the GAL?" asked the client.

"She'll interview both families and anyone the children routinely have contact with. Teachers, principals, church leaders, school counselors, and so forth."

From the office window, his client watched the cars pass outside while he continued with the plan. She cowered thinking of Olivia and Lennon's friends' parents knowing their family business. After the interviews, going to the Piggly Wiggly meant she'd have to take extreme covert measures.

"Just to clarify," she interrupted, "We'll be paying her by the hour too. Every interview, phone call, keystroke. All that comes at a price."

"Emily Cochran is fairly new out of law school. Her fees are probably half of mine," Tom said.

Kristin did the math in her head.

If Tom charges $250 an hour, "Legally Blonde" will be $125, minimum.

"All of this, so she can give an assessment of two children I've raised since birth."

"That's why your interview is crucial. You'll want to appear calm, collected—which I have no doubt you will be. Try not to bash the other parent or sound too possessive of the children, which I don't think you will. You want the GAL to believe your home is where your daughters belong."

Standing, she placed her hands on her hips and paced beside the former residence's built-in bookshelves browsing her attorney's display. Worn bindings of legal resources and framed accolades served as the backdrop for scattered pictures of him and other smiling faces she assumed were his family. The mother studied one in her hand. A slimmer Tom and a bright-eyed girl wearing a navy band uniform stood together on a football field. Lights shone down from the top of a stadium reflecting off his bald head; her dewy face radiated. With one hand nestled in the crook of his arm, the girl's golden plume jutted past Tom's wide grin. Her gloved fingers clutched a polished flute in the other.

"You'd think that would be obvious; I'm Mom." Kristin's voice softened, returning the picture to its place on the shelf.

"This isn't the eighties anymore, I'm afraid. Mothers don't always get the children, not even when it's a daughter. On the other hand, good fathers have a shot at being involved in their children's lives."

"When it suits the court," said Grey, giving his bottom lip a tug with his teeth.

"That's always the unknown," said the attorney from behind the desk.

"I understand Hutch's role in this. My actions alone show how much I, we, value the father–daughter bond. It's just that he—" The client collected herself and returned to her seat. "Mr. Camek won't rest until I'm erased from their lives. And there's no consistency with these judges' decisions. Grey's ex-wife got preferential treatment because she was the mom, but she had documented substance abuse issues and the dad didn't. Here, I'm absent these toxic behaviors, but I stand to lose my children to the father who is clearly manipulating them. Where's my favoritism?"

"That's what the GAL will need to hear." Tom coached his client as she reached for a tissue from the box on his desk. "She needs to see you're willing to go the extra mile to keep them in touch with their father even though he's the one who left them for money. The GAL will see the children in their natural environments. She'll attend events you're hosting, visit them at school, home, anywhere they interact with others. Be sure to keep her in the know. Her written assessment is vital to the judge's decision."

"Does the judge follow the guardian's recommendations?" Kristin asked.

"Not always, but there's a heavy emphasis on their perception of each parent. We need her to side with us." Her attorney's eyes glimmered, planning his attack. "With the GAL involved, your two girls may not need to speak to the judge. Her representation may lessen the trauma of this whole thing."

Grey stood to shake Tom's hand. "Then, I guess we'll hire her." His voice bridled as he looked at his wife, still sitting. "If it will protect them, we'll find the money somewhere. I have a retirement fund from my corporate days; we'll tap into that if we have to."

"I agree," she said. "Maybe Ms. Cochran can shield them from the circus Hutch's ringleading. Lord knows, I haven't been able to."

"Keep me posted on how things go this week," Tom replied, handing Kristin a collated stack of papers. "You need to complete these interrogatories and financial affidavits too."

"I'm sorry to sound dense, but these terms—?"

"It's okay. I forget not everyone lives in the courtroom like I do. These are legal questionnaires. It's the formal way to post your argument against Mr. Camek, and his for you. The financial form will expose all of your debts and assets for the court to evaluate the household incomes."

Kristin's lips puffed.

"My admin can help you if you have more questions."

Chapter Eleven

The bedroom was still dark when the previous day's events stirred Kristin. She drifted between bliss and the world-crumbling reality awaiting her. Fighting to stay in her head, she buried her delicate shoulder under the crisp sheets. Hazy visions of young Olivia extending her hands toward a rippling canopy of linens sent a warm sensation through her chest. Shaded from the hot Alabama sun, she danced in the grass; her blonde ringlets hovered like bees gathering pollen above her head. Her laughter poured from her open mouth filtering through her gap-toothed smile. Kristin's eyes fluttered open. Dim numbers through squinted eyes read 02:00; she flung herself on her back until a quiet house invited her to complete her homework for Tom.

Sitting on the edge of the bed, her feet dangled just above the slatted floor. "Come on, Champ. Let's get this over with," she whispered. Of their three dogs, he was the only one allowed inside. Her faithful friend had slept at her bedside since she was pregnant with Olivia. Years of chasing squirrels and escorting kids to the bus stop had stiffened his joints, but he relinquished his restful slumber for her. She waited in the doorway for her loyal companion. A shiver crawled her spine, recalling the day Hutch demanded she move out and take her pathetic pet with her. As the patter of pawed feet followed her down the hardwood floors, she again found a place of peace in her despair. Stopping at the girls' bedroom doors she touched her forehead to each, embracing the gift of knowing they were safe one more night.

I wonder what feels worse. Waking in the middle of the night remembering their beds are empty or realizing you've grown used to it?

"I'm not ready, Champ," she said through a whispered sigh.

She ran her fingers along the smooth top of the wooden desk to find the base of the lamp. Two clicks revealed the unopened packet Tom gave her still in need of her attention. The crinkling envelope resounded through the night's stillness as she unveiled her ex-husband's accusations against her.

Kristin adjusted her reading glasses and rolled her neck combing through the tangible reminder of her reality. Her shoulders tightened as the words on the page came into view. *Name, Address, Employer Information. She continued to read, Names of the children. Ages. Place of birth.*

Each line invaded her privacy, her soul.

Tension built in her neck with each bulleted interval. Blood rushed through her carotid arteries, spiraling to the top of her brain. Her fingers made circles over throbbing temples as her heart raced. Question number one read: *Why should you be the primary physical custodian of the minor(s)?*

Do they need to see my stretch marks?

For a week, she spent the pre-dawn hours defending her parenting decisions against a host of exaggerated attacks. Each emotional crucifixion left her greeting the sunrise with reddened, puffy eyes.

I know many married couples who use poor judgement daily. Where's their rectal exam of accountability?

Question 4: *Why was the oldest child not scheduled for an eye examination, when she complained of vision changes?*

Because I didn't have the money, and asking him for help meant listening to a barrage of insults.

Question 8: *Why did the mother refuse to meet the father at the half-way point in Florida?*

Because both governors ordered evacuations along the Gulf of Mexico for a category five hurricane.

Question 11: *Why was the mother present in the therapist's office when the youngest child expressed interest in a same-sex relationship?*

Did he just out my kid?

Can exaggerated grievances outweigh years served as a recognized parent on the student council? Will the judge allow his embellished storytelling to overshadow the multiple affidavits from school officials validating her character? Would written testimonies from integral adults in her children's lives be enough to carry her through any weak parenting moment she may have had?

She proceeded with the questionnaire. Why did the mother sign the child up for soccer lessons on his weekends?

Because the child wanted to play soccer. Why don't they base their decision on how the mother sliced the children's grapes, horizontally or vertically?

After absorbing repeated blows of insulting accusations in the interrogatories, Kristin's shoulders tensed as she flipped to the page reading *Financial Affidavit.*

Let's get this enema over with.

The documents questioned her salary increases, along with recording any accumulated debt. She sighed, documenting her credit card balance at its limit, given the recent influx of legal fees. Kristin complied with answering invasive inquiry after inquiry. Mortgage information, life insurance premiums, and tax records teed up for scrutiny by her ex-husband's legal counsel. Her shoulders tensed, knowing their accounting records were on full display.

Air blew through Kristin's lips. With minimal difference between their character, on paper, the only significant differentiator was the wealth she'd walked away from. By removing the girls from a society worshiping the gods of power and income, she thought she was protecting them. Her former friends were helicopter moms and their kids depended on antidepressants to make it through high school. Sure, they were married, but to husbands insisting on higher GPAs or improved performance on the field. Crushing their sons' and daughters' free will, all for scholarships to hide the parents' guilt for not saving for their child's college education.

Rather than groom her daughters into pre-planned personas, Kristin had offered them freedom to grow into self-defined success. Now, they were standing on the edge of the pit she'd crawled out of. One filled with sleepless nights, hidden anxieties, and an emotionally absent man who devoted his love to making money.

Pages of more questions remained on her desk as she started a fresh pot of coffee. The bright rays of morning grazed the edges of the kitchen sink where she stood watching sparrows flutter across their backyard. Her shoulders hung low as she suspected the courts viewed her simplistic homelife as a denial of opportunities for her kids. Society's expectations were trumping her desires for quality time by setting the standard that children needed more in their already busy lives. More extracurricular activities, more money, more networks; more of everything. In this world, a father's social status discounted a mother's nurturing. Kristin needed a shower to wash away the remorse.

***

It took a full weekend to prepare their home for the guardian's visit. The sweat on Grey's brow dripped under his wraparound sunglasses that held the misted back spray of the pressure washer. "This deck will be the death of me." He scowled at the clearing mildew stains.

Handing him a glass of iced tea, his wife said, "If you're at a stopping point, you should get dressed."

"Done." The husband smiled at his wife as he wiped his face with a towel. "Thank you for the excuse to end my torture. Maybe the guardian won't deduct points for stairs showing wear; I mean, we've lived here eight years."

"Let's hope."

Entering the home, the smell of fresh lavender invaded her senses, which was the greeting she aimed for with her all-day cleaning routine. She smiled watching Grey's chin tighten as he noted living room decor staged for display.

"Nice touch."

"I've cleaned corners in the house that hadn't been touched since we moved in. You could eat off those walls." She continued her way to the bathroom to finish her makeup. "It's sickening to think I have to audition for the role of mother."

"Spoiler alert—you got the part."

"Why don't married families go through this process? Every few years they should be subjected to a legal inspection of their parenting skillset."

"And have to pay for it."

"I know five families right now who wouldn't pass."

"Could you imagine Twila and Ches meeting with a GAL?" he asked, pulling a coiled towel from the triangle-shaped display in front of the shower entry.

"That needs to get refolded when you're done."

"Do you think she'll inspect our bathroom?" he asked, the splashing sounds of water garbled his laugh.

"The dogs are barking, that must be her. Would you hurry, please?"

"I'll be right there. Get started, Vivien Leigh."

Peering through slatted shutters, Kristin's eyes fixed on the silver SUV. A twinge of angst fluttered across her body, as the stirred dust settled. Yesterday, this person was a stranger to her, but after their interview the mother felt confident she'd complete a full psychological profile on the woman whose opinion of her was so heavily weighted. Favorite foods, hobbies, and especially pet peeves ranked high on the list. She longed to be inside the head of someone with the power to change lives. A glimpse of the VIP through the driver's side windshield made her call on decades of nursing experience. She'd proven herself in stressful environments before this girl was born.

A woman exited the vehicle, stopping her approach to calm the trumpeting dogs who greeted her. Her pale strands reflected sunlight as she approached the pebbled path to the front entry. The counselor's sensible slacks and low-heeled shoes appealed to the soon-to-be-defendant, a look she'd mimic in the courtroom.

Grey joined his wife lurking in the mudroom. "Can you button this collar?" he asked, stretching his neck, and lifting his chin. "She looks young."

"Yes, she does. Let's hope she's wise beyond her years," Kristin fastened the top button and patted her husband's broad shoulders as she scurried to the front door.

Opening the wooden door, she noticed the visitor's prominent cheekbones were marvelously delicate up close. "I'm sorry about the dogs. They are loud, but harmless."

"Oh, that's no problem. We've had dogs all my life. You

must be Mrs. Murphy. I'm Emily, the guardian ad litem. The other attorneys scheduled our meeting today," she said with the perk of a baby shower attendee.

"Please call me Kristin," she said. Her hand flared with the ease of a game show host as the door opened into the couple's living room. "Come inside and meet my husband, Grey."

"Hi there, Mr. Murphy."

"And good day to you," he said.

His wife's brow creased with a harsh glare at him, once the flawless-skinned attorney greeted Champ and walked into the kitchen.

"What?" he asked, in a whisper.

"Good day? What are we, Australian?"

His jaw dropped. Turning his palms upward, he asked, "Are you trying to be Martha Stewart?"

"Good grief. This feels so unnatural."

"I agree. Let's take a step back," the husband said, placing his hands on his wife's shoulders and looking into her eyes. "Every parent has flaws; we've got nothing to hide. Deep breaths."

Kristin forced a smile, greeting the youthful attorney in the kitchen.

"I've always wondered who bought this land after the previous owners foreclosed." Emily said.

"You're from Ellington?" Grey asked, taking a seat beside her at the table.

With a nod, she said, "My parents live just down the road. I went to Westfield High."

"That's where Lennon will go, if ..." Kristin paused, realizing her daughter's future was evolving, as they spoke.

"It's a great school. When I looked at this case, I recognized several teacher's names you have listed. Some of them taught me when I was in middle school."

And, I bet you still fit into your prom dress.

"We've been happy here," he said. "We moved outside the city limits for more space when we married. Our family was young, and we wanted space for them to play. My family raised me on a farm in the country; it was a good childhood."

The young woman tilted her head toward the ATVs parked under the carport outside. "I loved my four-wheeler too, at that age. Still do when I visit my parents' house."

"It's nice to meet a small-town success story. I'm sure your parents are proud." The mother removed her hands from her pockets and sat with the others. If she couldn't relate to the guardian, perhaps she'd strike a resemblance to the woman's parents. She hedged her bets, hoping Emily had a good relationship with her mom. "Are we okay in here?"

"This is fine," the lawyer said, placing the contents from her satchel on the knotted-pine table. "I understand your daughters, Lennon and Olivia, have expressed an interest in living with Mr. Camek. Have they ever talked to you before about a change?"

"No, they haven't. This is all news to me."

"They've always seemed happy with the arrangement we had in place," the stepfather said. "We make sure they see their father as much as possible. Kristin drove them to their dad's every weekend when he lived in Birmingham and does so, even now."

"To Florida?" the GAL asked.

"Yes, we meet halfway on Fridays and Sundays."

"How long has that gone on?"

"Their dad moved to Lake Tarpon in January, so it's been five, almost six months. It was a promotion for him and a move home for his wife. She's from the Miami area, I believe."

"That's a lot of driving. For the parents and the kids. Do they like giving up their weekends to be on the road?"

"I think all of us know it's temporary. We were waiting for summer break, to get a final plan in place. I, we—it takes his support too," she said with a glance to her husband. "We value the father–daughter relationship."

"Wonderful," Emily said. "Any idea why they've changed their minds about living with you?"

"Now that you mention it, there was a time when Lennon said something about moving." The mother's eyes widened, turning to her husband. "I may not have mentioned it to you. It seemed so insignificant at the time." Returning to Emily, she continued. "The oldest has had some issues with anxiety. The counselor says its common with gifted kids; their brains work faster in all areas. Anyway, on her twelfth birthday, just last year, she had a mini-meltdown after her friends left the party."

Emily's pen scribbled across a legal pad.

"She said she didn't want to turn twelve. Of course, I asked her why. She said she was worried her dad would pressure her to move in with him since she was 'of age.' " Kristin's fingers motioned air quotes."

"How did you respond?"

"I dismissed it at first and tried to help her see her age as something to celebrate. No mother wants their child upset on their birthday. It bothered me some later that night, but Hutch, that's my ex-husband, was living closer. At worst, I thought he'd ask for more time with the girls, but I thought nothing about her election for custody."

"But, you were taking them to his house every weekend already," the attorney said, pushing her cornsilk strands behind her ear.

"That was never enough for him," the wife said. "Hutch always wanted more. I assumed she meant he would ask for additional time over school holidays, spring break, summer, you know."

"Did you mention her concerns to Mr. Camek?"

"After a lot of thought, I approached Hutch like a sensible co-parent."

"Why do you say that?"

"Well, with him. He's—," the wife paused, looking over her shoulder to Grey. "He can get nasty, let's leave it at that."

The young lady's brow dented just above the bridge of her glasses.

"With you, or the children?"

"With me, but we never know how he reacts with the girls when they're with him. He's the type to take things out on people behind closed doors," the stepfather said.

Kristin held her breath, hoping he wouldn't go into more detail.

Emily asked, "How did he react to Lennon's statement?"

"Typical Hutch. He shrugged it off. Said he didn't remember saying that, and if he did, she must have misunderstood him," the mother said.

"Did the child bring it up again?"

"No, nor did I. I guess he was priming the pump then, and I missed it."

"So, you think this is his idea, not theirs?"

Handing her the printed text messages she and Grey copied from Lennon's phone, Kristin said, "We *know* it's his idea."

The guardian studied the documents, making notes on her legal pad, and shuffling through the copied messages between father and child. Kristin spoke to the top of the young lawyer's head as she filed papers in her portfolio. "We've had a good situation for almost ten years. I don't know how to explain my ex-husband," she said, leaning forward. Emily laid her pen down as the client ran her fingers over the table's surface, chipped from years of art projects and family meals. "If there was a pizza on this table, we'd likely take a slice, maybe two, but not before we made sure there was enough for everyone else. Would you agree?"

Emily squinted her eyes and nodded yes.

"Hutch would serve himself first, taking as much as he wanted and leave the others to fight over the remainder. He thinks of his needs, always," The woman stammered, recalling her attorney's advice for her to take the high road with every opportunity. "That's not a bitter ex-wife statement. He and I view the world differently, but we are divorced for a reason, right?"

"This has been helpful, thank you," Emily said, handing the copied texts back to Kristin.

"I bet you see some tough cases in this role," Grey said, receiving a forceful nudge from his wife for dragging out the painful interview.

"They are all tough," the young woman said, with a somber tone. The sky-colored flecks in her eyes darkened. "My role is to be a voice for the children in each case, and it's tough. It's easy for the ex-spouses to get caught up in their reasons for divorcing each other, and they forget they're still married to their kids. When you're the one who writes an assessment for the judge, everyone gets tense."

The husband and wife adjusted their backs in their chairs.

"Sometimes, the children don't have a good option. Those are extremely difficult, but I stay focused on the kid's point of view. Parents, you may have questions along the way that I can answer, but other times I may refer you to your own attorney. My clients are Lennon and Olivia and I represent their interests, no matter the outcome."

"Thank you for clarifying your place in all of this. I feel confident you'll provide comfort to our daughters while they're going through this difficult time in their lives. Grey and I are happy to provide anything else needed to help put the puzzle pieces together."

"You've been so helpful already." Emily collected her things. "I'll be visiting Mr. Camek on Wednesday. The attorneys are moving this along to beat the school calendar."

"You're flying to Lake Tarpon?" The mother's voice wobbled.

"Yes, since the girls are with Mr. Camek for summer break, I want to see them at his home. Oh, and this isn't an expense you'll split," she said, opening the door. "Mr. Camek is paying for the trip in full."

"Well, I hope you enjoy yourself." Kristin shuddered at her game show host persona reappearing. "I hear it's lovely right before hurricane season."

"Thank you, I'm such a sucker for the beach," she said, with a laugh. "Y'all have a good week; we'll be in touch."

She imagined the young attorney ditching her sensible footwear for a pair of flip flops in the Uber from the airport. The bikini-cladded guardian writing her recommendations poolside, while the palm trees swayed above her in the bicoastal breeze. The mother hoped Emily didn't spill suntan oil on the final dossier. Upon closing the door, she heard ice clinking behind her.

"Want one?" he said, tilting his glass toward his wife's blank face.

"No, thank you. I don't think I could keep it down. Did you catch that?"

With a loud sip, he said, "Sounds like she's a small-town girl about to head to the white beaches of The Magic City."

"Why didn't she meet Hutch at her office?" Kristin kicked a dog toy on the floor. "This is where the hearing is, they have to do it in the county the children reside in. Can't they do a Zoom meeting or something?"

"I think we both know the answer to that."

Her chest tightened watching the SUV's brake lights

fade into the cloud of dust, "It's like I'm standing on a sandbar, in the middle of the ocean, getting pounded by wave after wave. I can't catch my breath before he's hitting me with something else. He knows my every move."

"Honey, our attorney said he's probably been planning this for years . . ." the husband paused, watching her leave the room.

His logical response wasn't the answer his wilting wife needed to hear. Champ dutifully escorted his owner to the bedroom where she fell on her knees sobbing into the church-window-patterned quilt.

Chapter Twelve

She listened to the copier recording her life, soon to be on full display.

"How are you holding up?" The stout attorney asked, entering the room from behind her chair.

"I'm ready to end this, one way or the other." The mother wrenched her hands in her lap.

"Did you read the guardian's report?"

"I did; no surprises," her voice, toneless.

"There's a decent chance your girls are going to go to Florida after tomorrow's hearing," Tom said, matter-of-factly, as he scrutinized the report. "It appears the guardian fell for the trap they set for her."

Kristin remained silent.

"These cases are the toughest to predict. Even if there were safety issues, the child is almost of age to elect a custodial parent."

"*Almost* of age," the mother said. "There's nothing like playing horseshoes with children's lives."

"So, you're telling us even if this judge leaves the girls with us for another year, Lennon could change the custody arrangement at fourteen without argument from a judge?" the stepfather asked.

"Pretty much. It's rare a judge refuses a juvenile's election once they're over age fourteen. Even when they elect a parent who's less qualified than your ex. The state feels like at that age, they can manage the repercussions of their decision."

Kristin rolled her eyes, envisioning a group of old white men wearing dark suits, smoking cigars under the golden dome of the state capitol building.

All in favor of burdening middle-schoolers with life-altering decisions? Aye!

"We know Hutch would persecute her until she followed through," Grey reiterated.

"Like a dog on a bone. These types don't give up, easily," the lawyer confirmed.

The mother looked at the two men in the office. "We committed to see this fight to the end because we think the girls are being coaxed unfairly. This is a situation that best suits Hutch, not the kids. They're too young to see the impact on their futures."

"That's why tomorrow we're focusing on the youngest child's age and her fairly new medical diagnosis," Tom interjected. "In her report, the GAL depicted the youngest child as wavering. She documented, multiple times, that the child has a contingency plan on how to return home to Mom if she doesn't prefer living with Dad. Ms. Cochran recorded that the oldest child understands she may have to live there without her younger sister, and they support the split if it doesn't work out. Do you think the youngest is on the fence?"

"We have a tight bond." Kristin's voice broke recognizing the accuracy of Emily's assessment.

"We're leaning on the texts Mr. Camek sent both girls. I'll have him read those aloud to the court," Tom strategized.

"We'll also stress the existing parenting plan is the established norm for the children."

"All this time I hoped I was doing the honorable thing encouraging the girls to stay in contact with their father."

Tom nodded and organized documents into tabbed folders.

"So many times, I did more than the requirement. I extended Hutch's time in the summer or during school holidays beyond the court-ordered minimum. I communicated special events in hopes he'd attend. I'd remind the girls to call his family members on their birthdays." The mother's words left her empty lips as she stared at the desk. Raising her palms to the ceiling, she asked, "Where did all that get me? Nowhere."

"You are not the corrupt adult here," her attorney said. "These parents—hell, even grandparents—who overstep, they don't care about the children. They're usually seeking revenge on the other adult, fulfilling some egoic void from their childhood, or they're in need of money."

Facing down, her voice shrank. "He hates paying child support."

"They all do. Some want the tax deductions. Others want to save money. In most cases, it's about their need to have control. You'll make yourself crazy trying to rationalize an irrational person's motives."

With a jolt, the defendant opened her eyes wide. "I have something else to add. She dug through her leather bag on the floor and removed a white document. Handing it to her attorney, she said, "It's an interview the Lake Tarpon Equestrian Club did with Peyton Camek, Hutch's wife. She admits she planned her first pregnancy, so their birthdates fell during an optimal party planning month. South Florida's summers were too hot, but winter birthdays interfered with the holidays. Of course, the twins came early, but lucky for them they fell into the right season."

Tom peered over his glasses with raised eyebrows at Grey's frozen face. "You can do that?" "Plan a baby's delivery date?"

Kristin watched their exchange. Adjusting her presentation from lead investigator to nurse educator she said, "If the woman knows her basal rhythms, it's possible."

But, why would someone do that?" Grey asked.

"Exactly the question I hope Tom can uncover." The defendant sipped water from a plastic bottle, then returned it to the brief at her feet. "What type of mindset are you in if you schedule your conception date? And, if they shot for a bullseye once, why wouldn't they do it again? Most people wouldn't voluntarily take on a custody battle the same year they were moving across the country, starting a new job, and having a baby."

"When's the baby due?" Tom asked.

"During the Lake Tarpon school district's fall break."

"While all the kids are together," her husband said. "They're hoping."

"Also, Peyton says they are planning to have all the children in the birthing room when she delivers, so they can bond as a family." Both men's jaws gaped open. "This nut wants my preteen daughters in the front row. of one of the most gruesome natural events the human body can create. I can't count how many nursing students I've picked up off the floor during their OB rotation."

"I fainted when they took Browning out," Grey said.

"Not to mention, my kids will have a full-frontal view of their stepmother during a birth," Kristin said. "Tom, this is some Jim Jones level, Kool-Aid-drinking control. Tell me I'm not crazy."

"You're not crazy but being a control freak doesn't make you an unsafe parent." He turned to file the document in his arsenal of evidence. "It does show they've put a lot of time into this scheme. Maybe I can rattle her tomorrow, but not too much. No judge can resist a crying pregnant woman's testimony. If she'll admit to how long they've been planning this behind your back, the judge could view their actions as unfavorable."

"Is there anything we need to do for tomorrow?" Kristin asked. "I've Googled 'Custody Hearing,' but there's not a lot of examples matching our scenario."

"Here's the blueprint of the questions I'll ask both of you tomorrow," Tom said, handing Kristin a list of questions.

"Me?" Grey asked, resting his elbows on his thighs.

"Yes, you'll be a witness to Kristin's parenting and the girls' demeanor when they're at your house."

"I can do that, but shouldn't we have other live testimonies? Mine is biased, given I'm their mother's husband."

"Family court is loose when it comes to qualifying witnesses. We'll use the written affidavits as other sources of Kristin's capabilities," Tom said.

Grey shrugged his shoulders and flipped the papers face down on his lap.

The attorney coached his clients from behind his desk. "When answering, speak to me, not the judge. Don't get distracted watching Mr. Camek's reaction to your statements. He will try to unnerve you on the stand."

The key witness held her shoulders back and a legal pad in her lap, filling yellow pages with his crash course in family law. Her chest fluttered with each tick of his pre-trial checklist. The leather, padded armchair clung to her skin with each scratch of her pen. Until this day, her prerequisites were her stepchild's custody hearing and a viewing marathon of Law and Order episodes. The crime drama taught her the most believable witnesses wore low-heeled shoes and a dark-colored dress; she'd wait to see if Tom confirmed.

"Try to respond to the cross-examiner's questions with simple 'Yes' or 'No' responses. Be prepared for a long pause," he said. "This is where witnesses crack. When they elaborate on their previous response, they can get in trouble."

"I feel like I've done something wrong," Kristin's voice tightened.

"That's what they want you to feel. They want you to feel guilty, so you respond like a guilty person. Just tell the truth. We're all parents. We all make mistakes. Don't make it worse by covering up something."

Their attorney continued his lesson on the complex world of family law where the rules are in black and white; but the judges can be any color of the rainbow.

Why is the hearing an overcomplicated game of cat and mouse?

A foam board with worn edges hosted an enlarged replica of the state's domestic relations code. He used his chubby finger as a pointer, "Here is where we'll drill down."

In determining the best interests of the child, the judge may consider any relevant factor including, but not limited to:

The importance of continuity in the child's life and the length of time the child has lived in a stable, satisfactory environment and the desirability of maintaining continuity.

"And here," the attorney said, dropping his visual cue to the bottom of the board.

The willingness and ability of each of the parents to facilitate and encourage a close and continuing parent–child relationship between the child and the other parent, consistent with the best interest of the child.

"Mr. and Mrs. Camek have interfered with the emotional well-being of your daughters, repeatedly. We'll leverage their scheme to prove they're seeking personal gains." His forehead creased, looking at his silent clients. "I know this is a lot to take in all at once."

The mother looked to the floor, ashamed that her home state's legislation was devoid of evidence-based research.

"I think we're ready," said Grey.

"If you think of questions after you leave, just text me," the attorney said, accepting his client's outstretched hand.

"Thank you. We'll be in touch," she said.

Chapter Thirteen

"Len? Liv? Breakfast!" Kristin called while removing a bubbling casserole dish from the top oven and placing it on a quilted hot pad on the counter. She took extra care to preserve the dress she was wearing for the hearing.

Olivia appeared in the kitchen before anybody else. "My sugar was 121. How many carbs are we looking at here?"

Kristin surveyed the meal. "Baked French toast on high fiber, wholewheat bread, a side of turkey sausage, and some sugar-free syrup. If you don't go overboard on the syrup," she smirked through a sideways grin at her daughter, "plan for 30 grams."

"Who me?" The young patient joked, sticking the needle into the bladder of the medicine vial, and withdrawing insulin with precision accuracy. "Voilà! How's this, Nurse Mama?" she asked, holding the filled syringe up for Kristin's inspection.

"Looks perfect, Nurse Liv. Need help?"

"Nah. I'm shooting it into my belly," the child said, pinching the skin above the waistline of her pajama pants. She winced with the piercing needle.

Mom hid her grimace. She doubted she'd ever grow accustomed to watching her child inject herself with medicine that would kill the average human.

"When am I getting a pump?" Olivia asked while disposing the needle into a sharps container under the sink.

"Doctor Roland said soon." Kristin handed a stack of plates to her, "We're waiting for the honeymoon period to end, remember?"

"That's the only honeymoon she'll see." Lennon jeered her younger sister, swatting her hair from behind and positioning herself at the table.

"Whatever, buttface."

The mother pleaded. "Not today girls. RaRa is on the way over."

"Why so early?" asked Olivia.

"Moron." The oldest sibling sneered through clenched lips. "It's court day."

"Oh, that's right. Aren't we supposed to go with you?"

"I'm not allowed to discuss the case with you, remember?" the mother asked, placing plates in front of them. RaRa will stay here while Grey and I are at the courthouse. You both have ironed dresses hanging in your closets." The dogs alerted her from outside, prompting a pause in her instructions. "She'll bring you to the courthouse if you're needed. Otherwise, enjoy a pajama day."

She stepped to the side window. Her mother's red Mercedes pierced through the dust with no regard to the four-legged welcome wagon in her way.

Calling from the laundry room, she asked, "Are we good on the plan?"

"Good."

"Good."

Kristin's body trembled seeing her mother walk to the door clutching her Louis Vuitton purse away from the eager hounds. Her throat tightened, knowing Rosalyn's visit wasn't for the usual family gathering. She parted her lips, but her mother's entry silenced her.

"Why must you have so many dogs, Krissy?"

"We're dog people, Ma."

"One is one too many." She kissed her daughter's cheek smelling of white rose and Moroccan jasmine. Entering the kitchen, the grandmother said, "There they are—the most beautiful granddaughters in the world."

"RaRa!" they exclaimed.

Giving each a pecked kiss on the tops of their heads, she admired their full plates. "This looks yummy." With raised brow to the chef, she said, "Betty Homemaker to the end, I see, dear. Is that the same dress you wore to Dennis's funeral?"

"It is, Mother. Forgive me. I was never in the mood to shop for an elegant custody hearing gown."

"Love you, Mama. Good luck today," Olivia said, prompting a harsh glare from her sister.

Puckering her lips, Kristin blew a kiss and walked toward the door; her mother followed.

Balancing on the top step, she called to her daughter, "Krissy."

Her tapping heels stopped on the cement floor. She faced her husband's truck running in the driveway. With a deep breath, she turned to face her mother.

"I just—"

"Save it, Ma." Turning her back, the tapping resumed.

"Krissy, please," Rosalyn's voice cracked.

Her daughter froze, bracing for another scathing insult.

"I know how you hate to fight. I just— I wish I could go

for you," the mother said. "In our dynamic duo, I'm the muscle, you're the heart, right?"

Approaching the bottom of the stairs, Kristin looked up to her mother. "I fight when I have to. You taught me that much."

"Listen, I know I wasn't the best mother. . ."

"You're passionate about your family, don't apologize for that. This is just your Catholic guilt."

"I'm Irish. We always feel guilty for something," Rosalyn said with a smile, running her fingers across the wrought-iron railing. "I'm trying to say, I'm—," The mother swallowed. "I know I did things when you were growing up. My temper was more than I could handle, at times, but I always loved you. I should have done better." With a brittle voice, she said, "You. Now, you, my dear, are an exceptional mother."

The emotions of the day filled the daughter's eyes.

"Even when dealing with this jackass. You've never let your feelings toward him mar the way you parent your daughters. I admire that about you."

"You don't have to say this, Ma. I know you love me."

"I know I don't have to; I *need* to tell you this. For my own sake."

"That means so much to me." Kristin shook her head. "*You* mean so much to me. Listen, if there's one thing this experience has taught me, marriage, divorce, children, the whole lot. We do the best we can with what we know at that time. I've learned lessons and I've made mistakes along the way."

"We all have, sweetheart."

Her lip quivered. "Now I know, I've got to stand up to this bully. My kids need me to fight for them. Defend them. And, lucky for them, I learned from the best."

Rosalyn blotted the corners of her eyes. Her jeweled arm jangled. The vibrant, emerald glimmer had faded from her stare after years of revenge-filled visions. She smirked, "I got a cousin in Southie. Francis, he's a real head-breaker. He doesn't ask questions."

Kristin blew a soft kiss to her mother. "I should go. I love you."

"Okay, Kiddo. Give 'em hell. Remember, they can't eat you for supper."

Giving a one finger wave over her shoulder, she lugged her brief to the vehicle. From the passenger side windshield, the daughter watched Rosalyn flash her palm to the couple before re-entering the house. Kristin closed her eyes, in hopes her mother's tenacity would fill her for the day. The brutal legal world labeled peacemakers as weak. This was no time for compromise or negotiation. Hutch would bring her to her knees if she emerged as the agreeable adult he divorced.

It was the first time the mother had walked beyond the passport office window at the local law building. Passing through the metal detectors, people blurred. Voices muffled into a dull roar. A uniformed image motioned her through the archway to the lobby foyer. The beeping wand hovering over her bra strap served as an abrupt reminder: a battlefield awaited her arrival. Uncrossing her arms, the mother rolled her shoulders back, then climbed the stairwell to the second floor. Her breath slowed. She counted the seconds of each inhale and exhale to remind herself she wasn't suffocating.

1,2,3. 3,2,1.

Tom greeted his client outside the courtroom doors. "Thursdays are a little hectic." He looked around at the frenzied huddles of attorneys and clients scattered throughout the waiting area. "The judge hears all the cases, in a rapid-fire fashion. I'm not even sure how much time we'll have for our demonstration."

"It sounds like Hutch's man knew the schedule would rattle the judge today, should we reschedule?" Grey asked.

The attorney appeared intoxicated by the Derby Day atmosphere surrounding them. He removed a white handkerchief from the breast pocket and blotted his bald forehead. "He'll never agree to reschedule because they want this done before the school year starts in a few weeks. You're right about his selecting this day for a reason. This hot shot, Miami lawyer is as crooked as they come. I have some colleagues in that area, so I asked around. They said this guy is known to judge shop."

"Judge shop?" his client asked.

Returning the napkin to his pocket, he said, "Like he's building a Fantasy Football team. He researches each magistrate in the circuit before a hearing and memorizes their ruling record. Then he works the calendar to get a judge who will most likely agree with his client."

She blew a puff of air toward the ceiling and rolled her eyes.

So much for objectivity.

"You'll want to wait outside today," a suited man warned, emerging from the double doors labeled 'Court One.' "The air conditioner is crapping out, and the place was at max capacity by 8:15 a.m."

The pearls the mother selected as a tried-and-true display of a Southern woman's trustworthiness felt more like a tightening noose than a badge of honor. Her fingers adjusted the necklace around her collar before she claimed an open seat on the knotted-pine bench. Staring at the colorless floor, Kristin listened to the cacophony of chaos taking place around her. To the right, ragged work boots tapped while a male voice recounted his victim story to a pair of polished dress shoes beside him. An abrupt scurry in the room's corner caused the tapping work boot to take a solid stance within inches of the suit shoes. The polished pair served more like a referee than legal counsel. Across from her, a set of female athletic shoes, not recognized as a Law-and-Order-prepared patron, was close to a pair of camel-leather high heels. She overheard something about enforcing a restraining order. The presumed defendant wore the hiking boots wedged in the far side of the lobby.

1,2,3. 3,2,1.

She attempted to escape the rumbling agitation rolling through the room by squeezing her eyes tight. Her pulse throbbed along her temples. She questioned herself:

Why am I here? I'm not a criminal. Yesterday, I was a professional businessperson making reasonable choices for myself, my career, and my family. Today, I feel like a caged animal.

Her mind drifted back to an earlier point in the week. Olivia helped her make a new sugar-free brownie recipe. The two dotted each other's noses with almond flour and took selfies while nibbling chocolate chips. It was a stark contrast to sitting next to a man with visible coke residue around his nostrils.

Maybe yesterday, he was doing the same and today, his decision-making, and sanity are under a microscope like mine.

An elevator door dinged open, announcing the top of the hour had arrived. Clanging shackles silenced the bustling lobby. She opened her eyes as the parading grew louder over her shoulder. The wide-strapped, orange slides peeped out from dingy, white pant cuffs and held formation inches from her navy, low-heeled pumps.

One female officer's booming instruction tensed every muscle in Kristin's body.

"Hold!" All were silent.

"Gentlemen, wait here. Enter the courtroom one by one, on my direction," she informed the obedient group and strolled beside their lineup. "Do not ask questions. Do not skip ahead of the person in front of you. Do not speak unless the judge asks you to do so. Are we clear?"

"Yes ma'am," the gruff voices chanted.

The inmates' feet shuffled in and out of the courtroom. Observers' respect came in the form of stillness. Her chest ached with the reminder they were all there for some version of a sentencing.

Animalistic discussions lessened with the roundup underway. Deliberations were handed out like Tic Tacs to the shoes, shuffling through the same wooden doors they entered. She tried to distinguish the winners from the losers, but they were the same. Every loss exiting the room offered the mother relief from the stagnant air.

The lobby emptied. "Kristin, they're ready for us," her attorney said.

Her eyes panned the patina-green, stucco wall in front of her as she looked at her husband.

"You got this," he said, with a confident nod.

Standing from the benched position, she said, "I'm sorry you have to sit outside during the hearing."

"Tom says all the witnesses have to sit here until they testify. I'll be listening through the door."

Smearing the remaining lip balm over her mouth's parched edges, she followed the same path as the inmates. Two oak doors engraved with the city's symbol of justice opened as the clip of her heels dulled. She ambled along the worn, green, carpeted decline of the courtroom floor. Her gold bracelet glimmered in the faded lights. The defendant hoped the judge would note she followed the rule of six when selecting accessories to complement her role as a phenomenal mother on trial.

Positioned at the front table, she noticed her ex-husband's sandy blond waves blended with new silver ones as she approached the judge's podium. His expectant wife stood beside him. Both focused on their attorney's instructions. With each step, Kristin's peace-seeking soul gave way to her mother's rage boiling deep within. She felt a warmth in her cheeks as her lips tightened with each inch closer to the plotting pair. Her nose flared. Her breath hastened.

You're young, beautiful, rich. Why do you need to take my daughters from me?

Her fists tightened around the handles of her leather brief. For a moment, the defendant wholly identified with the tiny tennis moms rumored to lift cars off their children's limp bodies during traumatic events. The adrenaline surged through her veins. She felt as if she could run through the wall and come out unscathed. The rational thinker wondered if this was the time to drop the reins and make a statement.

"Kristin, we're over here," Tom directed, snapping her out of her leopard-like intensity.

Her cheeks cooled and her eyes fluttered, hearing another familiar voice behind her. "Hey, you."

She forced an exhale and turned her back toward her opponent's table. "Audrie? What—?"

"I knew Grey would have to sit outside," she said with a wink. "I'm no stranger to legal procedures."

A familiar face in the room was a welcomed sight. "You missed your calling as a legal advisor."

"No way," Audrie scoffed. "I hate heels."

After a quick embrace, Kristin took her seat next to her attorney at the table. A glance around the room behind them revealed a smattering of voyeurs still present from the morning's cases. Emily sat cross-legged a few rows behind Hutch's team, wearing a dark-gray suit and white ruffled blouse. Her luminant hair was pinned in a tight bun at the nape of her neck. Her piercing eyes no longer reflected the innocent country girl who visited the Murphy home. Her rigid jawline angled down as she reviewed papers on her lap.

"There was a change," Tom's voice lowered. "Last night, it seems Mr. Alvarez, pulled a fast one and sent the assigned judge all of his client's affidavits by email."

The key witness sensed her sister-in-law leaning into their conversation from behind, "Do you mind if she listens in? I may need help deciphering legal jargon today. My nerves are shot."

Nodding to Audrie he said, "Welcome to the party."

"Help me understand," his client said.

"Written witness statements of character are considered evidence," her attorney said. "The judge can't see any evidence before the hearing."

"Maybe he doesn't know Alabama laws," said Kristin.

"That's a universal law, honey." Audrie chimed in. "Any chance this was a rookie mistake?"

"Doubtful." Tom shook his head no.

"Did Snell remove herself from the case?"

Tom's jowls flopped, nodding his head in yes. "She had no choice. If she stayed on, and ruled in Mr. Camek's favor, it's automatic grounds for appeal. If she ruled in your favor, the same would apply for his argument. It was a no-win situation for her."

"I'm sure she didn't read it. I've known Judge Snell's family for years. I took care of her husband when he needed a heart cath. They're such nice people."

Audric raised her eyebrows in Tom's direction.

Seeing their exchange, Kristin interjected, "She wouldn't remember me."

"This is Ellington, Kris," Audrie said. "Everybody knows everybody."

"And Alvarez probably recognized Snell's pattern for being a mother-friendly judge," Tom concluded.

"Judge shopping," his client noted.

"He'd rather roll the dice with a quick replacement."

The doors at the front of the atrium opened, and the bailiff asked for all in attendance to stand. A middle-aged woman climbed the steps to a desk podium holding a Styrofoam cup close to her chest. Taking a seat in the pulpit, the collar of her black robe was illuminated by a bright-yellow, beaded statement necklace.

"It's Judge Lewis," Tom said with a whisper in his client's ear. "She can be a bit of a wildcard."

Kristin sank into her seat.

The magistrate adjusted herself in the high back chair at the top of the stage, fluffed her golden waves, and adjusted her glasses. Setting the cup on the desk, she announced, "Ladies and gentlemen, I know nothing about this case."

Chapter Fourteen

Judge Lewis continued with her introduction. "You're likely aware why we've made the change."

"Yes, Your Honor," the attorneys responded in unison.

"We're on a tight schedule, I'm supposed to hear criminal cases down the hall. Those are on hold for this case. The court reporter will serve as a timekeeper to make sure we don't run over schedule. I'm allowing 45 minutes for each side," she paused for the attorneys' confirmation.

"Yes, Your Honor," the lawyers chanted.

"With that, call your first," Judge Lewis announced. Her poised hand motioned in the air like she'd freed the gate latch releasing salivating thoroughbreds. Both sides were hungry for the flowered wreath of destroyed families.

"Your Honor, we call the plaintiff, Hutchins Maynard Camek, to the stand," his attorney said.

Her ex-spouse strolled to the witness stand with no acknowledgment of Kristin when he passed her table. A waft of juniper and rosewood seduced her nose as his arms swung past her. It had been years since she was this close to him. At drop-offs, they remained inside their vehicles while Lennon and Olivia lugged backpacks between trunks. At school events, she positioned herself at the opposite end of the venue, so she wasn't intimidated by his cutting stares. He still knew how to wear a 42" long, three-button suit, even in a listless Ellington courthouse. The border of his hemmed pants grazed his coffee-colored Cole Haans with each shift of his weight stepping into the witness box. Using his fingers, he combed his thick wavy bangs to one side unveiling the scar over his eyebrow. One she remembered him saying, he earned in a fight at boarding school. Edges of a forearm fraternity pledge, vanished with a tug of both shirt sleeves as he stood, listening to the bailiff's sworn statement. On this day, she found it hard to see the fawn eyes their youngest child had inherited. Kristin recalled how they used to invite her closer.

"I do," Hutch affirmed his oath with a booming response before taking a seat.

And she'd identified the first lie of the day.

His deep tone jolted her in her chair, triggering a rush of traumatic memories from their marriage and after. The salesman prepared for the ultimate pitch as she felt a cold panic creep in. Her breath shortened. Saliva thickened in her mouth like a paste. She reached for the copper pitcher on her table while keeping her shaking hands out of his view. Water splashed on the bottom of her Styrofoam cup; his eyes darted in her direction.

Mr. Alvarez concluded his softball toss to this client, then the defense attorney approached. Tom's questions seemed light as well, but Kristin recalled from their legal planning sessions, these benign how-do-you-dos are designed to loosen the client up. Hutch answered each, flashing his impeccable smile toward the onlookers.

"Mr. Camek," Tom said, approaching the witness stand. Handing the plaintiff a set of collated papers, he asked, "Will you read those aloud to the court, please?"

Hutch gleaned the documents while sipping from a plastic up. The mother's cheeks flushed watching his muscles push fluids through his throat.

"Mr. Camek?"

"Of course, I'll read them." He fidgeted in his chair. "It's a little difficult to jump in. I feel like something is missing from the conversation."

"Will you read what's on the paper, Mr. Camek?" asked the judge from her podium.

"Me. Be honest," he read, pausing to glance at the defense attorney over his glasses. Tom's jowls flopped with his nod. Hutch continued to recite the words like a table read for a play. "Child 1. So, I can tell her I'm okay with staying with her for the summer? Me. Are you okay with it? Child 1. Well, we are coming to live with you for the school year, it just seems fair. Me. Is it fair? Is it fair you've lived your entire childhood with her? Is it fair I've missed out on so much? Is it fair that I keep missing out?" Hutch paused and addressed the judge directly, "I don't think this is the complete text."

"Continue, please. It's complete," Tom said.

"Child 1. You're right. I'm sorry, Dad. I'll tell her we want this to happen now, not next year. Me. If she respected your wishes, she'd do it. Child 1. True. Me. She's putting herself before you. Child 2. I've been waiting a long time for this."

Taking the paper from his hand, the lawyer asked, "Mr. Camek? What were you instructing the child to do?"

"Listen," Hutch said, turning his shoulder away from Tom to face the judge, "I realize I could have handled that better. I'm not a perfect parent."

"Your Honor, we have several examples of Mr. Camek not only coaching the children on what to write in their affidavits but telling them what to say if you call them to serve as live witnesses today."

Judge Lewis accepted the bundle of papers Tom offered. "Mr. Camek, I'll ask you to address Mr. Peavy, given he's the one asking the questions. Gentlemen, proceed."

The witness continued reading the incriminating texts aloud, at Tom's request. Kristin's stomach churned hearing him speak his manipulating instructions line by line. She scanned the courtroom as her ex-husband's grating voice continued. The judge followed along with his testimony, reading the copies on her desk. Mr. Alvarez hunched forward over a legal pad, and scribbled notes after each message his client repeated. Emily stretched her arm across the back of the pew, relaxing into her seat. Returning her gaze to the front of the courtroom, she watched the court recorder's head bob and her keystrokes pause. Her fingers returned to typing after a sharp jerk of her neck capturing every fourth or fifth word he spoke. She shook her head, fading in and out of Hutch's script read. Kristin looked at her lawyer to tell him, but he was fixed on the plaintiff's testimony. The judge slid the paper pile to the side of her desk and skimmed her computer screen while he stumbled through justification of his interference.

Kristin forced air through her nose. The ruler of the court seemed oblivious to the recorder's misconduct. At the least, the mother hoped the magistrate was researching parent alienation syndrome. Scrolling mouse clicks from her perched stand sounded more like the honorable maverick was deleting old emails.

"Counselor, your 45 minutes are over," the court recorder announced in an orotund voice as she adjusted her headset.

Hutch coiled the papers in his hand and rose from this chair.

"Just a minute Mr. Camek, I'll dismiss the witness when it's time," the magistrate said.

With gasping breath, Kristin turned toward Audrie sitting behind her. Her legal confidant gave a resounding shake of her head at the court recorder's time assessment.

"That can't be right," said Tom. "I set my watch the minute I started. I have 18 more minutes to question Mr. Camek and call another witness."

"I'm sorry, Counselor. We're following the court reporter's watch, not yours. Wrap this up," she said, returning to her monitor.

Patting the tube of documents on his leg, the witness said, "This isn't the best of me, I agree. The girls needed some guidance on how to communicate their genuine desires. They knew their mother would have a harsh reaction to their request to live with me."

"No further questions, Your Honor," Tom said, turning to his client seated at their station. He approached the table with a jutted chin and clenched jaw.

"Mr. Alvarez, do you have any follow up questions for your client?" the magistrate asked.

"Yes, Your Honor, just one," he said, approaching his client on the platform. "Mr. Camek, do you love your children?"

"With my whole heart."

"If you love them so much, why didn't you have them live with you after your divorce from Ms. Murphy?"

"Kris—I mean Mrs. Murphy, will say I traveled a lot with my job, which is true of the past. Now, I'm dedicated to being more present in my family life. The girls see it and want to be a part of it. I'm not sure we can add much more than that."

"No further questions, Your Honor."

The judge dismissed Hutch with a glance, returning to her electronic activity as he stepped out of the raised stand. He passed in front of her table again, this time with a swagger she recognized. Flashing a sideways grin in her direction, his wink reminded her that a coward lived beneath his public persona.

"The court recorder mismanaged the time," Tom said, through clenched teeth to his client. Kristin watched the veins in his neck pulsate. "She cut me out of about half of my questions for Camek. Now, I won't get to call Grey in."

"She fell asleep during his testimony. Nobody noticed," Kristin said.

Hutch's attorney stood. "Your Honor, we'll call Peyton Amelia Alston Camek to the stand."

Accompanied by the bailiff, the stepmom glided through the lobby doors. Her hips swayed past the plaintiff and defense stations prompting a tight-lipped smile from the judge. The mother's stylish gold jumper wrapped her baby bump in modern fashion, only to be outmatched by her exquisite almond-kissed cleavage on display. Stepping into the witness area, Peyton brushed her golden hair behind her shoulders. With his gaze fixed above her jawline, the court steward swore her in. Scrolling clicks resumed from the court authority's mouse.

"Mrs. Camek, can you describe your relationship with your stepchildren?" Mr. Alvarez asked.

"I love them dearly." Peyton's plummy tone overtook the room as she rested her hands on her golden shelf. "It's been such a pleasure to watch them grow and their relationship with their father deepen. We are close. They even call me Mom."

Adrenaline surged in Kristin's veins again. She leaned forward, placing her elbows on the table.

"Wonderful," the attorney said.

"When is the baby due?" Judge Lewis interjected from her elevated seat above the witness.

"October. We just found out it's a girl. The kids are thrilled to have another sister."

"We understand you have a slide show you'd like to share," her lawyer said.

"I do." Her smile served as an advertisement for cosmetic dentistry.

On Peyton's cue, the GAL stood, dimming courtroom lights overhead. Hutch whipped out a projector from under their table, giving a tug on the attached drop cord.

A movie screen rolled from its obscure position on the sidewall. The court reporter turned her chair for a front-row seat at the impromptu viewing. Love ballads filled the stagnant room, while images of their sandy-footed family frolicking the palm-lined coast drifted through the hearts of a captive audience. There were photos of Olivia rubbing her stepmom's baby bump, still shots of all the children baking cookies together, and a picture of Lennon and Peyton together wearing matching white collared shirts, with the child's natural curls swirling. Kristin's throat tightened.

As the lights blinked on, the court reporter tapped her wrist and looked toward the judge. "That will conclude the witness's testimony. You may step down."

Kristin crumpled the stepmother's pregnancy interview in her hands.

Both attorneys alternated through her testimony where she defended her role as mother. During Mr. Alvarez's cross-examination, she considered sharing how she stopped eating deli meat or having her hair dyed the minute she discovered she was pregnant as examples of selfless acts.

Peyton's Tik Tok video can't compete with that.

She held her commentary, recalling Tom's pre-trial advice that the courtroom was no place for sarcasm.

The witness drew her prepared responses from the interrogatories she slaved over in the weeks prior. Upbeat pecks from the court recorder's keyboard indicated she had caught her second wind. When the lawyers exchanged positions, Kristin glanced over her shoulder into the judge's cubicle. Affidavits from school officials and community leaders, all written attestations of her infallible character, remained untouched on the desk. Her ex-husband's printed text monologues scattered across them. A variety of screens reflected in the judge's glasses.

"Let's take a ten-minute recess," she said, as the mother's testimony concluded.

Walking the inclined ramp to the exit, Kristin noticed her opponent's team in a relaxed huddle. The group laughed, as Hutch wound the cord to the projector in place, unconcerned by the truths she shared moments prior.

Grey left his holding place on the bench when her group opened the doors. Is that it?"

"No," said Tom. "We're on a break. The time limit is up for witnesses, so I won't be able to use you. You can come back inside when we return."

"That's fine. How's it going?" Grey asked, placing his hands on his hips.

"The judge doesn't seem interested in any of the testimonies. It's like she's already made her mind up," Kristin said.

"This is where the age of the child comes into play," the attorney said. "Unless she hears something horrific, I suspect Lewis will agree with the guardian's recommendation."

Audrie placed her hand on her sister-in-law's shoulder. "Family court is such a mess. You did everything right."

The group returned to the courtroom to see the guardian ad litem sitting in the witness box. Emily wore a gray suit and powder blue button up, appearing as comfortable in the conflict-ridden world of family court as Kristin did behind a ventilator in an intensive care unit. Everyone has their arena, and the mother knew this wasn't hers. She listened as the GAL summarized her investigation of both parents.

"I had the pleasure of working with both Lennon and Olivia Camek over the past few weeks. They are incredible girls," Emily said.

The anguish Kristin restrained all day rolled down her delicate cheeks, listening to a stranger's account of her two children. She acknowledged the compliment with a smile as she blotted her face with a tissue.

"Ms. Murphy and her husband live in a beautiful home here in Ellington. I interviewed them both. It's obvious they love the children and are committed to providing a solid foundation for their family. The girls respect all the adults in their life. This is a hard decision for them. Especially the youngest, Olivia."

"How old is she?" Judge Lewis asked.

Kristin lengthened her spine hearing the court authority's interest. It was the first clarifying question she had interjected.

"Ten," Emily said. "There were some tearful moments during our conversations. She has more reservations about the move than her older sister. Olivia said if this arrangement didn't suit her, she was comfortable moving back to Mrs. Murphy's home, even if the older sister stayed. They agreed to the backup plan."

"I traveled to Mr. and Mrs. Camek's home in Lake Tarpon, Florida. We met in one of their two living rooms. All four of the children gathered on the couches and shared their reasons for wanting Mr. Camek's daughters to live with them. It was sweet," she said. "While there, I met the school's vice principal and the church minister who are all familiar with the family's situation."

"Did you interview the school officials here, where the girls attend classes today?" Judge Lewis inquired.

"No."

"Why not?"

"Because I've lived in Ellington all my life. I felt like I had a good understanding of the local system," said the guardian.

Kristin's eyes widened at the women's exchange.

"Yes, but you're evaluating the school system from the perspective of the Camek children, not your past experiences," Judge Lewis said, peering over her glasses.

"True." She shifted her weight in the chair. "The lawyers were eager to move this process along. I was mindful that the school schedule resumes in a couple of weeks for both districts."

The court reporter signaled to the guardian her time was close to ending.

Leaning into her high back chair, the magistrate said, "Continue, Ms. Cochran."

Tom twisted a grin toward his client, then over his shoulder to Audrie and Grey seated two rows back. Kristin hung on every syllable leaving Emily's lips.

"Thank you for the reminder," Emily said, acknowledging the timekeeper. "My recommendation is for the children to live with Mr. Camek. Ultimately, this is the oldest child's election of custody. I believe the father subjected them to more legal information than necessary, and this should stop immediately. It's unhealthy for their development."

"Thank you, Ms. Cochran. You may step down."

Turning away from the witness stand, the robed superior faced the guests of her court. She removed her glasses and ran her fingers through wheat-colored waves. Rubbing the indented space where cartilage meets bone, her eyes closed. "Well, I won't lie," she said, stretching every vowel. "This has been a difficult case to hear." Her eyes opened. "Not because the children are in danger. Counselors, we can all attest to hearing much more tragic scenarios with cases presented."

Respectful nods stemmed from both legal teams, while Kristin pondered how long it took for the scars of mind games to become visible.

"This case is tough in its own way because both families have immense love for these girls, and they in return."

The mother rocked in her seat.

"Sure, there's the occasional squabble. Some things were mishandled, but the children have benefited from these parents' decision making. Overall, it sounds like you've both done a good job." She stood at her desk. "Let me take a break. Y'all stay here, I just need five minutes. My decision may surprise you."

This is no time for the circuit wildcard to go rogue.

Awaiting the judge's return, Kristin's peripheral vision blurred. She recalled a recent Behavioral Psych lecture she'd presented. Undergraduate nursing students learned how to help anxious patients identify subtle details of their surroundings. The technique was designed to alleviate mentally taxing tension—needle phobias and custody hearings alike.

Five sounds

Tapping *keystrokes* from the awakened court recorder, just a few feet in front of her; the gentle flow of *water* from the pitcher as Tom refreshed her cup; the *jangle* from the bailiff's belt when he rested his hands on it; *lights* humming overhead; and the zoom of *cars* outside in the distance. Kristin longed to be with those outside of this tomb.

Attendees stood as the judge reentered. "Thank you. Y'all sit."

Kristin's exercise continued while the magistrate adjusted herself in her seat.

Four sights.

Stranded gold marbles followed the neckline of the judge's robe.

One, two, three, four. Three feelings.

Warm tears glided from her blistered eyes down both cheeks; the judge cleared her throat.

One, two.

The breeze from the antiquated cooling system, finally catching up with the day's activity, cooled her neck.

Three. Two smells.

She inhaled the musty presence of deception and the stench of loss.

One, two. One taste.

A salty flavor escaped the contour of her lips to rest on the tip of her tongue.

One.

"She's struggling with this one, I can tell," Tom whispered, leaning toward Grey and Audrie behind him.

His client's chest fell with a final push of air.

"I'm a mother of six children, myself. I know kids," the honorable ruler said, with a gentle smile. "I like to think, on most days, I'm a good parent. Or, at the very least, my heart is in the right place. I believe that about both of you too, Mr. Camek. Mrs. Murphy. My concern here," she said, lifting her tone, "is that you're asking a ten-year-old child to make a decision, yet she has no clue how it'll impact her. Not in the short term, and certainly not in the long term. We could argue the thirteen-year-old has *some* awareness, but she's almost of age to make her election independent of the parents' preference. Regardless, the youngest is really just following orders."

Kristin's eyes widened while she mentally retracted

every negative thought she'd entertained about the judge.

With a tense stare at Hutch, the judge said, "The commands you're giving the children need to stop."

He offered no reaction, keeping his eyes fixed on her.

"This is a hard one, folks." She centered her chair.

Losing focus on the beaded necklace, the mother's head bowed.

"Therefore, it's my ruling, the oldest child be allowed to live with her father, in Florida. The youngest is ten. In Alabama, the child must be eleven to have a dog in this fight. She'll stay here with her mother, in Ellington."

Kristin stopped breathing.

Chapter Fifteen

The deliberation resonated throughout the courtroom, and her remaining senses muffled. Through a steady cascade of heartbreak, the mother gave a blurred scan over the room. All three attorneys sat at attention recording the judge's stipulations like an operating room scribe capturing a surgeon's orders. With his head low, Grey's shoulders rounded his back while staring at the carpet beneath his feet. Audrie's hand touched Kristin's shoulder as she stretched her neck looking for her ex-husband's reaction. It was the first time all day she didn't care if he noticed her interest. She was compelled to watch him absorb the loss he'd created.

Hutch remained seated at his legal team's table with his ankle rested on the opposite thigh, his hands clasped in his lap. She could see the corners of his eyes, reddened, as he stared at the city's symbol for justice behind the judge's podium. The unintended consequences of litigation had pierced even the hardest of hearts this day. He loosened his tie and unfastened his collar's top button. His wife's pink fingernails made a circular motion over his upper back as she listened to the judge's final statements.

"Mrs. Murphy, the children should remain with you for the rest of the day. They need to hear this news from Mom."

Unable to speak, she affirmed her understanding with a nod, "Yes."

Hutch uncrossed his leg and moved to the edge of his seat. "I'd like to see the children, Your Honor. This is a tough day for all of us."

"Mr. Camek, our state law allows children to elect custody, so they can explore living with both parents. Although your oldest daughter falls short of the age requirement, the guardian's report deems the teen a mature individual who can handle the change. I'm upholding the child's right today. Your actions, thus far, show your delivery of this message would serve your cause to belittle their mother."

Kristin sat taller in her chair, accepting a fresh tissue from her attorney.

The magistrate continued. "Mrs. Murphy has demonstrated she is qualified to discuss the court's decision in a manner allowing the children to grieve the loss of her, and each other. The oldest child can move one week from today."

"School starts in two weeks," the father said. "She'll need time to get her physical done before admitting her to the school system."

"Didn't I hear your ex-wife is a registered nurse?"

The plaintiff relaxed back into his chair, as his attorney tapped the table in front of him.

"Given Mom has accompanied your daughters on every medical appointment since their birth, I think she's capable of managing the pre-admission requirements for your—" she paused, reevaluating the paperwork, "—Lake Tarpon school system. Wouldn't you agree?"

Air returned to Kristin's lungs.

There is a place for sarcasm in the courtroom.

The lawyers finalized their notes as the court authority listed her orders for the arrangement.

"Neither parent will discuss the court hearing or the legal process with the children, so we'll need the guardian to stay in place. They'll both remain in counseling. Ms. Cochran, please be sure to monitor their adjustment."

"Yes, Your Honor," the young attorney said.

This will only make things worse.

"Counselors should carve out a visitation schedule that suits the split arrangement. Make sure the children get time with the other parent and each other during the holidays."

Olivia's desire to move will skyrocket.

"This is a temporary agreement. We'll have a permanent hearing over the winter break and make final arrangements."

Does she think the child will change her mind after she just empowered her to overthrow her mother?

The defendant's blood pounded through her temples while she played out the coming months in her mind. Lennon was living every 13-year-old girl's dream of moving away from her mother's reign. Hutch would award her loyal commitment to his plan with a new iPhone upon arrival. It would come complete with a South Florida area code to clear any remnants of past friendships in Alabama. In two weeks, she'd be a welcomed new girl, in a new school filled with curious teenagers. She'd finally get to smell the puppy breath of the Labradoodle he bought for her and her sister.

She imagined the girl bragging to her younger sister about trick-or-treating in million-dollar neighborhoods that handed out full-sized candy bars. Thanksgiving would serve as the opening ceremony for a lifetime of annual traditions with their new sister. And, a Christmas to remember would round out the child's "tour d'Hutch".

After more milestone events than a seasoned adult could process, the judge expected a child to return with a non-biased decision on which parent she wants to live with until adulthood?

Will she offer ice cream cones in her private chambers?

Kristin felt lightheaded as the attorneys asked their final clarifying questions.

Should I let Olivia go now rather than prolong the agony of the inevitable?

Her damp palms felt cool pushing on the tabletop as she adjusted in her chair.

Can I wrap my hands around Peyton's windpipe without harming the fetus?

She rolled her shoulders backward.

What if I walked across the room and slapped Hutch?

The mother inhaled, deeply.

1,2,3. 3,2,1.

"It's a lot to process." Tom's voice signaled the hearing had concluded. "I'm not even sure I know what just happened. Let's debrief outside."

The defendant, her husband, and sister-in-law followed the attorney down the stairwell through the center of the courthouse. The silence of the historic building was as deafening as the frenzied conversations that filled the room previously. His devastated client glared at the Cameks having a private conversation with Mr. Alvarez. Hutch paced within their circle while Peyton patted his shoulder with one hand and rubbed her baby bump with the other.

"Are we able to appeal?" Grey asked.

"On what basis?" Tom asked.

"The court reporter took a nap during your cross examination, and she mismanaged the timeclock," Audrie said. Her voice tightened. "What about that move Alvarez pulled? Are we supposed to think it was an innocent mishap?"

It relieved Kristin that someone's brain synapses were still firing.

Tom rubbed the nape of his neck and loosened his tie, "Family court appeals are expensive with poor outcomes. I wouldn't recommend it. We can talk more when you come to the office. Go home. Rest."

A late afternoon storm formed outside when they left the courthouse. Kristin struggled to open the door against the wind. The humidity thickened before the atmosphere released raindrops onto her back as she climbed inside. The wipers screeched, smearing dust and water, while the couple remained speechless. She texted her mother to let her know they were a few minutes away.

Kristin: It's over. The judge split them. We're on the way home.

Ma: How unexpected. See you soon.

At the house, her mother stood on the paved drive, holding a black umbrella over her head. The rain had turned to mist as Kristin joined her mother under the shelter. Grey's wipers squeaked in rhythm behind the two women.

"I have no words," Rosalyn said.

"Me either."

"You certainly don't need an audience for this," she said, with a glance toward the house.

"You want to grab a coffee?" Grey asked, through the driver side window.

"Coffee would be good. I'll meet you at Lou Ann's. They're the only place serving a decent cup around here anymore."

"Sounds good."

"Ask Audrie to come too," his mother-in-law said, as the window closed.

He acknowledged her order with a thumbs-up from inside the dry cab.

"Audrie?" Kristin asked. "How did you know she was there today?"

"She stopped by the house this morning to see you before the hearing. I told her you'd already left for the courthouse."

"But she was seated inside the courtroom when I got there."

"I'm sure your timeline is blurred, dear. Let's not relive this horrific day." Rosalyn handed the umbrella to her daughter and lit a cigarette. "They've been angels. We watched *Mamma Mia* 1, 2, and the Sing-along. If they're stressed, you'd never know it. You've raised resilient girls, Krissy."

"Thank you, Ma. I'm glad they didn't see that circus. The courtroom, the tension, everything. It's no place for kids."

"You don't deserve any of this. This stupid state and their backwoods laws. Why—" Rosalyn paused, taking a drag. "I won't ask anymore of you today, dear. You'll fill me in later."

Her sleek sedan followed the clatter of Grey's truck. The daughter smiled, knowing Roz would share her disdain for his mountain of a vehicle blowing mud on her hood as soon as they sat down in Lou Ann's.

The house felt hollow knowing the normalcy of her daughters' worlds would be forever changed with her next statements.

"Hi Mama," they said, in unison. Olivia returned her game controller to the coffee table while Lennon powered off the console.

Sitting between the two girls, she said, "RaRa reported a good day here. *Mamma Mia* was a hit, I hear."

They nodded yes, with fixed eyes on their court

messenger and positioned their hands across their laps. No cell phones in sight.

Roz did a good job of keeping them away from Hutch's updates.

"I'm sorry it took so long," she said, tapping both sets of knees.

"It's okay," said Olivia. "We had a good time with RaRa."

"We didn't have to go today, huh?" Lennon asked.

"No. Miss Emily represented your interests well."

Both girls looked like game show contestants awaiting the reveal of a million-dollar home makeover. The mother knew the ultimate gift of their devoted loyalty brimmed their anxiety.

"Well, you know nurses like to rip the Band-Aid," she said. "So, I won't give you a lot of fluff, but I'll answer any questions you have."

The children looked at the wall in front of them.

"Lennon goes. Olivia stays."

With no response, she studied her daughters' faces. Their dreams welled in the corners of their eyes, both reeled from the blow.

"How could this happen?" Lennon asked.

"The judge felt Olivia's age was too young to make such a big decision. You're really too young too, but she made an exception."

"My birthday is in just two weeks. I'll be eleven," said Olivia.

"The judge struggled. There was a lot of discussion around how your father handled this. He's coached you and planted seeds of distrust in your minds. You have a good life here; he wants you to think otherwise." Her stomach twisted, acknowledging their father's emotional neglect.

"I'm not sure I can go without Liv," the oldest sister said as her voice cracked. "It's just, we never would have done this if we didn't think it was a sure thing. Dad said it was a sure thing."

"I'm so sorry you're even in this position," she said, running her fingers across the ends of the teen girl's hair. "Your father misled you. Nothing's certain when a stranger decides the outcome of your life. We had two hours to explain thirteen incredible years to her. She can't possibly know your needs, but she made a ruling we're stuck with, for now."

"What's that mean?" asked Olivia.

"It's a temporary arrangement. Lennon can try living in Florida, but if she doesn't like it, she can come back. Miss Emily will check on the both of you. There's no shame in saying you want to move back home."

"Len, I want you to go. You're really the one that wants this. Don't let me stop you," the youngest sibling said.

"It also means when you're eleven, you can make the decision to move. This arrangement will give you time to make sure this plan is right for you. You may both decide not to change anything and that's within your right," Kristin said. "Any more questions for me?"

"Can I talk to Dad?" Olivia asked.

"Yes, of course. I love you very much." The mother removed her hands from their knees and watched her deflated children proceed to their rooms.

Outside, she scoured the garage for an old pack of cigarettes her mother left after a pool party. Spotting the wrinkled Benson and Hedges logo, she stretched her arm behind the bag of potting soil to reach them. Slow footsteps behind her forced her to abort her mission.

Her father-in-law's tall frame in the shadows drew a gasp.

"I'm sorry Kristin, I didn't mean to startle you."

"It's okay, Ches. I was ..." She pulled the pack out from

behind the clutter and lowered her gaze. "I'm a wreck today."

He smiled at his daughter-in-law's honest confession. "You know they'll smell it. And report it as one more sin to add to your list."

"It will be at the top, right above *can't braid hair* and *takes long naps*."

"All incredulous things for a mother," he said.

With a forced laugh, she dabbed her eyes questioning why she had to deal with another smug man.

Haven't I checked that box already today?

"Are you looking for Grey?" she asked. "He just left for coffee with my mother and Audrie."

"Yeah, he mentioned the court hearing was over," he said. "I just wanted to check on you. I'm sorry I wasn't there today. I felt like it was a private thing for you and Grey."

"No apologies, really. It was a mess; no need to subject yourself to that."

"Well, if you don't need anything, I'll head out and go meet the others," he said.

"We're good here. Thanks again for dropping by." She left the cigarettes to hide behind the potting soil for another crisis as the roar of her father-in-law's rebuilt engine revved behind her.

The sisters emerged from their closed doors. Lennon's tears had dried and her sister skipped into her room.

"Okay?" asked the mother.

"Okay."

"All good."

Entering Olivia's room, she asked, "You got the answers to your questions?"

"We did. Dad helped us understand this wasn't permanent. Len will go now, and I'll go in January," she said with assurance.

"That's not a guarantee. This is a trial period, not a

vacation. Moving to Florida is permanent, so you take your time making this decision."

"You said Lennon could change her mind."

"During this temporary period, she and you can cancel your requests to move. After January's hearing, the living arrangement you select becomes permanent. Florida state laws don't allow a child under 18 to decide which parent they live with," she said.

"I understand."

"Share with me your understanding," Kristin nudged.

"I get it. I'll be eleven and a half when the next hearing is scheduled. I'll speak to the judge, so there will not be any confusion about what I want," she said, stuffing her blanket underneath her.

"That's not information your father should share," the mother said, feeling her voice tremble.

"It's fine, really. This gives me time to say goodbye to all my friends and get my insulin pump. I'm cool with it."

Her older sister entered the room with an illuminating smile. "Are we playing?"

"Yep, here Leonard," the sibling said, tossing a controller to her partner.

The mother sighed listening to their laughter as they created another dream home on their Xbox game. Designing a fantasy family, creating new extravagant homes, and making babies grow up with the push of a button was becoming their expectation of reality. She feared they'd grown used to skipping hardships or dealing with real consequences. Kristin wondered if Judge Lewis served chocolate-chip cookie dough in her chambers; it was their favorite.

Chapter Sixteen

While the house slept, the withered remnants of an annual drought fell onto the sun-charred grass and Kristin presented the previous day's events to her mom. "So, that's it. You were right. They didn't eat me," she said. Forcing a smile through her tears, she doubted she'd ever be able to tell that story without breaking.

"How'd the girls take it?" her mother asked.

"Shocked at first. Followed by some humble confessions." She paused. "All of it washed aside the minute they spoke to Hutch."

"I'm in agony for the children and Grey, but especially you. You have no idea what you're up against with that man. He'll never change."

"That's coming into view for me."

"It's absurd these justice systems can't see alienation for what it is," Rosalyn said.

Active thrashers, on the pond, occupied Kristin's wandering mind while her mother ranted about the judge's decision. She agreed, the separating of siblings was unheard of, even in the unpredictable courts of family law. Kristin envisioned her ex-husband seething over the delay; ravenous to have his possessions under one roof. All in pretense it was in the best interest of the children.

The glass door opened beside her chair and Grey's face stuck through the cracked entryway. "Why did you post that for everyone to see?"

"People care," she said, holding the microphone away from her face. "It's easier to post it on Facebook than answer individual questions at the grocery store."

"I just didn't think we were going to announce it," his voice cracked. "Not yet."

"She's leaving today. How long was I supposed to keep this a secret?"

The springs eased the door closed, as her husband returned inside.

"Is he referring to the social media post?" Rosalyn asked, bringing her daughter back to the phone.

"Yes."

"I thought it was well-worded, Krissy. You missed your calling to be a writer," her mother said. "But why is she leaving today? Didn't you say the judge was giving her a week here?"

"She did, but Hutch insists the school requires her physical to be done in Florida and the pediatrician's schedule was filling up."

"Hogwash!"

"I know. The judge's signature hasn't dried yet, and he's already in contempt."

"This has to be hard on Grey. First Browning, now this," the mother said.

"He'll never admit it."

"Even the toughest oaks crack when their branches are

heavy, Krissy. Go. Talk to your husband. We'll chat when you get home from the airport."

Kristin held the cell phone in her lap, feeling her lip quiver as she admired the sky-blue hydrangeas in full bloom. She made Grey plant them the first month they lived there. He argued it wasn't a higher priority than building the greenhouse, but Kristin wanted the hedges to mature into the perfect backdrop for future celebrations.

Her cheeks tightened at the reminder of the first months the blended family spent together. Then, the school-aged girls took pride in helping her decorate the family's 'forever home.' Lennon believed the porch was a house's smile and each glass lantern was a tooth. The brightest lights sparkled through beveled edges for everyone on the dirt road to see her house was happy. Each of the girls delighted in having separate bedrooms. Olivia, the youngest, dreamt of the day she'd see horses grazing outside her window. Her stepdaughter, Browning, relished the privacy a basement suite offered when she visited her father's house.

Kristin's mother criticized the quaint farmhouse, deeming the meager dwelling too small. She advocated for them to join her in the country club estates, insisting her grandchildren use her dining account at their leisure.

"Why do you want to live in the obscure outskirts of the county?" she'd ask.

The new homeowner reminded the New England native how much she and Grey enjoyed the peacefulness of the countryside. A smaller home was a sacrifice they'd endure with visions of sharing the cozy, empty nest in their golden years. A forced compromise, the mother agreed to visit, forgoing all interactions with farm animals of any sort.

While she valued her mother's commitment to raising her as a single parent, living in a perpetual state of starting over was tiresome. Rosalyn's estate sales were the first indicator of an imminent move looming. Kristin routinely awakened to bundled strangers huddling elaborate displays of their personal effects. There was the time her mother sold the bed she was sleeping in and awakened her to help the customer with disassembly. When the teen balked, the auctioneer bubbled through her room holding a cigarette, seeking accompanying accessories to include in the purchase price.

"We'll get you another one, Krissy, at the new *apartment*. You'll love the modern construction and I'll love not having to cut grass anymore," she'd said, taking a drag.

As an adult, she had few keepsakes to show after spending her transitional years making sorted piles of "must-have" and "okay-to-sell" items. And, she couldn't forget the mementos that didn't fit in the station wagon on moving day. Despite identifying her childhood pets as "must haves," the new residents found Oreo and Pepsi Cat along with a mismatched selection of Tupperware bowls her mother discarded.

When she was married to Hutch, his sales career brought a whirlwind of new houses in different cities across the country. Each bigger and busier than the last. After Olivia was born, the mother's craving for steadiness surged. She wanted a grounding lifestyle for their daughters; but to him, prestige wasn't found in the hardened red clay.

Both Kristin and Grey agreed: constant reinvention of oneself burdened young children and adults. Sitting on the porch they designed to host a lifetime of memories, her heart panged for the dreams yet to unfold. There were at least five more years to be granted to them. Time filled with Junior and Senior Proms, band concerts, and wearing face-photo buttons on her jackets while cheering the home team. The mother and stepfather counted fireflies in the summer skies, laughed about his plans to intimidate hopeful boyfriends, and future first driving experiences on their dirt road. She dreamt of seeing grandchildren pick from the same muscadine vines she once lifted her daughters to reach. He hoped to pass down his farming advice to future sons-in-laws eager to learn the ropes. Now, the reality of their crushed dreams was in her husband's crosshairs and she hated Hutch for sighting-in the target.

The glass door re-opened. "Mom, I'm ready, Lennon's gentle voice announced. "I have my neck pillow for the trip."

"Okay," the mother said, clearing her throat. Her eyes took in every angle of her daughter's face like it was the first time they'd met.

***

On the drive to Hartsfield-Jackson International, Kristin pretended to read a magazine as the traffic whizzed past. Olivia's phone laid in her lap, she too seemed to avoid reminders of their new reality. The driver of the silent vehicle remained emotionless. His wife knew letting go of Lennon was more difficult than he cared to admit. Thinking of his pain, eased her own.

For the first time in his adult life, he accepted his vulnerability. Learned behaviors from his childhood dissipated as their marriage strengthened, but she feared he'd revert to reining in his emotions again. It was the safest option in his father's home.

According to Grey, loving anything meant putting one's heart in a guillotine with Ches Murphy holding the rope. His dad's lessons included making men tough, reminding women of their weaknesses, and using children as pawns when needed. Grey learned defending his mother resulted in turmoil for both. Adored pets went missing. Girlfriends remained nameless, to preserve tender feelings from ridicule.

When his 4-H project drew contest-winning praise, he awoke to a slippery sludge oozing under his bed on competition day. The countless hours he spent tending the watermelon from seed—cored, along with his pride.

Like his wife, the storms of Grey's family culture molded his parenting practice. Both agreed to end the cycle of selfish agendas with varied approaches. She overcompensated for her mother's psychological stronghold, forgetting to put on her own oxygen mask at times. He reserved his heart for moments when he felt safe.

With his blended family, he relished being a parent and provider for his daughters. He welcomed their differences and learned to see the world through their eyes. Although his preference was to remain out of the limelight, his steadfast love for the girls was a constant they leaned on. Like the time Lennon was sick on a camping trip, Kristin and Olivia returned from a hike to see the stepfather holding her hair while she regurgitated Skittles into a travel toilet. She watched her weak-stomached husband gag along with the child, but she never knew it. Her delicate, pale face showed her appreciation, and Grey refused to leave her side, even after Kristin offered to relieve his nursing duties. Then, there was the afternoon she was drowning in meetings and the school called alerting her Lennon had suffered a panic attack in class. Without hesitation, he left the store to rescue her from the vicious cycle of anxiety and shared his personal struggles to ease her concern. Fatherhood allowed Grey to feel the all-encompassing love parents experience; but this day was a reminder of how rejection fragments the soul at any age.

At the check in counter, the teen asked, "Why did we have to drive to Atlanta?"

"The flights from here are direct into Fort Lauderdale. It's not safe to have kids wandering airports looking for a connecting route," the mother said.

"Why are we here so early?" Olivia bemoaned.

"What else do you have to do today? Play *Fortnight*, dork?"

"It's her first time flying as an unaccompanied minor."

Olivia crumpled her face.

"Alone. It takes some time to check in kids who aren't flying with their parents, but we're ready now."

The stepfather stood from his leaning position on the baggage carousels as the group approached him. "Well, come here, girl," he said, holding his arms open wide. "Your mom is the only one who can walk you past security, so I'll take my hug now."

Admiring their sincere embrace, the mother's heart burned seeing Lennon cling tighter as he started to release. Soft tears filled her stoic husband's eyes before the child eased her grip.

Wiping her face with her shirtsleeve, the lanky teen stepped back to study her stepfather's expression. "Your allergies, too, huh?" she joked.

Family laughs eased the mother's palpable tension. She appreciated her daughter's ability to weave humor into any situation; a life skill that would suit her well.

With an annoyed hug, the siblings bid farewell. "See you soon, Leonard."

"See ya. Don't touch anything in my room. Ever," the teen said, before she and her mother entered the security checkpoint boundary.

Leaving their group, the mother chuckled overhearing Olivia ask Grey, "Can I get a daiquiri?"

"Negative."

"A virgin one?"

"Nope," he said. "And never say that word again."

Their banter faded into the bustling noise of the airport

atrium, as the sound of Kristin's heart pounding in her chest took over her senses.

The security screening was minimal with no luggage. Hutch advised Lennon she wouldn't need to bring anything. Peyton shopped for her and a stocked wardrobe awaited her arrival. The two boarded the concourse train with other passengers seeking a shuttle to the gate. Kristin admired her daughter standing tall, wearing black headphones around her neck, while holding onto the center pole on the train. Forcing a swallow, the mother turned to lose herself in the passing lights of the train tunnel. Her heart struggled between desperately wanting to feel needed and bursting with immense pride her child could blaze this trail without her.

At the gate, the hour-long wait felt like an eternity. She held back the urge to smother her coming-of-age daughter with tearful attention in the crowded airport. As the call for pre-boarding rang overhead, the mother clenched her fists in her lap.

The attendants at the desk verified their identities with a quick review of their documents. The uniformed man looked up from his feverish typing, "Given she's a minor, she can board early."

She gasped inside, hoping for a few more minutes just to hold her child's hand. "Well, kiddo. It looks like you get the best seat in the house. It's hard to believe you'll be starting eighth grade in two weeks—" Her voice cracked, words no longer left her mouth. She clutched her headstrong, first-born in her arms and Lennon folded into her mother's chest. The queue beside them inched forward, staring at the duo while Kristin recited their backstory in her head, as if she were sharing it with the onlookers.

Would you even believe it if I told you our story? An incredible mother, losing her oldest child to an outdated state law which disregards teen brain development, daughter/mother bonding, and common sense. How's that for drama?

"Mama, I love you." Lennon sniffled.

"My God, child. I love you so much."

Stepping back from their embrace, the teenager said, "We'll see each other on Fall Break, at the end of the nine weeks. I promise to stay in touch. Tell Olivia I love her too. I was just kidding about my room. Well . . ."

"You are the very best of me," she said through streaming tears. "You'll do great!! Remember, they can't eat you for supper."

And she released her hand with the same hesitation as she did the first time the nurses took her from the delivery room. The mother watched the back of her child's strawberry streaks shimmer in the lights of the terminal walkway and pass through the cabin doors. Passengers vacated the waiting area. She stood at the window, watching the aircraft inch away from the dock. Her sternum burned stronger with every rotation of the jetliner's wheels, taking the child farther away from her hedge of protection.

Meandering through the matrix of the terminal, she was numb to the onlookers witnessing her visible distress. At the top of the escalator, she refreshed herself before greeting Olivia and Grey at the baggage turnstiles. The teary-eyed child stretched out her hand in silence, which Kristin graciously accepted.

Approaching the van, "You can sit in the backseat with me, Mama."

The doors slid open to reveal the Starbucks cup Lennon drank from on the trip to the airport. The remainder of her favorite hibiscus tea pooled at the bottom like a fresh reminder of how quickly Kristin's life changed. She felt her pulse skip, climbing in behind her baby.

The somber ride home provided a few moments to clear

her mind from the stressful morning. She adored watching her child nap clenching her security blankets like she did as a toddler. Olivia's gaze jolted with the buzz from her mother's phone as they arrived at the house.

350-902-6638: Mom. Just landed. Here's my new number. Heart emoji.

Olivia reading over Kristin's shoulder, "I bet it's an iPhone 11XR. I hate her."

Chapter Seventeen

Howling dogs interrupted the nursing instructor's planning time and alerted her of an arriving visitor. Peering through slatted shutters in the laundry room, she noticed the guardian's SUV approaching the roundabout section of their drive. Kristin tried to recall if she missed a scheduled visit. She threw her tangled hair in a bun and walked to the door without concern for the half-empty wine bottle on her kitchen counter.

"Hi Kristin," the guardian ad litem greeted. "I was just in the area and I remembered you worked from home. Is now a good time?"

"Sure, I have a break between meetings. Just come through the gate on the side of the house. We can sit on the deck."

The Jasmine-adorned pergola provided shade over the refurbished wicker furniture Grey frantically painted before Emily's last visit. Kristin noticed the bluebird egg color already peeling beneath as her hands rested on the armchair.

"These early Fall mornings are lovely," she said, inviting the house guest to have a seat.

"It's been a few weeks since Lennon moved. I thought I would check in to see how things are going. We spoke on the phone last night and she said she'd made friends at the new school. Getting settled, you know?" Emily paused. With no reaction from Kristin, she continued. "I just met with Olivia at school. She said things are going well for her, too. How do you think she's doing without her sister here?"

"She has her moments. To be expected," the mother said.

"My biggest concern is their separation."

"Rightfully so, it was a decision Judge Lewis made from a position of power, not research. A blatant disregard for children's developmental needs."

Looking down, the guardian asked, "Have either of them mentioned they're interested in changing their requests about moving?"

"Hutch would never allow them to lose focus. He's too invested now."

"The girls both said things to me indicating they knew more than they should about the court case," the lawyer said.

"Why aren't we holding him in contempt?" Kristin asked. "He's violating a court order again. The paper is just that to him, there's no obligation to stay within the confines of a written document."

"I'd have to refer you to Tom for guidance. I'll say that it's difficult to hold up in court. This is such a common occurrence in family law cases, the judges just sort through it to get to the real issue. In this case, both girls have two good parents. This is an anomaly in the family court world," the youthful attorney said, as her narrow face tilted away from the sun streaming through the slatted roof.

"I'm so tired of hearing about good parenting. What does that even mean? Do we beat our children? No. Does he brainwash them? Yes. I guess it depends on which is an acceptable evil," the mother's tone flattened.

Emily dug through her brief removing several pieces of paper Kristin recognized as the newsletters Hutch, or Peyton rather, had created—the flowery communiques on cheerful templates complete with corkscrew arrows and neon colors. Each version number correlated with the week Lennon had lived there, denoted next to the title "Loving Lennon." Inside each pastel pallet square was a tidbit about her activities, upcoming events, and usually a picture of the teen swimming in their sparkling infinity pool or stretched across her vibrant-colored queen bedspread, her new puppy close by.

"So, you get those too?" asked Kristin.

"These are good resources. Mr. Camek must want you included in Lennon's day-to-day life. He hasn't shut you out completely," she smiled, handing the papers to the woman.

"I'm familiar with them," she said. Her hands remained crossed in her lap.

"Lennon added her own message, here." Emily read from the document, 'Mom, I'm having a great time. Today I walked the dogs and visited my school. It's so big and the lockers are half ones, not the cubes we used to have. I really like my church and I'm making new friends. You'd really like it. Love you – Len.' She sounds like she wants to stay in touch with you."

"Emily, this is all an act," she interrupted. Her tone, a strong indication she had finished auditioning for the role. She'd earned this gig when the guardian was in pigtails, and the mother tired of the director cutting her lines. "This is all an orchestrated show, and the girls are his puppets. He's not giving them facts; he's giving them lines to recite."

"I'm sure—"

"Do you know what Lennon's favorite Xbox game is?

"Well, no," the guardian said.

"It's a home design app which lets her create families, homes, careers—all at the whimsical click of a button. There are no consequences for deleting the digital mom in her world. Did you know Olivia's a gymnast?"

"I noticed the ribbons on her bedroom wall at one of the homes."

"Do you know what's involved in placing at these competitive meets?"

Emily shook her head, no.

"Memorizing foot placement and formations, also the physical commitment to strengthening exercises. In other words, my daughter follows direction quite well, and her father's betting on it."

The attorney returned the papers to her satchel. "Maybe I should come back another time, this is still so fresh for all, I'm sure."

"Neither one of them realizes once they become residents of Florida their right to decide custody is removed until they are eighteen years old. There's no changing their minds. There's no coming back, Emily. This move is as temporary as the tattoo on your ankle," the mother said. "You recommended this arrangement because why? He has more money. He has a bigger house. You've known Mr. Camek for eight weeks? I've known him for twenty-five years. I had proof of his coercion and manipulation, and you did nothing."

"I know this is difficult," she said.

"Difficult is hearing my daughters call his wife Mom." Kristin leaned forward. "Once this is over, these newsletters will end. His communications will return to demeaning emails reminding me he's the gatekeeper for *his* children. That's what power—custodial power—does to an adult."

"But you have joint custody."

"What does that even mean outside of the courtroom?"

"He has a primary physical placement because the children live with him, but your legal rights are equal. United parenting has better outcomes for the children. He should consult you for all major decisions," the GAL said.

"You're fooling yourself if you think that's how it works in the real world. The court order is a piece of paper just like those newsletters. He'll tell me what I'm allowed to do and when I'm permitted to do it. He'll scold me for opening his car door to help them with their luggage. He'll use the distance to punish me. I'll drive thousands of miles through storms to execute my allotted Mommy-time and he'll reprimand me for being later than the court ordered drop-off schedule. This is the world you'll not be there to monitor. This is the 'good parenting' you keep referring to."

"He doesn't have to be like that. You're a good mother; he should want you in his kids' lives."

"You're right, but you made a recommendation based on a surface-level assessment. There's only one parent looking out for those girls, and it ain't him."

The guardian tucked her documents into folders. "I'll keep your attorneys updated, Ms. Murphy. Again, I'm sorry this is the situation at hand," Emily said, standing to leave.

A dust cloud encompassed her vehicle, and Kristin sunk back into the house hoping her rant wouldn't reduce her to supervised visits. Her pulse slowed to its normal pace as she rested her hands on the kitchen island. In the living room corner, a piano's shelf hosted photographs she'd collected. Framed stills of space-toothed smiles, braces, and polished poses served as their family's timeline together. Scanning them, she considered the GAL's position. It was doubtful the young attorney would negate the truthful evidence she'd claimed at the original hearing. No number of interviews with teachers, guidance counselors, or church directors would give her enough information to change her proposal.

She knew the attorneys would fight as long as their clients paid them. Family Law was a billion-dollar industry in the US. Justice was deeming a father's income a substantial reason to change their original parenting arrangement and labeling a mother's objection as high conflict. Any long-term consequences for children of alienated parents were brushed under the rug. To the court, emotional and verbal abuse weren't crimes; rather, manipulation and coercion were merely a chapter in their white-collar civil issue.

The mother's hope for her children to have a revelation faded. She knew their father's propaganda filled their minds and his tug at financial purse strings kept them in line. If he could have that impact from five hundred miles away, he'd be unstoppable when they were under his roof.

She felt numb inside returning to work.

***

Tom walked around the desk to greet his clients. "Well, it's been almost two months since the hearing, how's the youngest one doing without her sister?"

"She's starting to have some resentment. I think we expected that," said Kristin.

"The GAL said the same in her interim report. I could tell Judge Lewis struggled with her decision. I think she hopes the oldest girl will change her mind. Do you see that as an option?

"How can she with a new phone, new room, new puppy, and a new sister all happening within a few months of her move?" Kristin asked.

Tom nodded. "They set the final hearing dates in January, during the break for both school districts. The folks that signed affidavits will need to be live witnesses on the stand."

"These are my friends. Most are teachers, administrators, and community leaders. I can't ask them to give up their already limited time off to sit in court all day," his client said.

"I'm sure they'd do it for your girls. These are good kids; they want them in their classrooms and their community," the lawyer said.

"What else is involved in the final hearing?"

"The children will definitely talk to the judge."

"Why?" Grey asked. We're paying the guardian to be their voices."

"For the final, Judge Lewis will want to talk to them directly. Any chance they'll change their mind by then?"

The mother shook her head no.

"What's the likelihood the judge would leave them split?" Grey asked.

"There's a good possibility. The youngest will be over eleven, but the court may lean toward maintaining what they established in the temporary. If both girls are doing well with the situation as is, then she could stay with you."

"And file for her own custody modification at fourteen," Kristin said.

"A fair assumption, I'm afraid."

"So, best case scenario is we do the dog and pony show again and they both go to Florida, as originally proposed," the mother said.

"It's not an easy one, I'll give you that." The lawyer removed his glasses and leaned onto his desk.

"Olivia and I are going to see Lennon tomorrow. I'll give everything some thought," Kristin said.

"In Miami?" Tom asked.

"Of course. You didn't think he'd facilitate visitation with me, did you? He's made it clear, if I want to see Lennon, I'll make the sacrifice."

"We'll be in touch," her husband said, with a firm grasp of Tom's hand.

The mother walked through the hallways of the refurbished ranch home for what she hoped would be the last time. Each encounter inside those walls ended in anguish. Even those whose verdicts were found in good favor had to give up their dignity at some point in the process.

Chapter Eighteen

Zipping the suitcase on her bed, she listened to drawers slamming in the neighboring bedroom. "Pack shorts. It's still hot there."

Olivia appeared in her mother's room wearing her fleece sweater, leggings, and boots. "What? It's like October. People have pumpkins out."

"The pumpkins are rotting under the palm trees. Florida isn't known for their seasons," she said with a smirk. "These are things you need to consider."

Kristin hoped something from Olivia's small-town upbringing would resonate with her. This was the sweet, sensitive child who relished in the brisk, evening air with her friends bundled under cozy fleeces cheering on the high school football team. Even not that she was eleven, how could she begin to know who she was or understand what she was giving up? It was natural for her to seek the excitement of something new, but Kristin questioned her commitment once the enthusiasm faded.

"Did you get your insulin? I have a cooler ready."

"Yep, I have my pancreas-in-a-bottle," Olivia joked. "I probably should take my flip flops."

Out-of-season clothes were stockpiled in the back of her daughter's closet. Kristin preferred to keep them close by given the transitional seasons in Alabama were a mixed bag of weather options. It was easier to retrieve sandals from a hidden nook than the attic. Entering the walk-in space, a calendar hung on the inside wall. The child had scribbled, *Aunt Vy's Halloween Party* over the upcoming weekend. "I'm sorry we're missing Vy's party. I know how much you look forward to it."

Olivia investigated her bag deeper. "It's okay."

"You've been going to it every year since you were three. She did a good job adding things to it as you kids got older. It started with apple bobbing and now we have a chainsaw murderer on standby. That's impressive," Kristin complimented her sister-in-law's flare for the dramatic.

"Yeah, my friends lost their minds last year on the hayride."

"Won't you miss them?"

"Yeah, but they understand," she said, sounding as if she needed the reassurance as much as her mother. "Dad is counting on me to come to Florida in January."

"You shouldn't feel pressured."

"I want to go too," Olivia corrected. "It's not just Dad."

Kristin wanted to keep talking and remind her of all the things she was leaving behind, but she knew that would make her as guilty as Hutch.

The mother stacked their things at the back door while her travel partner texted on her phone. "G, we're going. I'm supposed to be there by 6:00 p.m. to drop her off at his house." As her husband approached her, she whispered, "I have to look responsible, you know."

"You *are* responsible." Grey hugged his wife. "Traffic may be bad today. The snowbirds are migrating south for winter, and the evacuees are returning since the hurricane passed through."

"The joys of Florida travelers," she said. "Just one of the many things I'll have to account for now when I want to hug my child."

"Why don't' I get to fly, like Len did?" Olivia asked.

"I'm not sure we're ready to take on a blood sugar emergency from 30, 0000 feet. Soon though, I think we're getting the hang of it, don't you?"

On the way to the car, the child gave a quick shoulder shrug and said, "Glad we have movies and snacks."

"I'm sure you have everything. Drive safe." Grey kissed his pensive wife's cheek and closed the door behind them.

As her husband warned, the state's residents filled southbound lanes as they schlepped back to see what the hurricane aftermath left of their homes. Northerners made their biannual migration. The cars lined the interstate like ants going to a picnic.

Why would anyone want to live here?

"We'll be late," she said. "Can you text your dad, I'm driving?"

"He said *K.*"

Kristin's phone lit up out of her passenger's view. His texts flew in by the sentence.

Just Breathe: The court order says 6:00 p.m.

Just Breathe: This will not look good for you.

Just Breathe: You're sabotaging Peyton's plans for our daughter's welcome home party.

Just Breathe: This just shows you're an insecure parent.

Driving, Kristin peeked at the insults while keeping her focus on the RVs speeding through to make their campsite check-ins. She longed for a camping vacation again.

"Livvy, can you let him know we're looking at an extra hour?"

With no response from her normally attentive daughter, she asked again, "Liv? Can you text your dad?"

A glance in the rearview showed her youngest child holding a blank stare out the window. Traffic slowed to a dull crawl on either side of their vehicle. The mother repeated her request. "Liv?"

The child's eyes darted toward her mother's voice like a newborn responding to the ever-present stimulus they recognize from the womb. Her body slumped further into the leather seat.

"I think your blood sugar is low. Can you hear me?" Kristin asked, jerking her head around in either direction to lay eyes on her child seated behind her. She calculated for any opening in the flow of cars where she could pull off the road. "There are glucose tabs in the back of my seat, please Liv."

She continued to plead with drivers, as she helplessly watched her child's expression dull. With her voice breaking, she continued to keep her daughter oriented. "I'm trying to pull over. Stay with me, Livvy. Mama's here. I know what you need."

A narrow gap opened, and she angled her front wheels to veer from the traffic jam. The car inched forward toward the rear of the other vehicle.

"Let me out!" she shouted, slamming her hands on the steering wheel.

Her screams vibrated off the windows and Olivia's eyes closed.

Shoving the driveshaft into Park, she searched for a button she'd never needed. "Where is that thing?" Her hands hovered searching the dashboard for the elusive triangle-shaped symbol.

Hazzard lights clicked on, and she scrambled to the rear

passenger side.

Flinging the door open, the rose-colored blankets slid from the child's seat into Kristin's hands before dropping to the scorching pavement below.

With her stationary vehicle in the middle of the busiest travel corridor the Southeastern United States offered, she assessed her daughter. Her nursing experience reminded her to reduce pressure in the glucose-starved brain. She reclined the rear passenger seat to a thirty-degree angle. "Mama's here baby. Mama's right here. Liv, you're going to be fine."

Her child's eyes fluttered.

Kristin fumbled with the nasal spray, cursing her ex-husband for not giving her the intramuscular injection she'd administered 100 times in the hospital, like she'd asked him to do. The bright-yellow tube slipped through her hands and under the driver's seat.

"Liv," she said, stretching across the back seat for a liquid glucose gel packet she stored in the middle console. "Open your mouth, baby," she pleaded. Puncturing the plastic wrap with her teeth, she squeezed the sugary gel onto her fingertips and ran it across the child's pale gums.

Her brow dripped sweat while she stood half inside the car; the warmth from creeping traffic radiated the backs of her calves. "Olivia, this is sugar. You'll feel my finger. You need sugar." Sticky syrup dripped from the corners of her mouth and down the nurse's wrist as she rubbed inside the child's flaccid cheeks.

Seconds felt endless.

Tipping a fuchsia thermos over her hands, she doused them with water and patted Olivia's pale, clammy forehead. Cool drops rinsed her sticky fingers.

"Baby, you have sugar in your mouth. Try to get it under your tongue."

Desperate, she dropped to the floorboard again

searching for the yellow nasal tube. A sneakered foot tapped her head.

The mother jerked her body off the sandy mat.

Seeing the tiny jawline flex, she begged her child as much as the Divine. "Lick the sugar, Liv. Can you taste it? Please, please show me you can taste the sugar."

Her lips smacked together.

"Oh, thank God. Thank you, God. Thank you." Chills crawled the mother's arms, her body, oblivious to the tyrannical Florida sun beating on her neck. She used the clean side of her palm, to brush the wet hair from her child's forehead. "Can you open your mouth? Let's get the rest in?"

With eyes remaining closed, she opened her mouth in full trust of her mother's direction. Kristin squirted more fruity substance inside.

Dashing around the vehicle, she flung the trunk open. She hated the day her cooler became a travel-size code cart and refreshments turned into lifesavers. The ice pierced her knuckles digging through to the bottom.

"What are you doing lady?" A driver shouted from behind. "This isn't a parking lot."

Racing back to the sliding side door of the van, she said, "Here, baby. Feel the straw? Take some sips. It's apple juice."

Olivia's sucking reflex gained strength. Her eyes peeled open with each swallow causing the mother's head to bury in the child's lap. Kristin squeezed her tiny hips.

Honking from an angry commuter pulled her away from the embrace.

"Liv, you'll feel the cold alcohol swab," she said, holding the child's hand in hers. "I need you to give these mad drivers a finger."

The mother's middle school humor drew a smirk, and the child raised her callused fingertip into position.

"Here's the needle prick. The lancet popped and blood

oozed from the target. Beeps alerted them with completed results in seconds. "Low," she read. "Well, we knew that didn't we, kiddo?" Her heart rate slowed seeing a thin-lipped smile stretch across her daughter's face. Adjusting the passenger seat to a higher angle, she asked, "Do you think you can drink more juice?"

The line of cars inched beside her makeshift ambulance. One passerby stopped gawking to ask, "Do you need me to call 9-1-1?"

"No, I think we're fine now," she said. "Can you let me over?"

The woman nodded yes and blocked fellow drivers from moving forward while Kristin resumed her position in the driver's seat.

"Mama's got to get this wagon rollin', kiddo." She pecked her child's cool, dry forehead and pressed the automated button on the sliding door.

A loud sigh emerged from the backseat, easing the mother's heart like newborn cries in a delivery room. She waved to the woman holding her position and returned to the southbound lane.

"Are you awake enough to check your sugar? Or do you need me to?" Kristin asked.

"I can do it," Olivia said with her usual hypoglycemic irritability.

"Let me know what it is, please." She listened to the clicks and beeps of her daughter's new routine which reminded her to confirm the order status of the continuous glucose monitor and pump when she returned home.

"85. Does that mean its snack time?"

"Yes. There's a box by your feet. Get something with some protein and carbs. I have it labeled."

"What happened?" she asked, over crinkling wrappers.

"Hypoglycemia. Low blood sugar."

"But I wasn't even doing anything. Stupid diabetes."

"We're off our routine. It's hard to say what the cause is. Are you feeling okay now?"

Olivia remained silent.

Gripping the steering wheel, the driver raised her view in the mirror. The tween's wavy, blonde hair bounced over white headphones to a beat while she snacked and looked out the window.

Noticing their delay, Kristin attempted to call Hutch to give him a personal update. The rings stopped after two cycles, and she received his voicemail.

Just Breathe: Written communication only.

Using her talk and text feature, she said, "Liv just had a hypoglycemic episode."

Just Breathe: What?

"We're in traffic. Her glucose is rising. We'll go to the hotel tonight."

Another glance at Olivia's reflection eased her tensions. The tiny warrior had closed her eyes, her head rested on her coveted silky, pink pillow.

Just Breathe: Unacceptable.

Just Breathe: You'll pay for this.

***

An illuminated entry drew nearer as she drove through the hotel's dark parking lot. She exited her vehicle, feeling the air cling to her skin. The warm breeze, off the Atlantic, reminded her of the crisp fall evenings she'd left at home. To vacation there was one thing but living at the beach full time was another. Being away from the ragweed could offer relief from her seasonal allergies; she remained optimistic.

Olivia looked up from her movie, "Are we at Dad's?"

"You'll just stay with me tonight. Traffic pushed us back.

I'll take you to his house in the morning."

"Okie dokie, artichokie. I hope they have shower caps," the newly eleven-year-old said.

Checking into the only room her reward points would cover, she said, "There's a pull-out bed on the sofa. You're only here tonight. Tomorrow, I'll take you to your dad's for a few days."

"Can I sleep with you tonight?" Olivia asked, burying her head in her mother's chest.

Helplessness overtook her. Kristin, too, hated this disease. More so, she hated how extensive travel between two households complicated things for her child's battle against it. With precise timing, she knew Hutch would use this day as an example of how her selfishness puts their child's health at risk.

"Of course, you can sleep with me tonight."

"Cool," the child said, dropping her bag on the floor.

"Don't lay your things on the floor. Bedbugs can grab onto anything cloth and you can take them back to your house. You should always use the suitcase rack or place your things in the bathroom."

"So, my bag is cleaner by the toilet?" the child asked while walking her bag to the new location.

"I guess. It's all kind of gross if you think about it." It used to be easy to stay in a hotel room or use a gas station bathroom. Now, the travelers had a compromised immune system to consider.

Desperate to create a semblance of home, the mother unpacked her suitcase using the dresser drawers she usually avoided when on vacation. She questioned their new norm, as her fingers touched the bottom support. Who else's underwear laid there prior to hers? Whose skin cells were flaked onto hanging folds along the dusty windowsill? Whose hair wound through the fabric-backed sofa where her diabetic child rested her head? A sinking feeling rushed over her, entering the bathroom, and seeing the countertop anchored by a tray holding a single-cup coffee maker surrounded by foam cups covered in plastic. Comforts earned from years of adult sacrifices had been stripped from her lifestyle. Now, she was relegated to pushing hair products aside for caffeine filtered with sink water. Home-cooked meals replaced by takeout boxes crammed into a hotel minifridge. Her reality was a nomadic life she never asked for.

As the lights closed the end of an extensive travel day, she said, "Love you, Livvy."

"Love you, times 1000, Mama."

Chapter Nineteen

The morning sun darted through the middle of two blackout curtains as Kristin approached the tween cuddled in white linens.

Grateful both her children greeted mornings with ease, she said, "Livvy, let's get up, baby."

Stretching her arms overhead, she yawned, and stood at the side of the bed. "Where's my...oh yeah, in the bathroom."

Entering her ex-husband's address into her GPS, she smirked. The distance was farther than she preferred, but lodging prices reflected hurricane season was over. She'd noticed the trend of increased rates with the weather anchor's 'all clear.' This region differed from the panhandle where she and Grey vacationed as kids. Resting on the county line of Miami, Lake Tarpon's peak vacation season started mid-October to avoid the brutal heat of summer. Temporary residents seeking respite from frigid winters flocked to coveted warmth. All factors she'd have to consider when planning her trips.

From the bathroom, her child said, "I'm starving. My sugar is 95. Does this place do the breakfast thing?"

"Let's do two units. I'm sure you're going for the waffle station."

"You know it."

"Sugar-free syrup, please."

"Deal."

Downstairs, she watched her youngest daughter navigate a lobby crowded with chaperones and church retreaters in matching tees. Each hovered over Styrofoam plates of food while balancing off-kilter, four-top tables. The mother questioned what would come of her family's morning routines. Is this how they would spend quality time, sitting elbow to elbow with strangers, watching CNN? Warm pajama breakfasts by the fireplace replaced with sharing a table with hungry, traveling ball teams. Grey's "World Famous Pancakes" ousted by powdered eggs and plastic bowls of Lucky Charms.

Olivia was no stranger to the kitchen. She loved cooking her own waffles when on vacation and at home. Her mother passed over their whims for toy ovens and encouraged safe cooking skills in their kitchen at home. Instilling a need for self-sufficiency was at the forefront of everything she did for the sisters. Watching the steam rise from the in-use waffle iron, the mother questioned how long living VIP weekends at the Hampton Inn would enthuse her kids. Eventually, Lennon would want friends over as any teenage girl does. What type of parents would let their kids come to their friend's mom's hotel room? When would they lose interest in spending time with Mom and how much time did she have with them before Hutch pushed that agenda?

Making eye contact with the little chef, she tapped the outside of her wrist. Her daughter took the cue despite knowing no one who wore an actual wristwatch.

"Did you get everything you wanted?" Kristin asked, helping the hungry passenger steady her juice cup.

"Yep."

Her kids were seasoned car diners.

Palm trees lined the six-lane thoroughfare, adorned with new shopping centers at every block. Her minivan joined suburban parents embarking on their Saturday morning routines. Drivers herded honor students to quiz bowls and pitchers to little league games. Lacrosse moms' Porsche Carreras sported decorated rear windshields pledging allegiance to each child's team. Maseratis lined the grocery store parking lots where glamorous mothers shopped for Kobe beef flanks and entertained their grocery cart passengers with organic fruit snacks. She converged with seniors driving their mid-life crisis convertibles. Kristin suspected the flame-colored Rolls Royce was on its way to the polo fields.

When married to Hutch, she watched a small-town boy sell his soul for a lifestyle demanding late business hours, week-after-week travel, and the type of stress that killed middle-aged men. Each promotion fueled his materialistic engine. New bosses stoked embers of greed, power, and wealth. Soon he looked down on anyone who didn't wear a suit to work or had a high handicap. He labeled friends from Ellington irrelevant or ignorant. Simple life bored him. Real estate agents handed him fulfilled dreams with each new keyring, while she felt like a stranger moving into another wife's house. The life he chased motivated her to seek simplicity at every turn, even if it meant leaving her marriage.

She wanted her daughters to graduate with friends from kindergarten and go to prom with boys who pulled their pigtails on the bus. Her own childhood was a constant shuffle from rental house to apartment complex, but her children had security surrounding them. Here they were forced to separate the "have-nots" from a world full of "haves" and Kristin wondered what ranking she'd receive.

The GPS-highlighted destination drew nearer to her blue beacon. Palms towered over elaborate subdivision entryways adorned with the state symbol for relaxation. Spanish-style, tiled rooftops sprawled, and the ornate landscaping invited residents home.

"I read Vanilla Ice lives in that one," she said, pointing to the brick wall surrounded by an oasis-like entryway.

"Who's Vanilla Ice?" Olivia asked.

"Don't make me—" She searched the nineties playlist they created together.

"Oh, that guy," the passenger said, bobbing her head to the iconic intro.

Approaching a speaker box at the entrance to the subdivision, she adjusted the volume and signaled her arrival.
"Name and homeowner, you're visiting," a robotic voice instructed.

"Kristin Murphy visiting Hutch Camek on Crane Lane."

"It's Crane Circle, Mom."

"Whatever."

After a long pause a live attendant's voice projected through the speaker, "I'm sorry. There's no answer by Mr. Camek. We're not able to approve your entry."

A line of cars stacked in her rearview as she felt her blood pressure rise.

Well, someone's on a power trip already.

Circling the van to the back of the visitor's lane, she gritted her teeth and asked, "Liv, can you call Dad? Let him know you're waiting outside the gate, please."

"Okay. He says for you to try it again," Olivia instructed.

Easing forward, she called the attendant a second time. The ex-wife scoured the entryway fully expecting to see Hutch crouched behind a Sego Palm laughing at her expense.

"Proceed," the robotic voice replied.

The intricate metal arm swung open and reminded her

all parenting choices filtered through Hutch's discerning judgement.

"Dad's house is at the back of the neighborhood."

Houses increased in size with each passing side street and the manicured lots spread into putting green-worthy lanes. Athletic moms jogged, pushing sporty baby strollers. Sophisticated residents walked dainty pooches on glittery leashes. Older men walked behind self-propelled lawn mowers giving the appearance they contributed to their own lawn care regimen.

"That's it," the child said, unclasping her belt buckle.

"Which room is yours?" Kristin asked.

Over her mother's shoulder, she pointed to a second-floor window laced in white curtains. "That one."

"Looks like the best spot in the house."

Several children, aged from toddlers to teens, piled out of the house and surrounded Olivia on the sidewalk before guiding her inside.

Lennon emerged from the crowd. "Hi, Mom."

The new court order had reduced their interactions to video chats and texted pictures. Kristin's heart pounded against her chest standing next to the child who made her a mother. She appeared years older than the girl who boarded the airplane eight weeks ago. "Well, well. Look at those curls," she said. Her daughter's cheeks blushed, as the mother kissed one side. "Beach life suits you, Len."

"I see you brought my favorite blanket," the teen said, her slender body leaning inside her mother's van. "What else is in here? Why does your car smell like waffles?"

"You'll have to wait," she said, activating the automatic close feature on the minivan door. "I'll get you in a couple of days and we'll have some time together."

"Do you have one of those waffle stations at the hotel? Is that where I'm staying when I see you?" she asked.

"Back away from the waffle-wagon." Both Mom and daughter laughed. "Maybe you can show me around town later. I'd like to see what it is you like about Lake Tarpon. So far, I just see a lot of yuppies. They're more dangerous than the sharks in the ocean."

"I know, right?" Lennon giggled. "See you in a few days, Mom. Love you."

"See you in a few days, my love." Kristin stood at the van watching her daughter close the door behind her and the other kids.

A barrage of texts awaited her attention when she returned to the driver's seat.

Just Breathe: I can't believe you fed her before she got here.

Just Breathe: We moved the party to this morning because you failed to get her here on time yesterday.

Just Breathe: Now this food is wasted.

The cell phone clanged into the cupholder and she left the vehicle's engine running. Deliberately bypassing the stone walkway, she marched through her ex-husband's lawn to the tiled steps of his entryway. Her lips tightened, as she gave a firm push on the doorbell.

Olivia opened the door. "What'd I forget?

"Nothing, baby," Kristin said, peering into the marble foyer. "Where's your dad?"

"Dad?" The child moved out of sight, as her father came to the door.

"How's it going?" he asked. The walls echoed his strident voice to others listening in.

"I'm still here," the ex-wife said, with her hands on her hips. "You said something to me by text while I was sitting in your driveway. Did we need to discuss it further?"

"Not really," Hutch said, looking over her head at the yard beside his.

"Your diabetic daughter had to eat this morning. I wasn't sabotaging your party."

"I'm aware she has special needs."

"She had a critical low while traveling this agonizing road trip yesterday. Does your party really matter more than her safety?" Kristin's eyes narrowed awaiting his reply, but he continued to avert his gaze to anything other than his ex-wife. "You're such a coward. How do you expect us to co-parent if you won't even look me in the eye?"

"I prefer our conversations documented," Hutch said, giving a quick scan of his ex-wife's face.

"That's no way to communicate about real issues."

Stepping onto the front stoop, the father closed the door to his home. She could still hear the others showering Olivia with welcoming hugs and cheer.

When he bent down, his face went dark. "When will you realize the girls don't want you?" he asked, with a nefarious tone. "They want me. They want to live with *my* family. They want to live *this* life, not the pathetic one you live. You're holding them back by being here."

No sounds escaped her dry lips. She stared as he stepped back inside.

"Drive safe, Kris." His voice penetrated the foyer again for any lurking audience to hear. "I'll let you know if plans change for the band recital tomorrow night," Hutch said, closing the door in his ex-wife's face.

With her head hung, she slumped back to the van, his chilling words penetrating her chest. Her legacy danced inside with the others, as she hoped they were still blissfully unaware of their father's castigating agenda. Perhaps they would be better off with him there, with tropical weather, crowded neighborhood gatherings, and limitless luxury. The father's smoke-and-mirrors raced against her nurturing heart, and he was winning.

Chapter Twenty

The heat of the late afternoon lingered like a midsummer day, despite it was the start of a new school year. Kristin dabbed her upper lip with a tissue, as she walked toward the opposite end of the parking lot where her youngest child stood.

"Hi, Mama, you look nice."

"Thank you, baby. Mama thinks her light sweater and black jeans are still too hot for this climate," she said, noticing the other parents clad in Bermuda shorts and guayaberas. She felt like Meryl Streep in a world of Jimmy Buffets. "I like your off-the-shoulder shirt . . . very hip."

"Don't say hip," she said. "Lennon and her band geeks are warming up, but you can walk with me."

The mother smiled holding her daughter's hand as they walked through the cement archway together. Maybe it's because she doesn't know anybody here yet, or maybe she's a little scared; either way, she cherished feeling tiny fingers clutched to her own. Passing through a pentagon-shaped patio area, she noticed a line of royal blue lockers lining outside hallways.

"Do you like it? This is where I'd be going to school."

An open recreation area appeared to be a spot for lingering students to catch up with friends. The perfectly annoying palm trees framed even the drabbest corners into postcard-like settings.

"So, tell me what you like about this school," she asked her eager tour guide.

"It's big. There's a ton of kids here. The volleyball team is boss. They've won like a buttload of trophies."

"Let's not say buttload, please. It's a good sport for girls." The middle school in Ellington didn't offer a volleyball team, even though she'd met with the school athletic director several times about initiating a program.

"Mama, this is Mrs. Sutton. She's the counselor I met with when we signed Lennon up."

"Hello, Mrs. Camek, it's nice to meet you. Your daughters are a delight."

"Murphy. I'm a Murphy now," Kristin said.

"I'm so sorry, I shouldn't have assumed," said the counselor.

"No, it's okay. It was a good last name for many years. Olivia is excited about the school and Lennon seems as excited as an eighth-grader can be, I guess." The women laughed.

"That's good to know. Lake Tarpon Middle has a lot to offer students. I'd be happy to get you a brochure. Will you walk with me to my office?"

"Sure," she said. "Liv, why don't you save Mama a seat. I'll be there before your sister takes the stage."

"Okay. See ya," she said, giving a spin away from the women.

"Lennon is such a talented girl," Mrs. Sutton said. "Her

band instructor raves about her musical ability. You must be musically talented as well."

"Oh, thank you." Kristin blushed. "I haven't played for many years, but she's had formal lessons for a few years now. Music is her passion."

"I hear your accent, remind me again where you live?"

"Ellington, Alabama. It's close to Montgomery."

"I know that area," Mrs. Sutton said. "There's a KOA off the interstate we use as our half-way stopping point on the way to see our daughters. We try to go once a year during my Fall Break. You're lucky to have such a beautiful place to live. All I've known is summer and sand my entire life."

"You're from here?" Kristin asked.

She nodded. "Yes, both my husband and I are. Our girls are grown and living their own lives across the country. We take some vacations on our way to visit them. We have one in Huntsville, and the other in Ohio. As different as night and day."

Empty-nester stories were becoming relatable to the mother.

The women stopped at a blue, metal door in front of a small courtyard. "Here's my office, excuse the mess." Shuffling through folders on the corner desk, she retrieved a floral pamphlet complete with palm trees on the front. "This brochure has the most frequently asked questions. I'll put my business card inside in case you want to talk."

"How does it work with a student who transfers mid-year?" Kristin asked.

"With a school of 1000, there's quite a few transitions during the school break. Parents' jobs, moves out of the district, and such. We keep the child on track with the curriculum they are leaving and close any gaps before the end of the year. Children like your girls make the change without issue."

"And the school nurse? What are her hours? Olivia is a newly diagnosed Type 1 diabetic."

"She mentioned that to me when we met. The school would want you and Mr. Camek to have a 504 in place. This document helps communicate how her condition is treated when she's on campus. The school nurse is here every day. She'd have full access to medical care while attending classes."

At home, the school nurse worked multiple campuses, in two rural counties. "Thank you for making this quick visit," she said. "You've given me a lot to think about."

"Call me if there's anything I can offer." The school counselor closed her office door and returned to chaperoning lost students back to their rightful spots.

Kristin strolled through the open courtyard, now emptied from frenzied families corralling through to the band concert. She paused, hearing the opening applause inside. Smells of warm popcorn mixed with the salty air tickled her nose. Pointed shadows of palm fronds flapped against a pink and orange canvas above; how they differed from the towering loblollies at home. An elegant heron glided to its nest with one or two effortless pumps; a contrast to the fluttering chimney sweeps she watched in the evenings. Nightfall was absent the sounds of crickets or bullfrogs, yet the cheer of proud parents was familiar. Her years as a band parent allowed her an empathetic moment watching band directors and school administrators hustle well past the end of their workdays. The fading sun still set on honored families, dedicated school officials, and unappreciative middle schoolers, no matter the venue.

After the concert, she greeted her musician with a tight hug. "You were incredible. Who knew a Queen medley could have a flute solo?"

Lennon blushed. "Thanks. I'm starving."

"We'll eat at the house," her father said. "*Mom* has

cooked your favorite—lasagna."

Kristin's stomach churned.

"Where will you be, Mama?" Olivia asked.

"I'm going to hang out for a couple of days. Check out the town, you know. Then the three of us will have some time together later in the week. Maybe we can go to the beach." She hid her disdain for sand under her high-pitched tone.

"Awesome!" Olivia replied.

"See you then, babies."

She watched both girls follow their dad toward the glowing LED lights of a pearl Audi sedan idling in the parking lot. The engine was nearly silent when he raised a key fob to unlock the doors and dangled the single-key keychain with two dealer tags still attached.

***

The mother spent the next two days learning about the sprawling coastal community where her eldest child now lived. She visited the local libraries, shopping districts, and the clubhouse area for Hutch's neighborhood. Since his move, their daughters were convinced the only proper upbringing was in the pews of the church. Several congregation members submitted their written support of the girls' joining their father and stepmother's home; Kristin thought it only appropriate to visit.

Upon entry, the place of reverence looked more like a tropical resort. The bird-of-paradise flowers popped open along stone sidewalks, leading parishioners between the sanctuary to Sunday School classrooms. While admiring the tiled archways covered in vibrant hibiscus vines, a woman wearing a flowing, grape jumpsuit approached. Her hair was as brilliant as the lush gardens.

"Good morning, Kristin?" her voice tilted.

"You must be Dot." The visitor recognized the name from one of her ex-husband's affidavits supporting the children's election to move.

"It's so nice to meet you." Her brilliant smile gleamed as she cupped Kristin's hands on both sides. Pulling in closer, she said, "Lennon and Olivia are absolute treasures."

"Thank you for saying that. They seem to enjoy visiting your—" She stumbled for the right word. Kristin hadn't stepped inside a religious venue since the priest accused Rosalyn of offering Sunday Schoolers paid tours of Mother Superior's private quarters.

"We've loved every second of having them in our youth group. Can I show you where they like to spend their time?"

The mother followed the hostess's violet ringlets to a stucco structure surrounded by pristine yards and a renovated playground. Inside, walls hosted artwork from budding creatives of all ages. Classrooms were filled with tiny desks and colorful chairs, anchored by bright, patterned rugs.

Their walk ended at the last door on the corridor. Dot said, "The Youth Group area is here."

Upon entering, Kristin froze and turned backward. "Is this it?"

Clutching her keyring, her ringlets bounced a yes, while she motioned for her guest to step inside.

A chalked sign welcomed Lake Tarpon Teens, which reassured her they were in the right area of the church grounds. Corners huddled high-top tables next to USB charging ports. Navy-and-white cushions formed a floor pallet in front of a raised stage. Three microphone stands and an amplifier lined a performance area under strands of dimmed lights surrounded by a sparkling skyline backdrop. Kristin trusted her tour guide had not led her to the church coffee shop.

"How nice," she said.

"Lennon has a beautiful voice; she looks like a natural on that stage," the woman said.

Assorted snacks and sodas lined the shelves of a refurbished bar in the back of the room. The youth director's reflection beamed in the mirror.

Noticing a cabinet label with her daughter's name on it, she asked, "May I?"

"Go ahead, the kids put it together for her."

Inside the storage area, a shelf supported three glass jars, each with their own label. *Sugar, Sugar Free,* and *Emergency.* Two were filled to the brim, with a smattering of low- and high-carbohydrate snacks. She saw several of her daughter's favorite brands along the edge. The other jar contained medications, a pocket-sized schematic outlining diabetic emergency procedures, and a host of medical supplies at the ready.

"They fell right into the mix with the other kids. Since they were visiting on the weekends, Winter Break, Spring Break, you name it!"

Kristin recounted the back-breaking commutes in her head.

"The Youth made this for Olivia when they heard about her diagnosis. They didn't want her to be afraid to hang out with them." Dot's smile flashed again. "They've missed seeing Liv with the new arrangement."

A warmth radiated through Kristin as she blinked away emerging tears. "That was very thoughtful of them, and you, Dot. It's so nice when someone loves your kids as much as you do."

Placing her hand on Kristin's arm, she said, "As a mother myself, I know this is difficult."

Then how could you support a plan to move my daughters away from me?

With planted feet, Kristin stood firm clasping her fingers

together. This was the self-righteous moment she dreamt of. She lifted her chin, ready for a full apology on behalf of the Pope.

I wish I could record this.

The scorned mother leaned in seeking vindication in every syllable.

"You have done a wonderful job raising the girls."

Kristin's chin lowered.

"All I can tell you is …," She paused, centering herself on a stool behind her. "I'm new to this role and teenagers—well, they're not the easiest group to fit in with. The last director was a hard act to follow. I worried how I would meet their expectations. Your daughters—" Dot's ocean eyes watered, "—became my strongest allies. When they accepted me, their friends embraced me, too. They are the reason I've been able to live my passion."

The mother's jaw loosened.

"I knew it had to be their mom. Only a mom could have taught them that level of compassion. It's clear, they've grown up watching you and now they mirror you," Dot removed her hand from Kristin's arm and placed her elbow on the table beside her.

"Dot, I'm-I'm humbled, truly. My daughters are lucky to have this church family." Grabbing her purse from the bar, she said, "You were too kind to meet with me on short notice. Please, don't let me take up too much of your day."

"If you're ever in town, please stop by again. The Youth would love to meet Liv and *Leonard's* mom." Dot gave a playful wink to the mother and helped her find the exit.

An incessant sun blanketed the pavement between her, and her minivan parked in the shade of a fiery, royal poinciana. She twisted her hair into a bun while walking. Beads of sweat released down her neck stopping at her blouse's collar. The steaming humidity of the morning, already intolerable, justified a prolonged rest with the air conditioner on High as she processed Dot's compliment.

Every bend of her journey to expose the inexplicable existence of Hutch's corrupt plan was leading her in a different direction. From the school administrators to the church leadership, she had yet to find one person who was judgmental or shocked by their nonconforming situation. The fast-food customer service and the carwash attendants were all polite, welcoming, and friendly. Maserati moms, the lacrosse kids eating organic fruit snacks; each offered a welcoming smile in her direction. If this was the world Lennon and Olivia were experiencing, maybe they had a genuine desire to transition. She knew there was a strong possibility the judge could approve for the girls to remain separated. Hutch's relentless approach was executed against her, but her daughters appeared unscathed. Like Dot suggested, maybe Kristin had imprinted a model of kindness that protected them from their father's detriment.

***

Later that week, with their chairs aligned, Kristin and both girls sat mesmerized by the rolling waves of the Atlantic.

"I hope I can get a tan this year," said the oldest.

"You need to keep sunscreen on; the sun is relentless," the mother said, adjusting the umbrella over her pale-skinned daughter.

Dropping her boogie board at her mom's feet, Olivia said, "Wow, the waves are gigantic."

"Let's take a break and check your blood sugar." Kristin held the child's wrinkly, wet finger for a sample.

"I've spent a lot of time here this week," she said, wiping the finger with an alcohol swab. "I can see why you like it."

"It's not that we don't like home, Mama." Lennon reared

her defense.

"Here's the stick," the mother warned, and the child closed her eyes on cue. She didn't think she'd ever get used to purposefully causing her child pain.

"We just want to try something different," said the eldest daughter.

"I get it," the mother said. "I do. You have to understand, this was a complete surprise to me."

"You're not wrong. We could have said something sooner," said Lennon.

"Well, thank you for saying that." Her mind raced, searching for the words that pierced her heart the least. "Livvy . . ." her voice thickened.

I can't do this.

The young child's eyes widened watching her mother struggle to complete the sentence.

Clearing her throat, Kristin continued, "If you want to be here with your dad and sister, I'm okay with it."

"Really?"

"Really," the mother said, forcing a smile. "It's 110. Eat something small to keep it up after your swim."

"So, you won't fight it in court anymore?" Lennon asked.

She handed the child a purple insulated cooler to select an item. "Nothing good will come out of going back to court. The lawyers and judges don't know my babies. I know you'll do well anywhere you live."

"Mama—" the teenager wrapped her sandy arms around her mother.

The grit on her back sent a slight cringe up Kristin's spine, but she welcomed her child's embrace.

Olivia sat with a stunned look on her face as her mother explained further. "Mrs. Sutton says they can add you to their rosters over the rest of Fall break. You'll fit right in; I just know it." She was relieved the crashing waves in the background, masked her brittle voice, and hoped they'd drown out the deep ache in her chest.

"Mama, I want to leave my blankets with you. I think I need a clean start with no baby stuff."

"You'll still be a dork," her sister said.

The mother's mind wondered, would they forget childhood memories with her and Grey? What would their future relationship look like? How far would their dad go with his attempts to erase her existence?

After wiping their feet and legs with baby powder, they climbed into the family vehicle. She helped the girls wrap damp towels around their waists while recalling many family beach trips they'd spent together, hauling sandy wagons filled with neon shovels and patterned molds, each used with the delicate touch of their fingertips. A climb into the car still meant a popsicle for the road. Although Olivia now got a sugar-free version, which was well accepted.

"Thank you, I love these things."

Juice-stained lips and sun-kissed noses followed by a comforting nap on the car ride home; this had been their beach routine since their early trips to Gulf Shore beaches. For the first time since her daughters announced plans to move, she was off her knees. She was no longer succumbing to her ex-husband's desire to punish her. Kristin met them with a proposed solution for peace. He may find other avenues to crash and collide with; however, for now she breathed in the serenity of acceptance.

At their father's house, the girls embraced Mom with heartfelt farewells. She sensed their father watching from inside, but she didn't release their warm bodies from her arms until each tear had dried.

Slipping one of the silk blankets behind her back. Olivia said, "I may need one if I have a sick day."

"Good plan."

Her brave children walked past the lush, green leaves along their father's walkway minding the grasses' razored edges. She knew, from that point on, he'd make her beg to remain relevant.

Chapter Twenty-One

Timing the drive home from her daughters' new residence was getting easier for her. After four months of making the commute, she had mentally broken the ten-hour drive into segments. Each completed stage meant less time agonizing her loss on the lonely journey.

Before she could exit the gated community, the mother felt her chest thundering and offering no sign of regression. Master classes aired by The Brené Brown, whom she lovingly referred to as B-Squared, helped her recognize this as a sign of her 'personal shame storm.' Like a tidal wave building momentum from the base of the ocean, the disgrace of being a non-custodial mother crashed on her soul's shore as soon as the girls closed his front door behind them. The first stage was spent driving while sobbing tears into a t-shirt quilt she had sewn for Lennon's fifth-grade graduation. It was always within arm's reach in the rear passenger seat, making it an easy grab during the drive. By the time she made it through the heavy suburban South Florida traffic, her tears were streaming across cotton-laced memories of birthdays, first sleepovers, and the scribbled signatures of childhood friends. Her pain buried in the very trophy of her joy. Being a parent to this beautiful, fiercely independent individual, she longed to stitch many more milestones into the seams.

The second phase usually meant trading the t-shirt quilt for a pair of tattered-edged, satin blankets left on the rear driver's side passenger seat. Olivia had been in her mother's rearview mirror since her car seat was first cradled there. Deemed a self-soother as an infant, Olivia spent many of her early years comforting herself by sucking her right two forefingers, gently cradling them with the soft sweetness of her blankets clutched with her left hand. Fussy after a long car ride, Olivia would often assume her position of soothing relaxation. Kristin's eyes flashed in the mirror, watching the hazel eyes of her sensitive child peer over the screen of pink pastels. With a brief reassuring exchange of glances, Olivia would drift into a peaceful slumber. Pride pooled from every cell in her body, seeing her children adapt, overcome, and push through discomforting times. Over the years, the blankets were demoted from being in Olivia's hand 24/7, and dragging across kitchen floors, to being reserved for bedtime routines. Then finally, to a safe spot on the top shelf of her closet where she knew they were close by, but out of the camera angle for her Tik Tok videos. By eleven, Olivia was well past her oral fixation needs, but the blankets were still her go-to comfort item, which mostly served as a gathered pillow when traveling between parents' houses. It was hard for her to tell why the tears soaked through the material at this leg of the trip. Was it the material wicking capabilities of satin or was she crying twice as hard?

The sobbing lessened in stage three, as the exit signs for the "The Happiest Place on Earth" came into view. Usually, the pinnacle of any family's road trip was seeing these beacons of fun along the roadside. The symbol of reward for the sacrifice of multiple hours riding in the backseat, with every living family member listed in the ancestry database. To Kristin, the directional cue was nothing but a stark reminder of one of Hutch's many sales pitches to Lennon and Olivia on how life with Dad would be more fun than at Mom's house. Forgoing any notion of a decade-long routine they had established and disrespecting relationships with doting grandparents, he minimized after-school ice cream runs together with promises of horseback riding lessons in the heart of South Florida's equestrian epicenter. He overshadowed Rosalyn's adoration with illusions of carefree days on white sandy beaches. Hutch trumped his own mother's commitment to be another loving face in the audience of every school award program, with the enticement of unhinged excitement at premier amusement parks. He had no regard for the friendships that budded in kindergarten, nor their connections to their nurturing families. These were all casualties of Hutch's war, soon to be forgotten memories like the mouse-ear headband under the seat.

Her self-diagnosed sciatica radiated through her lower back and leg by stage four, forcing her to make a NASCAR-like pitstop in Central Florida. After finding respite in too many undesirable locations, the driver starred a specific convenience center in her GPS as a favorite. It met her requirements of being off the arduous turnpike, which trapped weary travelers into paying exorbitant prices for gas and Doritos. This one offered gas stations visible to the cashier, which she knew from a guest expert on Oprah's podcast, was the safest pump position for a solo female traveler. While cleaning her bug-splattered windshield, she wrenched her spine in all directions. A considerate traveler, she returned the gas nozzle to its holster, wiped her hands with a Sani wipe and eased her van forward to make way for another solo female to take her spot. Clearly, she too, was a fan of Oprah's safety episode. Kristin took caution not to limp or wince through the pain when walking into the store, Oprah safety tip #9, deter would-be attackers assessing her weakest links. The bathroom was the key requirement, which met her checklist. It offered a long corridor entry way, touchless sinks, and a hand sanitizer dispenser outside for that extra bit of cleanliness on the go. The sharps container on the wall caught her eye. Returning to the car, she gave her back and feet a final stretch rummaging through a snack satchel for any snacks left behind. A handful of Hot Cheetos with half of an Otis Spunkmeyer muffin would have to do. Within twelve minutes, her minivan was easing out of the tow-friendly driveway where she entered.

The area was a prime spot for a panhandler to catch traffic headed in both directions. She'd grown accustomed to seeing one posted on the corner curb near the truck stop. The ones with the dogs pulled at her heartstrings. Today, there was a woman whose baggy green pants draped over her black shoes, almost touching the well-manicured patch of grass where she rested her backpack. Her hair was tucked under a dingy, red ball cap and her blue, long-sleeved shirt hung like a scarecrow's wardrobe over her frail arms. Kristin slowed the minivan, and the woman left her corner perch. She adjusted her hat and gave a tight-lipped smile, while her feet shuffled her low-hanging pants toward the driver's side door.

Kristin returned a smile, relieved she didn't see a tethered dog.

With a quick check of the rearview mirror, she reached behind her feeling inside the chair pocket. Fumbling past a tube of glucose tablets and crumpled straw wrappers, she felt around for the homeless handouts she and the girls created as a community service project. Her thoughtful children included a pack of crackers, some loose change, and one or two toiletry items wrapped with tissue paper, twine, and a small tag with a handwritten message. The pink packages included sanitary products; however, blue was the first available. There was no time for customization. She offered the gift through the window.

The woman softly cupped her hands to receive the wrinkled wrapper; Kristin tried not to stare at the dirt under her fingernails.

Ready for her return trip, the driver made a quick safety check of her vehicle. But the woman lingered, holding the package.

Oh, dear, what's she doing?

The stranger peeled back the note's edges revealing a scribbled message in hot-pink ink.

Kristin cringed. *Who reads the card?*

As the woman's mouth opened, she refused to make eye contact, darting her view to the bustling interstate just a few feet away.

The disheveled woman's surprisingly clear tone read aloud these two words, "You're cute."

Kristin froze.

Blood flashed in her cheeks as her mind returned to the hotel room where her goodwill ambassadors spent a rainy afternoon making the gifts. She didn't proofread Olivia's penwork that day; however, she assumed her direction was sufficient. "Write something cheerful. Happy. You know, keep it light."

The mother hoped her good-hearted daughters would conjure up a "God Bless You" or "Hang in There." Now, she was faced with looking at a woman who lacked all comforting resources and had just been likened to a small Pomeranian. She positioned her finger on the wood-grain window control, out of the woman's site.

She sensed the panhandler looking at her.

"Tell her," she paused. "Tell her, she's cute too."

With her eyes wide, Kristin peered under the tattered bill of the woman's ball cap to see her chocolate eyes watering. Her thin lips inched into her drawn face exposing faint cheek dimples that had likely been hidden for some time. With a tug at her lip, the panhandler gave an affirming nod to the driver and Kristin shifted into Drive.

Merging into the streaming flow of traffic on I-75 North, the mother pressed pause on her sadness recalling the encounter. Here she was, a parent without the sole token of worthiness the world recognized, living day to day in a fog of depression. Her despair lifted only by the intermittent phone calls with her daughters. She questioned how she could offer hope when she, herself, was hopeless.

Stage five included the remainder of the trip. It was typically a blur of self-help podcasts: Oprah, Dr. Phil, and B-Squared blasting her speakers, refilling her soul, and rebuilding the shattered glass heart she housed. She drove through blowing sheets of rain, passing family cars filled with sleeping teenagers pressed against the windows. The wife longed to go on a family vacation again. She'd lay on her rolling counselor's couch for hours desperately seeking a way to climb out from the smothering layers of loss she felt trapped under. The occasional lip quiver from a profound statement from her guru lineup was all that kept her heavy eyes from closing on the painted roadway lines ahead.

She often contemplated her new role as a mother without custody, or MWOC, for those who knew the term intimately. She thought it would be easier to be a female panhandler.

Now those women know how to shuck societal reign.

Carefree, no rules, no conscience, they had life figured

out. These gals weren't lingering in the Barnes and Noble's self-help section, scanning B-Squared covers for quick advice. They were rarely found perusing the astrology section for celestial insight.

Panhandlers knew their life couldn't be understood through words on a page, and they didn't waste time self-assessing their past failures, like MWOCs did. Panhandlers already had a place in the world. If this was the Wild West, they were the ones whose coats grazed the spurs on their boots.

This group of renegades were nothing like Kristin's fellow MWOCs, voraciously seeking resilience coaching from a host of podcasters. She didn't see them fighting traffic to pick up their children at the precise time a judge deemed acceptable to start parenting. Although, if they opted to listen to one of her top-ranked audio books, the panhandlers would be reassured by B-Squared's recommendations to own their shame and embrace their imperfections. Panhandler life comes with a graciousness not granted to MWOCs. Society assumes their nomadic lifestyle stems from a traumatic past, likely the result of a diseased mind. Perhaps they were abused as a child, lacked role models, or watched too much television, each a plausible reason for their corruption. If only MWOCs were wandering souls, seeking salvation from their psychological demons. The DSM practically gave them a hall pass. Rather, most were navigating a life they never dreamed of. There's no diagnostic crutch for this group and even the coats and spurs wouldn't keep judgment from overtaking their self-worth.

There was a voice change in her audio line up. Kristin vaguely recognized the formerly obese nutritionist, now a Certified Diabetes Educator, giving diet tips for Type 1 diabetics. She dialed the volume down, just low enough to be able to hear anything that indicated there was a cure fast approaching for this inexplicable disease. Her mind wandered, recalling her days as a charge nurse, hosting panel interviews for applicants to join her team. Only this time the candidates were panhandlers and MWOCs. How would she objectively screen for the best? There were some similarities. Both took their positions seriously. There were no preceptors to guide either if they get the job. Both lifestyles were defined by circumstance rather than intent. Kristin doubted these women, as dreamy-eyed little girls, asked to be misunderstood by society and labeled as a human deserving of a 'less than' life." It was unlikely they established SMART goals, or of having their identities overshadowed in a world with little compassion for women not meeting the gold standard.

Neither the panhandler nor MWOC needed performance evaluation, but the go-getters used the occasional critique to perfect their craft. Team building was minimal for either candidate. Both ran parallel to other groups, never intersecting. There wasn't time in their hectic personal lives for sincere relationships. If the panhandler or the MWOC experienced a close moment with someone in a similar plight, they might share best practices, or words of encouragement. Heeding their own advice, sometimes they looked like a professional call-girl, other times they're a virgin in the back of their mom's Suburban. There's no grace period with either role, but there's no termination either. It was an endless hell of trial and error.

Like fathers without custody, there are male panhandlers out there, but an empathetic society offers them a safety net. With this group, the popular opinion is they just couldn't conform to the family model. It's not their fault; if anything, women withheld the right resources from them. The world assumed female panhandlers failed somehow, while male beggars were deemed as being failed by the world.

Much like the dichotomy between non-custodial mothers and fathers. Nonetheless, all of these "criminals" emptily stared into blurred headlights on dark highways, grateful for any glimpse underneath their pain. Kristin accepted her title as a solo gig; ultimately, she was her own charity case.

As the lights of Ellington's downtown corridor came into view, she remembered the woman at the truck stop earlier in the day.

How did she recognize a child's handwriting so easily? Where are her children?

She wondered if the mysterious woman's ex broke her financially, emotionally, and mentally too.

It was always on the last mile when the demons took over.

Kristin veered right onto the exit, envying the woman's courage to live anywhere she could be nameless.

Chapter Twenty-Two

As a parent, Kristin admitted she'd become lost in her children's lives, a common occurrence with several of her friends. It was acceptable her socks had holes if her kid's Nike Air Ones were creaseless. Even as a divorced parent with child-free weekends built into her routine, it was still difficult to stay connected to her own needs. This is supposedly the time divorced mothers pamper themselves with facials and massages to relax from the daily stress of parenting. Kristin's friends probably thought she basked in the sun by the pool, reading, and being fanned by a pool boy while the girls were at their dad's. The truth was, her coveted "free time" was spent running errands she didn't want to do when the girls were home, because she didn't want to lose a fleeting minute with them. Of course, this method meant she stockpiled tasks for every other weekend. Her two days "off" became a forty-eight-hour sprint of shopping for school supplies she couldn't afford, cramming in car maintenance, and making sure to give her second marriage some attention.

Grocery shopping was one chore the mother actually scheduled for her kid-free weekends. As a divorced parent, other people's perceptions become written affidavits. One bad day at Piggly Wiggly could result in a witness claiming she shoved a Dum-Dum in her daughter's mouth for no reason. She knew divorced parents lived under a microscope; select public outings had to be chosen with care.

As soon as she returned from dropping off Olivia and Lennon for the weekend, the clock ticked for her to get everything done before their return. Having one hair out of place at pick-up time could have triggered Hutch to find the most minute clause in their parenting plan and file a motion for contempt. The only time she slowed down was to clip a hangnail from snagging on her sock hole.

Though her child-free weekends were not the glorious mini vacays everyone imagined, she now found herself pining for every worry of those days. When custody was awarded to Hutch, she was left staring at an abyss of loneliness. Empty nest was no longer a distant concept for her. Most parents had years to prepare for the day their child moved out of the house. By the time it occurred, the family felt the crunch of having too many adults living together. With the custody change, there was no warming up to the idea of her children living somewhere else. Family court issued a cold slap across her face. There were no last dinners together, farewell parties, or proper send-offs. Justice's knife sliced her, the targeted parent, and left a gaping wound with no first aid kit in sight. Even after the initial shock eased, Kristin's wound wept, oozed, and festered around the edges.

Self-care was becoming a priority for her. With delicate care, she cleansed the wound, but it took time. Aggressive treatment could scab the outside but cause it to rot from the inside out. She knew a dehiscence would bring more excruciating pain. With care, she packed the gaping hole in her heart with kindness, praying it healed with minimal scarring.

In her quest to expand beyond the role of mother, Kristin followed the experts' advice, leading the charge of reclaiming her own voice. B-Squared talked about finding those Marble Jar friends, and she knew her Mason glass was empty. She set out with the intention to surround herself with others that inspired, encouraged, and emulated the life she wanted to live. A peaceful, hippie-chick at her core, the former tennis player and critical care nurse was uncomfortable with the idea of Oms and monk-like chanting. No spacey world of wellness was going to do it for her. She needed some badassery in her life, but in a non-limb injuring way. Somehow, her Zen was found in the world of back-bending, hamstring-stretching, pelvic-thrusting yoga in an 88-degree room.

Hot Yoga appealed to many athletes and has-been athletes, like herself, who sought the adrenaline rush without the joint replacement. Several strong women in the group introduced themselves to the newcomer validating she was on the right path to reclaiming herself. Brooke and Kristin would often commiserate together when a particularly sadistic teacher would add Happy Baby Burpees to get the pain really flowing.

"She's brutal," the redhead said.

"She should be ashamed of making this relaxing stretch a form of torture." Brooke's short hair matted across her brow line from perspiration.

Along with their mediocre standing splits, the women shared a lot of like interests. She was a talker, which initially tickled Kristin's nerves on days she was there to prepare her mind for uncomfortable bliss. On the other side of the mat, she was trying to meet new people which meant letting others be heard, even when she wanted to zone out.

One day, she took her usual spot in the back of the class, just to the side of the ceiling heaters, yet close to the door so she could savor the occasional wisp of room-temperature air.

Brooke slapped her mat alongside her while she used the wall as a prop. "Jackson is really off the rails today," she said, smoothing her plastic, ¼-inch thick barrier over the rigid floor.

"Jackson? Your ex?"

Nodding yes, she said, "He likes to play these games of making me wait at the neighborhood entrance gate before giving the Security Guard his all clear."

"Sounds familiar." Kristin adjusted her headband in the mirror.

"He says that he doesn't get the call, but after 15 minutes the guard makes me circle back through. He said it was because I was early for my parenting time," Brooke huffed.

"They get off on the power." Her confidence was boosted knowing she could employ her hard-earned wisdom.

The two shared their individual situations. Brooke's voice cracked at times when talking about the love she had for her daughter. Her heart wrenched not being able to help with her own coming-of-age struggles.

"It's never easy knowing they're not with you," she'd say. "I mean, you know you're their mother, no matter where they lay their heads, but—"

"There's no panic like waking in the middle of the night, realizing your children aren't in their rooms asleep." Kristin finished her new yogi friend's thought.

Peace had arrived after court hearings, legal atrocities, and months of enduring the shame of losing her kids to her ex-husband. Brooke's story was hers. It was validating to have someone understand her pain, yet she wanted to help her new friend avoid some of the pitfalls of this new world. The mother's courage was restored by a mentoring opportunity with the novice divorcée. Marbles clanked in her Mason Jar.

Old hippies glared at the two giggling schoolgirls interrupting their pre-workout stretches. "Don't they know there's time built into class for that?" Kristin whispered.

"The human body can only bend so much so far, why overdo it?"

Here was Kristin's moment to shine her shame light on her imperfections. Brooke had been so open with her, it was the least she could offer. Seated on the mat, she leaned over prepared for full disclosure of her newfound life situation. An unbreakable bond was on the horizon when she felt a succinct bundle of pressurized gas bypass the well-placed seam of her new Fabletics yoga pants. A flappy echo bounced off every corner of the silent studio and the perpetrator cringed.

Kate Hudson has failed me!

Even the old hippies broke their supported bridge poses to see who dared to commit such an atrocity. Her future best friend and elementary school teacher didn't even dart her eyes. It was clear Brooke had concrete experience with overlooking bodily sounds.

In shock, Kristin dragged the side of her foot across the plastic mat beneath her, desperate to recreate a similar sound. She stopped only to prevent Brooke from adding Tourette's to her mental list of physical ailments. "So, yeah, exes," she said, through a nervous grin. "We have a similar story."

"We could write a book." The new friend turned away from Kristin executing an unusual lower back stretch.

B-Squared's words flooded her head, *Own it. Speak your shame. Your imperfections are what makes you desirable. This is my "marble jar" moment!*

In her desperation, she sought any connection that would catapult her from "non-custodial parent" status, to an acceptable circle of "women with a past."

A lean, twenty-something woman, wearing a Lululemon ensemble, glided into the darkened room and started a soothing playlist. Brooke immediately went into Downward Dog. The hippies unwound their vined poses and held Ragdoll until further direction. The last yogi to fall in line, Kristin lifted herself into position and clenched her cheeks together for the next hour and fifteen minutes. She was determined to not replicate the original incident. With her circulation rushing through her upside-down posture, she considered how she could salvage their budding relationship.

I'll DM her later. Maybe even throw in a few prayer hand emojis.

Chapter Twenty-Three

Grey had insisted the couple get away for the weekend to one of their favorite hotels in the city. While they enjoyed the simplicity of the countryside, a spa weekend was exactly what Kristin needed to erase the yoga fiasco from her memory. Prayer hand emojis were an ineffective marketing tool for her "Marble Jar" ad, she noted.

"Good call on leaving before rush hour," Grey complimented his wife's planning. He held the steering wheel with one hand and gave an approving nod to the suburban traffic moving at a decent pace beside him. "Did you load the app for the scooters?"

"Sure did. I can't wait to try them."

"Thanks again for making this weekend happen. I know you were looking forward to the medical conference with Vy," he said. "It sounded like a big one."

"They have lots of vendors and cutting-edge stuff, I've

been before. Vy goes every year with friends from work. Besides, with this virus popping up in big cities, I wasn't sure I wanted to travel to Boston."

"I agree, let's see where it goes before we make too many travel plans this year."

"It all worked out. Wey is using my ticket, and he'll make a fine nurse for the weekend."

His hearty laugh relaxed them both. "My brother sure knows how to get himself into a predicament, doesn't he?"

"Let's hope she doesn't make him sing karaoke at the closing ceremonies," she chuckled.

The husband and wife held hands as she watched the pine trees blur outside her window. It had been a full year since her daughters unveiled their plans to move to Florida. After spending seven months consumed with court timelines and legal jargon, Kristin was forced to make an emotionally gripping decision. One she hoped would be easier to accept with each passing day. Rosalyn's disapproval was as bitter as winter's wrath. Their porch-side coffee chats were abandoned soon after the first frost blanketed the pastures. Fumbling through holiday traditions, Kristin masked her dark sadness for family photos and gatherings. Her intense crying jags were limited to the shower, so no one could hear. The mother struggled to match the sisters' contentedness given the looming expiration date of their time together. She felt like a prisoner allotted a family visit in jail. Every passing hour sentenced her.

Poised in the center of Midtown, the Colonial was considered the queen jewel of Atlanta and had been a fixture of elegance since 1911. Grey stayed there on business trips when he was working in the corporate realm. His wife would often tag along to relax by the rooftop pool as he worked in a nearby office. After his day ended, there was time to indulge at a Michelin restaurant within walking distance. He loved the regal hotel's history; she loved the architecture and ambiance.

Her husband pumped the valet's hand by the cherrywood podium while uniformed attendants directed extravagant cars under the hotel's famed stone canopy. Kristin watched guests unload the trunks of their vehicles. A team of women hoisted a white bag with the label *Jean and Hall's Bridal* over their heads. As they maneuvered through the revolving glass doors with Navy Seal precision, Kristin tried not to imagine what beautiful brides her daughters would make.

She could tell Grey was revived by the pulsating frenzy of check-in; meanwhile, her enthusiasm was sedated. This was her first trip to Atlanta since she had said goodbye to Lennon at the airport. Her usual heart-skipping reaction to seeing the Colonial's iconic glass pinnacle was tempered by faded memories of chaperoning school field trips to the aquarium. In the distance, banners fanned a performer's concert dates where she and Lennon were once swooned by Harry Styles. The corner café where Olivia first expressed interest in the Pride movement was two blocks away. Kristin recalled her fascination watching the vibrant floats parade through the streets one summer afternoon. It was the moment she realized her little girl was evolving into a free-thinking woman. The historic theatre, directly across from the Colonial, was where the girls experienced their first love affair with stage performances. The mother could still hear six-year-old Olivia's patented leather T-bar sandals clicking across the mosaic tiled entryway to meet the young actress who portrayed Annie just minutes before. Every beat of her blood pulsing through her veins reminded her of future memories stripped away by her ex-husband.

"Kris," Grey's voice broke through the bustling road traffic. "Are you ready to go to the room?"

"Absolutely!" She forced her eyes open and gave a single, firm nod to her husband.

Revolving doors guided them to the lobby where the hotel's signature foyer spiraled through nineteen stories of cascading ivy overlooks. The encompassing glass windows sifted sunrays through every beveled edge, sending prisms onto guests below. She envisioned the gala premiers held here in 1939 when *Gone with the Wind* opened.

Maybe this was the exact place Vivien Leigh and Clark Gable posed for pictures.

Grey waved the keycard in the air, signaling her to follow the bellhop.

The smooth-skinned, black man admired his uniform in the mirrored panels of the elevator. Adjusting his name badge, he asked, "Are you here for the weddings?"

"Weddings? As in multiple?" Grey inquired.

"Always." The bellhop's fist steadied the brass luggage rack as the elevator came to a stop. "Everyone wants to get married at the Colonial."

"I bet," Grey replied, staring at the numbered marker. "We're just here for a weekend away."

"The grandparents are watching the kids, I see," the bellhop said.

Kristin darted her eyes toward the velvet floor.

Rocking on his heels, her husband fidgeted with the keycard before answering, "Spoiling them every second, you know."

The bellhop's question wrung in the mother's head as she peered down the endless hallway. The two men discussed game time programming behind her.

Will I always have to defend my character to strangers when I show up somewhere without my kids?

She considered confronting the man about his insulting assumption. There were plenty of fortyish women who chose not to have children.

Or, maybe he'd be more interested in me spilling my guts. 'Sir, my young daughters were manipulated by their father and they now live as residents of Florida.'

Everyone knew Floridians and Alabamans were inherently unable to like each other. Then again, she wondered if she was meant to answer these questions at all.

Maybe I'm not supposed to endure the aftermath.

The bellhop opened the door wide and inserted a rubber wedge between it and the floor. Black, hardwood planks lined the suite's entry. Kristin followed the path through the well-appointed living area to a bedroom with a majestic view of the city. The luxurious, white bedding complemented the muted pallet and represented the contemporary sophistication the hotel was known for. She laid her purse on the comforter, spilling the contents from inside. Joining Grey in the living area, she separated the drapes to reveal the balcony's view. Her eyes scanned the buildings stacked around her. Closed umbrellas stood like drawn swords along penthouse rooftops, ready for the coveted al fresco dining season. Pristinely manicured, topiary gardens lined the edges of courtyards in neighboring complexes. Her mind wandered through a fantasy of what the families' lives were like inside. Were they cuddled on the sofa with their loved ones or, like her, were they longing to feel whole again?

Standing over the metal track of the balcony entry, she let the buildings' shadows cloak her. The theatre's marquee vividly spanned the famed silhouette of Elphaba. She closed her eyes and felt the warm flicker on her face. Green. White. Black. Theatre patrons would surely fill the Colonial next week for a post-show experience.

Wicked was the girls' favorite musical since their family trip to New York the year prior. Lennon left the show aspiring to be a Broadway star. Olivia questioned everything she knew about the classic movie she and her mother watched each Thanksgiving. Kristin's brow creased remembering Hutch proclaim, at the hearing, the children approached him just days after returning from New York to initiate conversations about moving. Where was Emily's account of the children's Christmas vacation? Did Judge Lewis see the exuberant smiles on their faces at the Statue of Liberty, Macy's on Fifth Avenue, or under the lights of Times Square? If she had, she never would've believed they were searching for a life outside of the one ripped from their tiny hands.

Kristin bit her nails. Would every experience she encountered be a constant volley of joy and sorrow? Will pleasant recollections always turn into harsh reminders of how she was betrayed? A life of second-guessing every thought reframing her self-worth was no life at all.

Sitting on a small, modern couch Grey stretched his legs onto the leather cube in front of him. "This is the only thing I miss about corporate life," he said, crossing his arms behind his head.

"I'm going to step outside for a minute, before it gets too cold," she said, her palms pressed against the frigid barrier.

"Feeling brave today, I see," he joked.

On all their previous visits, his wife's fear of heights prevented her from experiencing the balcony's view. "I think so," her voice tightened, pulling the door behind her.

A cold gust struck her, drying her eyes, as she approached the ornate wrought-iron edge with caution. She blinked to clear her vision of the bustling thoroughfare 20 stories below and counted the thuds in her chest.

1,2,3. 3,2,1.

A confession to her therapist, during the custody hearing, prompted him to share that 85% of people consider suicide in their lifetime.

"It's the brain's way of trying to fix the problem," he said. "We're designed to solve things and the brain doesn't like turmoil, so its immediate reaction is to fix the issue."

At the time, her medical brain was satisfied with a neurobiological explanation. But, today she found it difficult to rationalize her mind with science.

The pain will end as soon as you're dead.

Her eyes squeezed tighter while tracing the icy rail with her fingertips. The therapist was right; she could solve the problem. She would no longer be subjected to Hutch's scathing emails of putative lectures. There'd be no more guilt for using Grey's 401K to pay family lawyers. Death meant no more answering questions in hotel elevators or faking smiles to brides on their wedding day. She would no longer find guilt in Rosalyn's rejection. Her friends would stop wondering; they'd know the pain she was hiding.

It would feel so good for someone to know.

Kristin's gaze locked on the tree-lined sidewalks while her engulfing agony untangled logic.

You don't deserve this pain.

The flicker of the theatre marquee grew louder, and her stomach pitted.

How long will I feel nauseated plummeting through the atmosphere?

The sensation was already numbing.

Will I hear their gasps?

Her desires drifted between being the responsible mother, wife, co-parent, employee—her list continued—reliable, predictable, unwavering Kristin she'd always been. Or, becoming the mangled torso she envisioned on the paved road below.

What will I regret when I hear my skull crush?

A shiver ran through her as the iron grazed under her shirt pressing onto her belly button. Her gaze drew upward.

Airplanes departed the runways where she cut her own umbilical cord.

This will solve the problem because you are the problem.

Adrenaline surged through her veins erasing any traces of her phobias. She unlocked her elbows, gasping as her body lightened its resistance.

I'm not jumping. Physics is a murderer.

She rooted her foot on the bottom railing and gave a firm lift of her hips.

The endorphins will take over. Nirvana erases remorse.

An inhale pierced her lungs when the church youth director's warm voice repeated in her head: *They've grown up watching you, and now they mirror you.*

1,2,3. 3,2,1.

Her chest deflated with a forced exhale and she relaxed the muscles in her neck.

Who'll care for them when I'm gone? Rosalyn? Grey? Audrie?

Their love was genuine, but nobody who knew her daughters better than her. She knew the real work was about to begin, this wasn't over.

The wind whipped her autumn locks forward over her shoulders. She felt her stomach twist again, and her vision narrowed as she stepped back from the icy rail.

"Honey?" Grey called from inside.

She repositioned her foot on the concrete pad and faced the suite's entrance.

"Honey?" he repeated. This time, poking his head through slatted blinds and shoving the door open.

Bending down, she swiped away rusted specs along her cuffed pants leg. "What is it? "What's wrong?" she asked.

"Lennon's blowing up your phone."

"Okay, I was just about to go inside," she said. Her knees quivered causing her to brace herself with both hands on the metal door frame.

"You okay?" Her husband backed away allowing her to enter the room. "It's odd for you to be on the balcony this long."

"It felt good for a little while."

"Your phone's buzzing woke me up. Teenagers," he huffed and rolled his eyes.

She furrowed her brow reading the illuminated texts from the vibrating device.

Lennon: MOM

Lennon: MOM

Lennon: I NEED YOU

Dismissing the message, she took a seat on the couch next to her husband. "Olivia probably unplugged her phone."

Kristin: What's wrong?

Lennon: Call me

Kristin: I'm out of town, what's up?

Lennon: It's Dad. Dad's dead.

Chapter Twenty-Four

"Death isn't funny," the mother said on the phone.

"Mom, I'm not joking. Dad is dead!"

"What?" Kristin asked, feeling her chest empty with her child's wails.

"He's . . . dead," Lennon said, pacing her words through sucked air and harsh sobs. "The police—called Mom, Peyton—earlier."

Hearing her daughter correct herself to appease her mother's ego, made Kristin's stomach churn. "Do you know how this happened?"

"He was on a business trip…" She continued to suck air through her nose. "He didn't show up at some work thing today."

"Lennon, I'm—" She paused as a twinge of relief rushed over her followed by immense guilt. "I'm so sorry this happened. I'm sorry I'm not there to hold you right now. My heart breaks I can't see you. Where's your sister?"

"She's here."

"Watch her. Stress can—"

"I know. Make her blood sugar go up," the teen said.

"What did the police say?"

"I don't know. All Peyton said was they found him dead in his hotel room," the child's voice cracked again.

Leaning forward with the phone in her hand, she rested her elbows on her thighs. The nurse coach asked, "Do we need to SIFT?"

"Now?"

"I'm worried about you. Remember, control what you can control."

"And to heck with the rest," she said, completing the phrase her mother taught her to repeat when feeling overwhelmed.

"S. Sense." Pacing around the bed, her lip trembled from stifling her own need to grieve, losing the father of her incredible children. Coaching her daughter to manage her pain helped her process her own.

This is the hardest lesson I've ever taught.

"I don't want to feel anything." The child cried.

"What does your body sense?"

"My chest hurts, hard. My throat burns. My fingers, they feel numb."

"Len, honey, take in a deep breath with me and release it slowly. I want you to pretend there's a flame in front of you. Don't take the light out, just make it dance." Kristin demonstrated, forcing air through her nose then releasing it with a soft sigh.

The teen copied her mother's example.

"I. Image. What do you see?"

"I can see him. Dead." Her thirteen-year-old voice broke into a forceful cry.

The mother covered the phone mic muffling her sobs. As they both regained control of their emotions, she continued her session. "Let's get this out, keep talking to me. The panic attacks come when you hold onto your emotions. Tell Mama, what do you see when you close your eyes?"

"I see him . . . lying on the floor." The daughter took quick breaths through her nose. In a soft voice, she said, "He's still. He looks like he's asleep."

"He's not in pain, honey. He's at peace."

"F. Feel. I feel scared."

Her mother struggled to hear her tiny voice on the other end of the call.

"I'm scared for me and for him. How did this happen to my strong Daddy?"

"It is frightening. When our world changes, we feel shaken. This is normal."

"I'm scared for me. And Olivia. What will happen to us?"

Chains from a porch swing tinkled in the background. Voices scattered with the sounds of slamming car doors. "Are you outside? Should we continue?"

"Yes, I'm feeling better. Let's keep going."

"T. Thoughts. What are you thinking inside that precious mind of yours?"

"I think—" Lennon hesitated. "I think I want to be dead, too."

The mother's legs buckled. A cupped hand over her mouth held her horror inside, as she guided her trembling body down the edge of the bed. Her knees burned, pressing into the grooves of the hardwood floor. Her husband's warm, callused palm rested on the back of her neck. The light of the theatre's famed marquee, now a rushing beam of electricity, flickered on the floor illuminating the bedroom. Syllables gripped the air, leaving her larynx as she spoke to her first-born child. "You. Are. Necessary. This pain will go away, trust me. But, *you* are a force in this world nobody can replace."

Sniffles echoed on both sides. Grey walked around the

bed, returning the spilled items to her purse. She pretended not to notice him studying a black compact device before tossing it into the satchel.

"I think I need to help with the littles," Lennon said.

"Helping others often helps ourselves."

"That must be why I like being with them. They don't know anything has changed."

"And that makes them feel safe. This is you, turning your pain into purpose."

"I love you, Mama."

Just as the tide rises and falls, she knew her child's anguish would come in waves. Sometimes crashing on the shore of her soul. Other times, trickling through the crevasses of sandy seashells. If ever grief masked its sinking sand as a tidepool in her child's life, the mother vowed to sit with her until it emptied back into the ocean.

"Are there any adults at the house with Peyton?" she asked.

"Her mom is on the way. Aunt Inez came up from Boca. You want to talk to her?"

She counted the years that had passed since she'd spoken to Hutch's aunt. "Sure, and I'll be there as soon as possible."

Feverish pecking stopped, as her conversation paused. Looking to his wife, Grey mouthed without sound. "What the—?"

She responded with a slow shake of her head and took a sip of water.

"I'm working on a flight now," he said, ducking behind his monitor again.

Squeaking door hinges called Kristin back to the phone. She heard a smattering of conversations in the background. "Aunt Inez? My mom is on the phone." Lennon's voice called in the distance. "Can you talk to her?"

"Of course, dear," the wobbly voice said. "Is this the hole

where I speak?"

The phone fumbled through the speaker. "Aunt I-?" Kristin cut her greeting short: mildly embarrassed she didn't know Emily Post's advice on what titles to give your ex-in laws.

"Kristin?"

"Yes, Inez. It's me, Hutch's, uh—"

"It has been a long time," the old woman said. "These girls you have are just beautiful."

"Thank you for your kind words about Lennon and Olivia. They impress me more each day," the mother said. "Please accept my condolences. I'm shocked about your nephew."

"It is horrific." Inez clicked her tongue against the roof of her mouth. "An absolute tragedy."

"My daughter gave me some information, but it was too difficult for her to discuss. Are you able to share anything about his death?" Kristin paced in front of the oval mirror in the foyer, holding the back of her hand to her forehead. "My head is spinning trying to put the pieces of the puzzle together."

"I'm happy to share what I know, dear. It's difficult for this old woman to say out loud."

"I understand. Thankfully, these are not words we speak often."

"So true, dear." A long pause precluded Inez's statement. Waiting for her response, the ex-niece-in-law held the phone face up, checking the connection, then returned the speaker to her ear. "Suicide. It's hard to say, but the police said they think he overdosed on drugs."

"I—" Kristin stammered.

"His wife said my nephew was traveling with work this week. You know, he does those conferences all over the world for the medical company he works for. I think he sells those heart monitor things that, you know, the ones that tell your doctor what your heartbeats do. I've never had a cardiar- cardio-. Oh, you're a nurse, I remember. What's the word I'm looking for?" Inez asked.

"Cardiologist. A heart doctor," the nurse said.

"I like that better. A heart doctor. I've never had a heart doctor. Oh, there I go again. An old woman rambling. I used to hate when Rosemary would do that to me on the phone and now look at me." Inez's chuckle threw the former two-pack-a-day smoker into a raucous coughing jag.

Covering the phone mic, she asked, "How's the flight coming?"

"The first one out in the morning is all that's available, but it's reserved," he said.

She nodded and returned to the phone.

"I'm sorry, dear. I got choked. Where was I?"

"Hutch was out of town for work."

"Yes, Nephew was at a conference. It was the last night of the event, and his work buddies said they went to eat together and stayed for cocktails in the lobby. I guess they were celebrating selling a bunch of those heart monitors." Inez snorted. "It seems all too expensive to me."

"So, he went to dinner last night." Kristin nudged.

"Yes. This morning, the kids said he never showed up at the airport."

"Kids?"

"The kids, well, I call them kids. Anyone is a kid compared to me." The old woman's hoarse voice chuckled. "I mean, work buddies. They said they called him on his phone multiple times. Sent those messages through the phones, you know?" Inez asked.

"Texts."

"Texts, yes. They sent Hutch texts, but no Hutch." Inez's voice strengthened. "They had to board their planes. They had families to get home to, too. Missing their own flights would have been silly."

"Sure, I understand."

Sweet Jesus, I could have flown there by now and had the police answer my questions.

"The work buddies didn't worry too much. They said Boston has a big airport and thought he may have taken a different flight, leaving later, maybe. They didn't fret. I've never been there, but I take their word for it. When they got to the office, still no Nephew." She clicked her tongue, again. "Well, that's when Hutch's boss called Peyton."

"Did Peyton call the police?"

"Well, she called the hotel first, dear."

Her face flushed recognizing her lack of crime knowledge. The ex-niece waited for the woman's next statement like she was watching a bobber tickling on the water's surface.

"The hotel manager checked the registry. He confirmed no check out this morning, like the work buddies said. I think they sent a security guard to the room, or maybe it was the cleaning lady who found him. It gets foggy for me."

"My goodness."

"The cleaning lady." Inez gasped. "I say lady. I should say crew, you don't know if it's a woman or a man these days. Anyway, someone saw him lying face down on the hotel room floor. Colder than a stiff fish. Still wearing his work shirt from the night before. Well, of course the hotel called the police after that."

"Did Peyton speak with them?" Kristin asked.

"Yes, they were the ones who called to let her know her husband was dead," Inez said.

"An overdose? I—"

"I know. I didn't realize he had a drug problem."

"Me either. It's hard to say what's going on in people's minds," she said.

"So true, dear."

"I guess they'll do an autopsy?"

"Yes, I believe Peyton gave the police her permission."

"Have you spoken to Rosemary?"

"Yes, my sister knows her baby boy is with the Lord," Inez whispered. "She won't be able to drive down. It's just too far for her to drive, but the funeral will most likely be there, in Ellington."

"I'm sure. Where Hutch's father is buried," the former wife said.

"Most likely. Well, "Inez blew air through her lips into the phone receiver, "I'm pooped. This has been an emotional day for an old grandma."

"I'm sure it has. Again, I'm so sorry. He was... a good man."

"Thank you, dear. I have a precious beam of light next to me who probably wants to speak to her mommy," she said, in a baby voice.

Kristin imagined her pinching Olivia's cheeks.

"It was nice to talk to you. Of course, I hate the circumstances."

On mute, she whispered to Grey with widened eyes and exaggerated lips, "Hutch killed himself."

"Unbelievable." The husband shook his head.

"Hi, Mama." Olivia's tender voice answered. "Mom? Are you there?"

She tapped the glass face with her finger a few times. "Hi baby. Sorry, I was on mute. Tell me how you're doing with all this."

"Yeah, I don't know what's happening," the child said, mumbling her words. "It's all so weird. Like, I'm sure Dad will walk through the door any minute, but everyone is crying."

"I wish I could see you. Hold you." The mother's nose tingled as her tears returned. "What questions do you have?"

"Is it weird, I want to see the body?" Olivia asked.

"I don't think anything is weird about how we process death. There's no wrong way."

"I feel icky just saying that out loud."

"It's good to live out loud. Don't hold in your feelings," said the mother.

"Do I have to leave soon?"

"I'm flying out early in the morning to be with you. We'll stay there as long as we need to, okay?"

"Okay."

"How's your stress? Are you focusing on what you can control and nothing else?"

"I am. I did that deep breathing thing you showed us. You know the one where you cross your legs and sit on the pillow with your pinkies pointed up."

"Meditation?"

"Yeah, that thing. I think it helps my blood sugar," the child said.

"You're doing everything right, kiddo." Kristin joined her husband on the couch and stretched her feet onto the black cube with his. "This is a lot for anyone to handle. I'll be there soon, and we can talk more. I love you so much."

"I love you, too."

From her seat, she peered through the balcony window watching pops of light appear in apartment homes across the street. Again, she wondered what those families' lives were like this evening. Was the mother cuddled tight under a blanket watching a comedy, while her children spilled overflowing popcorn kernels onto the floor? Or was she intercepting news that the man who caused her so much turmoil was out of her life? If the latter, was she wrestling peace and pain in a ring with her children sitting on the ropes?

Chapter Twenty-Five

Tapping shoes resonated through the Spanish-style archway, announcing her arrival to the place they had their last face-to-face conversation. A flutter through her chest appeared with the memory of his snarling intimidation. Her bracelets clanged together as she extended her trembling hand to tap the illuminated doorbell. The tepid humidity felt like Hutch's hands around her throat. She steadied herself with the reminder her ex-husband would no longer be on the other side of the door. A barrage of his insults and judgmental glares wouldn't follow the swoosh of air in her face. He wasn't there to torment her sanity with gaslighting and false accusations, nor could he deem her unworthy to enter his home, rear his children, or live a cooperative existence. Tears brimmed her eyelids; emotions played tug-of-war between relief and anguish. She had been labeled as the crazy ex-wife for ten years telling his friends, family, and countless others intrigued enough to listen to fabricated stories. How would she parent without wearing a heavy cloak of unworthiness on her shoulders? Chest pressure eased, understanding time restrictions with her beautiful daughters had been obliterated. They were done being used as pawns in his vicious game of revenge. The mother's begging had ceased.

Staring into the diamond-cut inlets of Hutch's front door, a buzz from her purse startled her eyes open. Audrie's name scrolled across her phone's screen and sent her call to voicemail. She noticed several missed calls from Vy too, occurring during the flight. The sisters-in-law would have to wait; now was not the time to hear their interpretation of what transpired. Reaching for the doorbell again, she was still curious if Hutch's voice would be heard from inside.

"Kristin?" A stout elderly woman with black-and-white hair stood before her with a welcoming smile. "It's been—"

"A long time," the niece said, smiling wide. She leaned down to embrace the woman holding the door. "Aunt Inez, you look so good."

"Tragic circumstances, but I'm grateful to see your face again. We've missed you at the family reunions. You know, Uncle B.C. passed."

Kristin nodded, "I believe Rosemary told me, I'm so sorry to hear it. He was a good man."

"Mom," a voice called.

Kristin's oldest daughter rose from a seated play area on the carpeted floor. She recognized the room as one of the two living rooms the guardian referred to in her deposition.

"Len!" The mother grunted as her child squeezed the air from her body. Stepping back, she said, "You've grown so tall. Look at you."

"I'll leave you two. There's a lot to say, I'm sure," the elderly woman said.

Holding her teenager's hands, she said, "Inez, it was good to see you. Maybe we can have coffee before I leave town."

"That would be nice, dear," she said, shuffling away.

"Mom, how long are you here for?"

"We need to work a few things out, but we'll be leaving together." A strong thud on her back forced her final words.

"I haven't felt like crying until now when I saw you," the youngest child said, her head buried in her mother's shirt. Through muffled sobs she asked, "This is really happening, isn't it?"

Squatting down, Kristin felt her knees click, as she looked at the brown-sugar eyes of her youngest child. "This feels like a bad dream. It does for me, too, but we'll get through it together, I promise." Standing, she asked, "I need to talk to Peyton, can you help me find her?"

"She's back here." Olivia said, pulling on her mother's hand.

Kristin followed her daughter through an immaculate, white granite kitchen, embellished by sparkling fixtures and a mosaic tile backsplash. The brilliant cabinetry towered over her as she wound her way around the center stovetop through to a small room in the back. There, a woman sat on an elegant, linen sofa next to a companion wearing a rust-colored cardigan.

At the doorway, the ex-wife paused, recalling the last time she saw Peyton she resisted the urge to dismember the pregnant wife in the courtroom. Now, she was the one at the bottom of the food chain. This woman's husband was dead, and she'd made her disdain for the couple evident. How could she approach the widow with genuine compassion? Her feet turned inward, watching the woman's golden ponytail tip the tops of her thin shoulders. The competitor's back muscles jerked in rhythm with her sobs.

"Make sure to include a thank you to my followers. They've all been so concerned," she said to the woman next to her. "That one. Yes, post that picture. Let them know I'll be sharing all the details from our travels through Southern Alabama on our way to the funeral."

With a freshening tug of her blouse, Kristin said, "Peyton." Her eyes followed the woman next to Hutch's widow as she stood and walked toward the door. "I'm sorry to interrupt."

Walking past Kristin, the woman in the cardigan whispered, "She's had enough pain for one day."

Haven't we all?

"What do you want?" Peyton asked. Her tone reminded Kristin of the nuns interrogating an unannounced parochial classroom visitor.

"I'm here for the girls," she said. "I'm sorry for your—"

"Of course, you are." Her youthful eyes narrowed. "You didn't waste any time getting here, did you?"

"I don't want to add pain to the situation. I have children who need a legal guardian. Let me get them and we'll all be out of your way."

"Of course, they're *your* children, aren't they?"

"Yes, they are. They're no longer a prop for your brand."

"They would be so lucky."

"I trust you'll send the funeral arrangements to me," the ex-wife continued. "They want to be included in anything appropriate for their age. Inez mentioned the family is meeting in Ellington prior to services. Just let me know the details, and I'll make sure they're there." Her palms sweated, gripping the leather straps of her purse.

"Let's be clear." the lean woman stood, using a tissue to blot her nose. "You're not welcome at the funeral."

"That's fine. Now's not the time to present your issues about me. Hutch was a father to my children, and you were his wife. That's all the respect I have for either of you."

"Respect." Peyton scoffed. "That's funny."

"I should go—"

"You respect him, and I hate him for loving you until the day he died." Her lip pulled tight.

"I'm not here to argue. He's your husband, you remember him however you choose."

"My husband spent the better part of our marriage climbing rung after rung of the corporate ladder trying to get an 'at-a-boy' from his pal, Kris." Her lean legs stretched walking to the edge of an armchair, her hand ran atop the rounded edge.

"I doubt that, seriously. Hutch was always in it, for Hutch."

"When his money wasn't enough to impress you, he went for your daughters. If they showed interest in Dad, maybe you would too." A school aged child brushed past Kristin, running in the room and clutched Peyton's thighs. The widow rubbed the child's soft curls never breaking eye contact with her rival still standing in the doorway.

"Peyton, I won't pretend to understand what you're going through. I just want my kids."

"He got up every morning and went to bed every night thinking of how he could get your attention. Your memory drove him insane. To the point of overdosing on drugs."

"There's no way in hell he killed himself—," Kristin forced a swallow. "—over me. At the end of the day, we're all just kids from Ellington trying to figure our lives out as ill-equipped adults. I understand you're angry and want to blame somebody or something. But we may never know what was going through his mind."

"He told us," she said holding a leather-bound book. The white tips of her French manicure showcased the gold embossed monogram, *HMC.* "His words are here."

"May it bring you closure, but I don't want to see it," she said, turning to leave.

"You don't have to read it. I did, and it sickened me."

Kristin remained in the doorway with her back turned to the scorned wife. Listening to Olivia and Lennon in the distance, she recalled several times she desired a connection with their stepmother. She wanted to co-parent with her, share ideas, and include her in decisions about Hutch's daughters they were raising together. Her efforts were overshadowed by the influencer's desire for a coveted "blue check mark" by her name. Over time, it became clear Hutch's wife was more concerned with appearing to have a happy family, rather than putting in the work to have one. When her persona deemed it acceptable to play the role of Mom, she did, but today the role of grieving widow was gaining more "likes."

She knew Peyton's accusations were as empty as her desire to be a stepmother, but if hating her dead husband's ex-wife brought new fans, Kristin would serve as the scapegoat.

"I can tell you this will be burned with everything else he left here. Don't think for a minute those girls will get a memento from Daddy. Why don't you just take your bratty children and leave."

Stepping to the kitchen, Kristin rested her hands on the marble island, her palms cooled on the surface. With a deep breath, she walked into the living room where her daughters entertained the younger kids. "Girls, get your things."

"Mom, we can't just leave," her teenager said, planting her feet.

"You stepmom has people to help watch the littles. The funeral will be at home, in Ellington. I'll make sure you're involved in every detail. Let's go home."

With her medical bag in tow, Olivia joined her mom standing in the room. Her sister's shoulders slumped as she started collecting her things.

"Inez, we're leaving. The girls and I should be able to

catch an evening flight home. Can I get that coffee chat with you when you're in town for the funeral?"

"I understand." Motioning for Kristin to lean down to her level she whispered, "The lioness is unchained today."

The ex-in law stepped back from the elderly informant.

Inez continued, "I told my sister I won't be making the trip for the funeral. These bones are too weak to go that far. I'm sending my condolences to my sister from sunny South Florida."

"I appreciate your understanding," she wriggled her mind to find a neutral response. Sincere, yet not incriminating. "It's a complicated situation."

With a last farewell to the oldest patron of her fan club, she pushed her bag onto her shoulder. "You should tell Peyton goodbye."

"I tried, but her mom said she wasn't in the mood for a visitor. She said she would let her know we were gone," Lennon said.

With quivering legs, the ex-wife walked down the steps of Hutch's home one last time. Her daughters at her side, she said, "The Uber is on the way, let's walk. I could use the endorphins and we'll save him a gate pass."

Their trio ambled along the palm tree-laden sidewalk; mansions shrank behind them with each step forward. Kristin's stomach pained, imagining her ex alone in his hotel room, battling his mind as death's impending sense of doom crept in. Were his breaths labored? Did he lose control of his bladder? At what moment did his powerlessness come into view? And, did it make him pitch a plea to his Creator, bargaining for his salvation? Like so many terminally ill patients she'd cared for, did he feel the surge of adrenaline that comes in the final hour? Hormones push the body during crisis, and the senses peak. Was there a glimmer of his survival, seconds before the potent odor of his demise took over? Her curiosity beaded on her forehead.

"Mom, are you okay?" Lennon asked.

"Yes," she said with a jolt. "Are you okay, is the question." The mother gestured to the driver of a small black sedan.

"I'm okay, I guess." The teen slid across the backseat behind her mom. "I don't see why we had to leave today. I feel better just being close to him, his stuff. I could have helped Peyton at the house."

"You're a thoughtful person, Len. Don't worry, she has a lot of people helping her today. Let's take care of you now, okay? Staying busy is just a way to avoid the pain," she said.

"Are we ever going back?" Olivia asked. "I just want to see my little brother and my sisters. They'll miss me not being there."

"Me too. I just want to see them again," the other child said.

The commute was spent watching the luxurious convertibles pass and remaining silent while her two daughters talked about their dead father. Sitting arm in arm, the sisters reminisced about his Dad jokes, banana nut pancakes, and Christmas mornings they shared with the man who made their mother's life a living hell. Her chest burned.

She interrupted the steady stream of fondness. "This is us."

They climbed out of the car and arranged their bags onto the crowded concrete walkway. "So, Mom. What's next?" Lennon asked.

"You'll live with me again. We're going home," she said, handing the driver a tip.

"Can we see our little sister again?" Olivia asked.

"We'll work something out with your stepmother, so you can see the kids. Let's just get settled. I'll check on her in a few days, if I haven't heard any details about the funeral."

"We should have done it," the sisters whispered to each

other.

"Done what?" Kristin asked. In the heat, she struggled remembering the last time she'd eaten.

"We can tell her now," the youngest said through clenched teeth. "It's not gonna happen."

"What's not happening, Liv?"

"Dad and Mom—I mean, Peyton—wanted us to think about letting her adopt us," she said.

"Adoption?"

"You were still going to be our Mom, but Peyton could've done things with us. Like parent stuff, you know. Doctor's appointments, school papers. That kind of boring thing. She continued, "We told them we needed to think about it, but now. . ."

The mother's peripheral vision blurred.

"Mom?"

"I need to sit down." Chills rushed her forearms, as her neck sweated in the heat.

A broad-shouldered, uniformed woman walked toward them. "Are you okay over here?" "Ma'am, are you sick?"

Dropping the handle of her rolling carry-on, "I'm not used to this heat."

"We're from Alabama," the child chimed.

Picking up the dropped luggage, the security guard helped the mother and children to a bench next to the security office. "Sit here as long as you need. I'll get you a bottle of water from the breakroom."

"Are you okay, Mom?" the oldest asked.

Leaning back, her head against the wall, she closed her eyes. "I will be."

"You want to count things, Mama?" Olivia asked.

"No baby, Mama's fine. It's just been a long day."

Olivia's eyes widened holding her palm open. "I can start. I see *five* things: pilots, and airline attendants—"

“Idiot,” Lennon said, with a scowl. “Mom’s the one having the panic attack, not you. She has to focus her brain.”

“It’s okay, girls, really. Mama will be fine as soon as we get back home. I just needed to rest a bit.” The mother lifted her head, digging in her purse. Handing the phone to the oldest daughter, she asked, “Can you do this for me? Grey made reservations for a return flight home. We just need to check in. Just follow the application.”

“App, Mom.” the teen’s merciless sarcasm thickened.

“Sorry. App. Thank you,” the mother said, feeling the blood pulse through her neck again.

Olivia proceeded with her own anxiety awareness treatment plan. “I hear *four* things on the overhead speaker.”

“Len, I know today has been overwhelming,” the mother said, as the teen tapped on her phone screen. “It’s normal to cling to what we know when we’re frightened, so I get why you want to stay. Your entire existence is up in the air right now and that’s scary. Familiar things bring us security; I’m clinging today too. Your father and I didn’t have the most agreeable relationship, but it was predictable, which made me feel safer, in a weird way.”

Tears touched the child’s eyelids, prompting a swipe with her shirtsleeve.

“I respect your relationship with your father’s family,” she said, taking a sip of water. “As for the adoption, you have a legal guardian. Your mother. Courts put adoption in place when the parent is not active or desires to let go of his or her parental rights. That was never the case with us, so it wasn’t a valid option. I understand it’s difficult to leave today, but your life is at home with me.”

“We’re checked in,” she said, handing the phone back to its owner.

“Thank you, here’s your facemask. This virus has everyone on high alert.”

"Three things I *feel.* One: this seat sticking to the back of my legs. Ouch! Two: . . ." Olivia recited as they inched their way closer to the security checkpoint.

Chapter Twenty-Six

Independence Day's notorious heat burned the back of her neck, leaving the shaded canopy of the trail. Cicadas hummed awake in the thick humidity. On the last leg of her hike, she stopped to blot her neck and face with a cloth. Water from her thermos spilled onto her chin while taking a sip. It dripped down the front of her throat, but she didn't wipe it. Life-giving blood rushing through her veins was welcomed.

"Champ?" Kristin called as her trail guide traipsed across a well-worn path in the brush. "Don't wander too far, the snakes are on the move." The tractor clambered on the other side of the hill. "Come on, buddy. We're almost there."

Grey wore his oversized straw hat giving an occasional glance behind him, while turning the earth with his bottom plow. She was grateful his biggest worry was keeping the rows straight for soon-to-be-planted crops.

"Good hike this morning?" he asked, shutting the raucous engine down.

"Champ approves," she said, as her partner cooled his belly in the freshly tilled dirt. "Thanks again for cutting that trail, it's a great stress reliever."

"Anything for you," her husband winked, taking a sip of water from her thermos. "Today's Sunday."

"I'm heading to the house now," his wife said, looking at her watch. "I've got time for a quick shower before she calls. You know she still likes her weekly coffee chat, even on the holidays.

"Odd, how it didn't take her long to get back on track, after—he died," Grey said.

"You know Ma would never miss an opportunity to tell me 'I told you so,'" she smirked, giving Champ a gentle prod with her foot. "I'll send the girls down to pick a watermelon for the cookout."

"Sounds good, I'll supervise." The farmer removed his hat and wiped his forehead with a towel. "I won't be much longer."

Water sprays massaged Kristin's aching muscles as she watched the suds puddle over her toes and down the drain. The solace of their lives echoed like the pattering stream that cleansed her. Both girls finished their virtual school curriculums from their mother's home, which saved them from transitioning coursework yet again. On track with grade-level requirements, the fall would bring Lennon into high school, while Olivia looked forward to navigating seventh grade with friends she'd known since kindergarten.

A flick of the towel released her thick hair onto her freckled shoulders. She slipped a teal tennis dress overhead with her wet hair still dripping.

Gliding down the hall, she paused at each bedroom door, placing her palm on the outside panel. Her chest fluttered.

The sound of her phone pulled her away.

Audrie: I'm coming over so we can ride to Vy's together.

I'll bring a watermelon.

Kristin: Got one.

Audrie: Okay, plates. See you in a few.

The mother held her phone at her side in one hand, a fresh cup of coffee in the other as she used her hip to open the front door. This was the setting where hers and Rosalyn's passionate, sometimes strenuous relationship found a common place week after week. Seated in her favorite chair, her eyes followed dust from the fields until it encircled the clouds. Feeling her lungs stretch like loblolly boughs greeting the sun, she closed her eyes. Opening them to release her hold, gazing into the vibrant hues of bevel-edged hydrangeas that would serve as the perfect backdrop for decades to come.

Peaceful recollections were interrupted by the sound of howling dogs, forcing her to step to the side overlook. Her mother's car peeled onto the paved roundabout blasting dust from the gravel entry into the air. Kristin smiled watching her mother step out of her low-profile vehicle, balancing her position atop her Louboutins.

"Well, this is a welcomed surprise," she said.

"What's that?" Rosalyn peered over her white-rimmed sunglasses. "We talk every Sunday."

"On the phone. But, an unannounced visit is always fun. Aren't you looking festive today?"

"I'm going to Wey-Vy's party this afternoon," she said, justifying her red, white, and blue ensemble as she stepped onto the wooden risers.

"You are?"

"Yes, why the surprised look? Please consider a baby Botox injection. At your age, your face should not show that much expression. You're an open book, dear."

Cold fingertips on Kristin's forehead caused her to pull away as if her mother had moistened her thumb to clean her face. "No reason, it just seems you have an inside line to the

Murphy family these days, that's all." She turned to go inside.

"Maybe I wanted to see you in private, before we were there," the woman called, taking her daughter's seat outside.

Returning with two steaming hot beverages, the daughter said, "A pre-party, then?"

"It's hardly a party, Krissy. Discussing how my fatherless granddaughters will be raised is much too delicate to discuss by phone."

Kristin shuddered. "And, she's back, ladies and gentlemen. For a minute, I thought you were having a small stroke, Roz."

"Strokes are no laughing matter at my age." The woman held her head sideways, pinching a cigarette between her red lips and flicking her lighter. With a deep inhale, "I wanted to see how you're holding up. It's been almost four months since Hutch's passing."

"I'm okay, I just keep a close eye on the girls."

"My namesake, how is she?"

"She finished her school year strong, virtual of course. Her friends welcomed her back home, which helped," the mother said. "I think they've got her excited about 9th grade."

"Well, the disaster that occurred at the funeral couldn't have been easy for her to forget. Peyton really showed her true colors," Rosalyn hummed.

The daughter's view drifted over the pond in search of an active thrasher.

"And, Olivia?"

"She seems to be back to normal for the most part. Her blood sugars have been much better with the insulin pump." Kristin held her phone screen at an angle, toward her mother. "Here's her glucose level now," she said, pointing at a bumpy white line ticking along the bottom graph.

Howling came from the side yard causing her grandmother to fling her hands in her lap, "The dogs. The incessant dogs, again."

With a laugh, Kristin said, "It's just Audrie. She said she was coming by—for the pre-party."

"I'm not wearing a mask around Audrie," Rosalyn said, adjusting herself and brushing a tiny speck of dirt from her white pants. "I only brought one for Vy's house."

"That's fine, Ma. It's a small crowd and there will be hand sanitizer everywhere."

"Hello! I'm getting coffee," Audrie called from inside the house.

The sounds of her cupboard doors opening and closing made the sister-in-law smile in awe of their familiarity.

"Good morning, Audrie," Rosalyn said, tilting her chin to scan the new arrival's hairstyle. "I love your braid; you should teach Krissy one day."

Patting her fishtail she pulled the end forward over her shoulder. "Thank you. Kristin, you don't know how to braid?"

"Now Audrie, where would Roz have fit that into my childhood?"

"Between running with scissors and cocktail mixing 101." The matron's thin lips turned inward as she gave a short huff through her nose, sending the group into a rowdy cackle.

Grey leaned onto one leg propped on the first step. "Well, isn't this a hen party?" he asked, before guzzling the remaining water from a plastic bottle and crunching the empty vessel into a ball.

"Do *not* call it a party." Kristin joked as her mother bristled beside her. "Are you finished in the fields?"

"Yes, I'm about to grab a shower."

"Join us, son-in-law. My clever daughter was just giving us an update on the girls."

"They have good days and bad days, to be expected. I worry about them probably more than I should." Her voice dropped as she glanced over her shoulder through the window behind her. "I'm concerned they may battle depression too one day, like their dad."

"You have nothing to worry about, dear," Rosalyn said, through forced breath.

"Depression is inherited. Children of parents who commit suicide are at high risk of the same."

"Don't lose sleep, my child."

"Are they in counseling, now?" Audrie interrupted.

Rosalyn's mouth drew closed, as she leaned her back into the chair crossing her arms across her chest.

"Yes, we went back to the therapist they saw during the custody hearing," the mother said. "He says they are coping, asking the right questions, and doing what they need to be doing. It just takes time."

"Have they asked you anything about him?" Audrie's voice tilted, as her fishtail braid dropped behind her shoulder.

"We've had good discussions about life, death, the afterlife." Kristin paused. "Father's Day was tough."

"I bet," said Audrie.

"We did a lot with Grey in the morning." She flashed a grin at her rugged husband still standing on the ground below. "Then in the afternoon, we planted a dogwood tree in the yard, in remembrance. He dug the hole and I stayed with the girls while they whispered a special prayer their dad taught them. It's right over there."

The women stretched their necks to see over the railing. A sapling fanned its white budded branches in the warming sun.

"I think the girls needed some stability after everything that happened," the stepfather said.

"Have they asked about their stepmom?" asked Audrie. "Are they still living near Miami?"

"As far as I know, they stayed in Lake Tarpon to finish the school year. Len said she DM'd her stepmother after the funeral, but she never responded. The mother's eyes darted toward the wooden slats below her feet. "Not much contact on their end." Her nose tickled, smelling a freshly lit cigarette.

"It sounds like things are going well, dear," Rosalyn said. "It makes it all worth it."

"Worth, what?" she asked, leaning her ear toward her mother's voice.

Audrie pulled a large sip of coffee through her lips; her face hidden by the rising steam. Grey's boots stomped the stairs to the top of the porch as the discussion quieted.

"What was worth it, Ma?"

"A mother knows what her children need." Her words dripped with smugness like the sweat on the farmer's brow.

"This is extravagant even for you, Roz. Why the dramatic intro?" Kristin angled her chin down.

"I'm sorry about your ex, but it wasn't a suicide," she said, leaning toward an ashtray beside her then resting onto the cushioned chairback. Rosalyn's bangled wrists crossed over each other with a clang.

"His autopsy said otherwise. The toxicology report is delayed because of the COVID-19 testing, but the police were confident of its results."

"It's beyond me." Rosalyn's midnight nails tapped on the armchair's rounded edge.

"Would you like to share what you know? Or is this what you wanted to tell me, in private?"

With a long breath, the grandmother leaned forward stretching her neck toward the door, "Audrie, could you close that?" she asked. As the lip sealed shut, she said, "It seems that Penny—," her daughter didn't bother to correct her. "—was in a tizzy after Hutch left her with all five children during such a busy time of year. It didn't help matters one that of them is an infant." She pressed her lips together and looked to the others. "Well, my namesake let it slip Daddy had an upcoming business trip to—"

"Why would she share that with you?" her daughter asked, with an abrupt interruption to her mother's feature show.

"She told me," Audrie said, with a tone that sliced the humidity around them. Grey stepped toward the wall behind the huddled group of women to flip the ceiling fan switch. His wife's eyes followed the sister-in-law's coffee cup from her lips to her lap as she continued. "We've been in touch since around the holidays. I made a point to check on her at least once a week."

"Is that right?" the mother asked, running her finger across her cracked bottom lip.

"They were feeling the strain of a new home, new family, all the things you warned them about before leaving. I think she was scared you'd say, 'I told you so.' You know teenage girls, they never want to admit Mom was right."

"I would've liked to have known my daughter was having difficulties," the mother said, wrenching her hands in her lap.

"When she mentioned her dad was planning a trip to Boston for work, I remembered you and Vy planning to attend a health conference there. So, I researched medical conventions scheduled for that week. There were a couple of different ones around the city, but it wasn't hard to find his company's itinerary."

"Well, who's Nancy Drew, now?" Kristin asked.

"With that, I made a call to the family," the sister-in-law said.

"Whose family?"

"*Your* family, Krissy," Rosalyn said, with a tone reminding her daughter what she was capable of.

With eyes wide, Kristin pressed both hands together over her mouth. "What in God's name is happening?"

"As I was saying, when my little angel shared that Daddy was traveling to the homeland, I made a call."

"Please, no." Her "shame storm" bubbled up.

"Your Grandfather Kelly migrated to America as a young boy. He grew up under the hood of cars, tractors, anything with an engine. During the height of the war, he worked in a machine parts factory; it was a coveted skill back then." The proud descendant raised her fingers to her mouth pinching an invisible cigarette; only to puff air through her cotton bangs, realizing she was empty-handed and trying to cut back.

"I remember, the kid raised some eyebrows after you helped her with a family heritage project," Grey said.

"Well, she got an A, didn't she? Anyway, my father's brother was not the righteous workaholic Pop was. My uncle found his money gambling, bootlegging, and a little side income doing jobs with, let's call them *investors*."

"How were they able to assist you?" Kristin asked.

"Today, most of the Kellys live off the radar, in Worchester, but it seems they still have a business near the financial district." Raising her palms to the ceiling, she said, "The opportunity was too good to pass up. I made a call. I'm not sorry."

Kristin's body folded onto her lap.

"Honey, just wait," her husband modulated.

"After the hearing, we met with your mom at Lou Ann's to debrief her," the sister-in-law said. "We were devastated for you and Grey, but really for our entire family. Olivia and Savannah are close in age. Lennon is so smart and needs you more than she'll admit. They were leaving our family, too." Her eyes pointed at the others. "Roz made a suggestion about how we could remedy the issue."

Raising up from her crouched position, she brushed the dangling red strands across her swollen eyes and reddened nose. "*We*?" she asked, slamming her fist on the side table. "Grey, are you part of the *we*?"

Audrie jerked her hand to her cheek, then twisted the end of her braided hair along her collarbone. Rosalyn looked down her nose at her daughter while gesturing the universal sign for "calm down."

Biting his lip, he said, "I was angry, Kris. We had just left the courtroom and I … I wasn't thinking clearly."

"He didn't know when we gave the go ahead," Audrie said. "We didn't want him to have cold feet about it, so we left him out, on purpose. I told your mom about the business trip and she made the arrangements."

"Thanks to Grey's father, the retainer was sent as an anonymous donation to a worthy Catholic charity," Rosalyn said, watching her son-in-law drop his head. "Our part ended there, we know nothing about the details."

"Newsflash, my ex-husband is dead from a suspected overdose. How'd your guy pull that off?"

"Francis always was the creative one on the playground." A devious grin inched across the mastermind's face.

"We know this is hard," Audrie said. "But think of the possibilities now. I wish my ex could have been removed from the picture long before we divorced." Leaning toward Kristin, she placed her hand on her sister-in-law's knee. "This ends the cycle of abuse you've lived in for so long."

Rosalyn dug in her purse, emerging with a tiny breath mint she popped into her mouth.

"We'll get through this together, I promise," the husband said. "But right now, you just need to help the girls grieve the loss of their father."

"The dogwood was a nice touch, Krissy," she said, sucking her lips together.

"I allowed Olivia to stay in Florida because I knew I could make it work. For *me*, not you. And it was working for all of us, until you meddled."

"You missed your chance to stop this nonsense," the grandmother glared.

"Things have changed since your divorce," Kristin said. "Moms don't always walk out of the courtroom with the children. Dads want to be more than just a signed check on the 1st and 15th."

"You're weak. Just like your father. You stopped fighting."

"I *was* fighting."

"You were *losing*."

"That's great Roz, you've always been the judge and the jury, haven't you?" Kristin asked, throwing her hands in the air. "Man, what my life would be like without you in it."

"I'm sorry you feel that way, dear. I've only loved you since the day you were born."

Grey squatted next to his wife's chair. "We didn't deserve any of this. Not Browning's death, not Hutch's mess. You and I are good parents and decent people. The courts don't work in our favor."

"So, it's okay to serve our own justice now?" the wife asked.

"Kris, now the girls are free from that prison they were being raised in with him. He had them so uptight; now they have peace," Audrie said, her eyes watered.

Others on the porch leaned in to hear the mother's voice almost disembodied. Her gaze lost in the blooming hedges below. "You have no idea what it's like. Parental alienation. It– It's like watching your child drown in the ocean. Every wave pushing her close enough for your fingertips to touch, only to lose your grip with the undertow's surge. Each crashing wave plunging her deeper and pulling her farther. Just out of your reach."

Clanging bangles chimed as the mother reached for her

daughter's hand. "I did a lot of things wrong when you were little. You must trust me when I say, I know what Hutch would have done next because I've done it. I've committed the same crimes, and God knows I regret it. Getting the girls to live with him was just the beginning. Alienators don't quit where healthy parents normally would. They just keep pounding the child into submission."

"Len told me they were pushing for adoption," Audrie said. "He wouldn't have stopped until you were erased."

"Seeing you pay for my sins was unbearable. I had to do something," Rosalyn said.

"I just can't believe you did that." The daughter accepted her mother's reach. "What if they find out?" she asked.

"So, what?" The mother's voice was gentle. "They have a little ruck on my account, who cares?"

"What if they think it was me? I had all the motive, right? Revengeful ex-wife, rejected mother."

"I won't let that happen," she said, the red soles of her heels tapped the space between the two women.

"They're already asking Vy questions, since my name was listed on the registry."

"When they don't get answers, they'll stop. You were with Grey in Atlanta. Vy was with Wey, it's all accounted for."

The glass door opened onto the porch, revealing her teenage daughter, wearing a red, white, and blue bathing suit. "Mom, what's wrong?"

"Nothing," she said, letting her mother's hands go and wiping her face. "Is that what you're wearing to the cookout?"

"Yes, I'll get my mask. Are you sure nothing's wrong?"

"Positive." The mother's chin tightened looking at her child. Warm gratitude flooded her chest seeing her at the same door where so much pain took place a few months prior. "We're ready too. I'll get my things."

As the girl left, the adults disassembled. Rosalyn and

Audrie's cars exited the drive in a dust cloud together. While her husband showered, Kristin swiped the steam from the bathroom mirror studying the woman's reflection. The bags under her eyes were barely noticeable. Her rose-polished tips dabbed pink balm to her bouncy lips bringing her round, plump cuticles into view. The person in front of her was deserving of the life she had been gifted.

A buzz drew her attention.

Giving a quick glance at the shower, she slid the vanity's top drawer without sound. Her hands below the lip of the countertop, she flipped back the palm-sized device's cover. A black-framed screen glowed in the shadow of the half-opened space.

367-448-6337: They're here again.

Kristin: They'll stop asking questions when they don't get the answers they want.

367-448-6337: They're asking new ones. The tox report is out.

Kristin: Relax.

367-448-6337: ??

Kristin: I'm bringing a watermelon for supper.

***

Acknowledgments

To the parents, grandparents, stepparents, and loved ones of alienated children, your stories lifted me when I was at my lowest. Thank you for sharing your perspective and pain, your victories, and defeats, and most of all your authentic courage. Our voices are being heard and we can change the narrative.

My husband. He makes me want to be a better wife. If ever the Universe graces me with half of his character, I'd feel like I accomplished something in life.

My mother is a voracious reader. Of no surprise, she encouraged me to read when I was younger. A single mother working full time, as so many of us know, she faced the challenges of childcare during school holidays. There was a library close to her office. She'd leave me with a bagged lunch and tell me to read until she could get off work. Mind you, the Dewey decimal system was housed in index-card files and a computer was a distant dream for future media centers. Although I rolled my eyes or begged to stay with a friend, it was one of my favorite places to lose myself. I'm sure she felt horrific guilt leaving her daughter there, but she should know I was soaking up every syllable.

My long-time friend from college whose creativity and warmth breathes new life into teaching. Her passion for education and learning is contagious. She was willing, or maybe guilted, into being an alpha reader for me and yes- there's a place in heaven for her.

Through the power of social media, I reconnected with my high school pal who shared the secret sauce for successful self-publishing. Beta reader, copy editor, and killer of commas. I'm grateful for his guidance and his brilliant, author-wife's ongoing encouragement.

Editing is a glorious craft, and I have the highest regard for those who dedicate their careers to it. Especially those who treat new authors with kindness and welcome debut novels to mold. Write Your Best Book and Line Upon Line, your critiques and gracious patience were well received.

Thank you to Tatiana Vila at Vila Design who took six emails and one blurry screen image and made a killer book cover.

Also, I have to give an enormous virtual hug to my nursing team at work. They suffered through my storytelling on morning emails, lunch-and-learn memos, and even a brief newsletter phase. What started out as focused recognition for outstanding performance evolved into anecdotal blurbs and sometimes dissertation-like narratives over the years. Sometimes, there'd be no reply. Then there were those that sparked a message in return. They'd tell me how much they appreciated my note, laughed out loud, and my personal favorite, spit out their coffee while reading my words on a screen.

They told me to write more, so I did.

About the Author

Roxanne is a nursing graduate from the University of Virginia who spent most of her career caring for critically ill patients. Her passion for writing started early in life thanks to her mother's encouragement.

Today, she lives in the Southeastern US with her husband. They enjoy spending time with their three daughters and three dogs.

Other Books

If you enjoyed *They Can't Eat You for Supper,* please consider Pre-Ordering the sequel, *They Didn't Eat Me for Supper* today:

https://books2read.com/TheyDidntEatMeForSupper

Lennon and Olivia are older now, and they've got her own story to tell.

Thanks for reading! Please add a short review on the retailer's site where you purchased the book. Let me know what you thought!

Printed in Great Britain
by Amazon

64536948R00166